Buffalo Soldier

TANYA LANDMAN

WALKER
BOOKS

First published in Great Britain 2014 by Walker Books Ltd
87 Vauxhall Walk, London SE11 5HJ

2 4 6 8 10 9 7 5 3

Text © 2014 Tanya Landman
Cover photograph: image of battle © Chuck Pefley / Getty Images, Inc
Image of girl © elkor / Getty Images, Inc

This book has been typeset in Bembo Educational

Printed and bound in Great Britain by Clays Ltd, St Ives plc

British Library Cataloguing in Publication Data:
a catalogue record for this book is available from the British Library

ISBN 978-1-4063-1459-5

www.walker.co.uk

TANYA LANDMAN is the author of many books for children and young adults including *Apache*, shortlisted for the Carnegie Medal, and *The Goldsmith's Daughter*. Since 1992, she has been part of Storybox Theatre, working as a writer, administrator and performer – a job which has taken her to festivals all over the world. She lives with her family in Devon.

You can find out more about Tanya and her books by visiting her website at www.tanyalandman.com

This book is dedicated to the Buffalo Soldiers who inspired it.

"He who fights the battles of America may claim America as his country – and have that claim respected."

Frederick Douglass
(Former slave, abolitionist, author, orator
and advisor to Abraham Lincoln)

Two covered wagons are heading out into the open, slow and steady, like little ships afloat on the ocean. Axles are greased, wheels barely creaking. The oxen are well groomed, their hides glossy as polished wood. Gaily coloured ribbons are tied to their horns and silver bells hang around their necks.

The faces of the people driving them are freshly washed, their clothes starched and pressed. Crisp linen shirts; pretty flounced dresses. Blue-eyed women with hair of dazzling blonde; square-jawed, clean-shaven men; and the children – rosy-cheeked and plump – are just as cute as they come. Smiling brightly, their hearts are full of courage, their heads full of hope. They're planning on settling down in the wilderness, carving a homestead out of nothing, making a little piece of heaven right here on earth: it's their destiny. The Almighty has given them the vast, empty land of America just as surely as he gave Paradise to Adam and Eve.

Only the land isn't as empty as it seems.

Whooping screams rend the air, chilling the blood and freezing the marrow. War cries.

Indians! Savages!

A dozen painted warriors, naked save for their loincloths, come riding bareback on spotted horses, feathers in their hair, tomahawks in their hands, scalping knives at their waists.

They circle the wagon and the settlers are fighting back but there are too few of them and too many Indians. One of the men takes an arrow in the chest. Falls. His wife runs to him. He dies, his head cradled in her lap.

The savages' blood is up now. Their yelling gets wilder. Ear-piercing shrieks, going on and on and only stopping when all the men are slaughtered.

And now the Indians are coming for the women. As they leap off their horses, terrified mothers shield their weeping children behind their skirts. They're all looking at a fate worse than death.

But then a bugle sounds. In the blink of an eye panic shows on the savages' faces. They try to run. Too late.

The cavalry are riding in on snowy-white chargers, uniforms of deep blue with scarlet neckerchiefs, buttons polished, boots shining, sabres gleaming. Soldiers slash at the Indians until every one of them is lying dead.

The cavalry ride a lap of victory. Once, twice, three times around the wagons while the rescued women and children cheer and jump for joy. Then they're pulled up onto the horses. Away they all trot, back through the curtained entrance and out into the darkness.

Where a stablehand is waiting in the shadows to lead the horses quietly back to their stalls.

1.

I guess Ma died. Or she was sold. I don't know which. By the time I got around to wondering there was no one I could ask. All I got from her was a name. Charlotte. Darned fool fancy thing for a slave girl. Didn't no one never call me that.

If I felt her loss I have no recollection of it. My life began in the cook-house. Seemed I'd just grown there, like a seed from a crack in the floor.

Child's heart got to attach itself to something. Mine attached itself to Cookie, winding around her like bindweed on a post. So long as she was there I could stand tall. When she was gone I was left sprawling on the ground helpless, twisting and twining every which way, not knowing how I was ever gonna get up on my own two feet.

Me and Cookie was the property of Mr Delaney. His plantation was three miles outside of town, but it could have been three thousand. Until the war come, I never set one foot off the place. My world was the cook-house, the attic above it, the bare earth yard around it, the vegetable garden beyond it: that was all. I never got as far as the fields, even. My only aims in life was pleasing Cookie, not getting noticed by the master and avoiding Jonas Beecher. That boy was three, maybe four years older than me: the overseer's son, with a streak of mean running through him that was wider than the wide Missouri. Seemed the sole purpose of his life was to make mine a misery. Punchings and kickings was the very least of it.

When I was around about eight years old I got me another aim in life: not offending Miss Louellen.

Master must have been close to forty years old when he got himself a wife. Miss Louellen arrived in a carriage with her mammy, followed by a cart stacked high with trunks all shapes and sizes. She was a dainty slip of a thing: dark-haired, white-skinned, blue-eyed, pretty and delicate as a piece of painted china. The belle of three counties, she was sixteen years old and as empty-headed as they come. Ham told Cookie there wasn't nothing much running between her ears but notions of balls and parties and where her next dress was coming from.

If Miss Louellen been left alone I don't suppose me and Cookie would have hardly noticed she was there: it was just another mouth at the big house table was all. But one fine day Mrs Beecher pay her a visit. After that there was

12

all kinds of ideas in Miss Louellen's head causing us a heap of trouble.

The first we know of it is when Miss Louellen starts yelling for Cookie one morning. She come out of the house all on her own, her big old hooped skirt swishing, sweeping grass and leaves aside as she storm across the yard. She carrying a pen and ink and a pocket book and she come right into the cook-house. Suddenly she got a bee in her bonnet about how every darkie on the plantation was a lazy good-for-nothing who been cheating the master for years.

"I know what's been going on," says Miss Louellen. "And you can't fool me. I'm the mistress here now and things are going to be different. I'm going to be keeping a close eye on you all."

She give me a real particular look, though I don't know what for. I surely ain't done nothing to offend her. Not that there needed to be a reason. Existing was enough.

"Now, I have a fancy for some gingerbread," she says to Cookie.

"Yes, Miss Louellen," says Cookie.

We was both expecting her to go back across the yard to the big house and leave us to it, but she don't. Miss Louellen just stands there. "You better tell me what you need to make it."

Cookie's keeping her eyes on the floor. "Well, Miss Louellen," she says slow, "first I needs some flour."

"Flour," says Miss Louellen. "Where's that?"

"In that jar. Shall I fetch it down?"

"Yes. Put it here. Now, how much do you require?"

"Three cups."

The mistress takes Cookie's old tin cup and scoops out the flour. There's a set of scales in the cook-house, rusting in the corner. Cookie never weighed nothing in her life – all her baking is done by hand and eye and feel. But Miss Louellen weighs the flour, real careful. She does the same with the butter and the sugar and the molasses. She does it to the eggs and the raisins. She even weighs the buttermilk. She writes down all them numbers in her little pocket book and adds it up. Takes her a while. Her ivory-white forehead goes crinkling into lines with the effort. Finally she says, "I'll be weighing the gingerbread when it's baked, you hear me? I'm not having you stealing, no siree. You're not thieving so much as a raisin from me."

It was the middle of summer and the cook-house was hotter than hell. Sweat was already making dark circles under the arms of Miss Louellen's dress. She didn't stay around to watch us do the baking. Calling for Kissy to bring her some lemonade, she went to sit on the porch.

Cookie starts beating up the butter and the sugar, working real fast to get it creamy-white before it melts, her wood spoon pounding so hard against the sides of the bowl it seemed both would break. She sets me cutting up raisins, taking seeds out, dusting them with flour.

14

I'm scraping them seeds into a pail for the hogs when a thought hits me hard in the head.

"Should have seeded them before she left. Cookie, they gonna weigh less. She gonna be mad at us."

Cookie frowns. "You right, child. Better save them. Heap them up there, so she can see we ain't eaten nothing."

So I pick them seeds back out of the pail, every last one. When I break the eggs I save them shells too, just in case.

When everything's together in that bowl Cookie starts up beating again. She whacking that mix around and I'm watching that arm of hers, wondering if mine will ever be as strong. I see the sweat coming up into beads on her brow and the smell of them spices got me drooling like one of the master's dogs.

When the beating was done Cookie adds in the raisins, then scrapes that bowl out clean. Every last trace of that mix goes right into the tin and that tin goes right into the oven.

But there was just one itty-bitty smear of molasses left on a spoon. Looking over her shoulder to check Miss Louellen wasn't watching from the yard she give me a wink and, without saying a word, pop it right in my mouth for me to lick clean.

That sweetness is so good it's making my head spin. I'm thinking I've died and fetched up in heaven. Then I hear a whooping and a voice piping up, "Nigger's licking a spoon. I seen it! I seen it!"

15

Jonas Beecher been hiding all this time, watching from the branches of the cottonwood tree, waiting, just waiting for me to do something I shouldn't. I see a flash of his golden curls catching in the sunlight as he shins down and streaks off across the yard, yelling his head off. And then all I see is Miss Louellen. She come in a whirl of skirts, fussing and fuming. She cussing Cookie and *slap! slap! slapping!* me across the face.

My head was still pounding by the time night come. That dainty slip of a thing had hit me so hard with the back of her hand the rings on her fingers cut into me. My blood gets smeared on that dress of hers. I got me diamond-shaped holes punched into my cheek. And me and Cookie, we got ourselves a whole new heap of rules we had to abide by. Didn't matter none that the gingerbread come out weighing right. As far as she was concerned neither of us was to be trusted. That suits Jonas fine. I see him standing, leaning against the cottonwood. I hear him laugh: a high-pitched squeal that bring to mind a hog at feeding time. I see him mouthing, "Got ya!"

But Jonas is the least of my problems. Miss Louellen ain't finished yet. She says, "I want you to whistle."

"Whistle, Miss Louellen?" Cookie can't believe her ears.

"That's what I said. Whistle. I want everything weighed. Everything accounted for. Any time you're cooking, I want to hear you. If you're whistling you can't be eating." She looks at me. "You too. And every time you're carrying food across to the dining room, I want to hear you." She gives me a prod with her little white finger, jabbing it so hard into me she breaks the nail. "I'm watching you. I can have you sold any time I choose. Don't you forget it."

The thought of being sold – of being sent off someplace without Cookie – just about makes my knees give up on me. My head is filled with fear. It squeezes out every thought. Every thought but one. Her finger's bleeding where her nail broke. A streak of her blood is smeared across her dress right next to mine. Ain't that strange? Can't tell whose is whose.

2.

Whistling all the time makes your face ache. Whistling all the time makes your throat dry and your lips crack. If you whistling all the time you can't eat. But you can't talk neither. Can't hardly think, even. And it ain't like all that whistling makes Miss Louellen any happier. If anything, it makes her madder than ever. And it irritates the hell out of the master.

For weeks me and Cookie had them both yelling at us. Her hollering for us to whistle louder, him hollering for us to shut up.

Then come the day that Miss Louellen drop down in the yard and lay there like she dead. Had to be carried back up to her bed by Ham. My, did that cause a stir! There was whispers of typhoid fever and shaking sickness. But there wasn't nothing too much wrong with her. When the doctor come from town he say she with child, is all. The way she acted you'd of thought it was something shameful. She wouldn't have no callers after that. Her mammy was the only one allowed into her room. She wouldn't see another living soul, not even her husband.

"What's wrong with her?" I ask Cookie. "She sick in the head?"

"No," says Cookie with a smile. "She a lady."

According to her, ladies was way too delicate and refined to acknowledge such things as breeding. As far as they was concerned cows didn't have no calves, horses didn't have no foals and chickens most definitely didn't lay no eggs. Ladies didn't have no babies neither. The way they told it, they found them under rosebushes.

I never heard such nonsense. It made me wonder how the heck she'd ended up getting that baby inside her in the first place but when I asked Cookie that, she burst out laughing and told me to hush my mouth.

The baby growing made Miss Louellen tired and sick. She slept most all the time. She couldn't hardly keep no food down. Took to her bed and lay there like she was dying.

While Miss Louellen was confined to her room we didn't need to whistle no more. Her window overlooked the yard. Instead we had to tiptoe around, quiet as mice, try not to disturb her.

Jonas had himself a whole heap of fun with that. I slept in the attic right above the cook-house along with Cookie and a bunch of house slaves. One time he come creeping in the dead of night and pile a stack of pans by the ladder so I kick them when I come down in the morning. Another time he fix a length of twine across the doorway so I go flying with a pail of swill. Each time Miss Louellen sent Mammy down to give "that clumsy nigger" a licking. That woman had hands like frying pans – just as big and twice as hard. My ears was always ringing after she done with me. I figured the only thing keeping me from getting sold was that Miss Louellen was too tired and sick to get around to organizing it.

Cookie kept fixing treats to tempt Miss Louellen's appetite but didn't nothing work. Them plates would come back hardly touched. The first time it happened, my eyes was popping and I was drooling like a dog. If Miss Louellen didn't want it, why, there was plenty of room in my belly. Well, hey, I was happy to give that food a good home! I check the cottonwood tree to see no one's watching. I'm sitting on the floor, and Cookie's telling me to tuck right on in. But then I give that plate a closer look. A gob of green spittle is squatting right in the middle, like a toad in a swamp. Hell, it's so big it's practically blinking its eyes at me. Miss Louellen didn't have the strength to eat, but she sure had strength enough to spit. I couldn't touch none of it. After that, all her leftovers went to the hogs.

When the baby come it darned nearly tore Miss Louellen in half. It was put right out to a wet nurse and she was in bed another two months, recovering. When she finally come out of her room I didn't hardly know her. That pretty, empty-headed slip of a girl had become a woman but she was like a dried-out rose: withered, faded, fragile, likely to crumble into dust if you breathed too hard on her. She'd kept her thorns though. They was as sharp as ever, and just as like to draw blood.

She was only back on her feet a few weeks before she was with child again. It was strange. Seemed to me she didn't much like her husband. She didn't much like her baby neither. Nor the one that come next. Yet she spent her entire time dropping babies, one right after the other. All that breeding was sucking the life right out of her, but I wasn't complaining. It kept her from landing on me like a duck on a bug every time I put a foot wrong.

3.

Time passed and things went on much the same. I got by. I stayed put. Miss Louellen's threat was always hanging over my head but I didn't get sold on.

Ask any slave on the Delaney place when they was born they'd give the same answer: sometime. The day? The month? The year? Didn't no one know. So I can't be precisely sure of my age but I figure I was maybe ten, eleven, when the United States of America decided to rip itself to pieces. That small world of mine was about to be blown right apart.

Now there must have been talk about it in the attic night-times. Whisperings about Abraham Lincoln and freedom and when and if and how it might come and what it would be like if it did. But if there was, I didn't hear them.

Seems to me life is all about big things and little

things. Sometimes you standing up so close to a little thing you can't see nothing beyond. You don't realize there's a big thing standing right behind it until it's too late.

See, I had me a problem. Besides Miss Louellen and Jonas Beecher there was something new to worry about. It was just a little itty-bitty thing, truth be told, but it filled my head so full I couldn't see nothing else.

A month or two back, Ezekiel, Mr Delaney's smith, been kicked when he was shoeing the master's horse. Hoof catch him in the face, cave his nose right into his head. I was sad when I heard, but I hadn't known Ezekiel so I can't say I took it personal. He been mortal sick for more than a week before he upped and died but the master hadn't never sent for no surgeon. Why would he? He was more concerned for his horse. As soon as it was plain where Ezekiel's soul was heading Mr Delaney took himself off to the auction house in town to buy a new smith. He come back with a man by the name of Amos.

New arrivals on the plantation always caused something of a stir. When Miss Louellen come she brung half a dozen house slaves with her that just about turned me and Cookie's life upside down for weeks. But I didn't pay much attention to Amos – the smithy was beyond the limits of my world. He was no concern of mine.

But Cookie sure noticed him. She's mashing up potatoes

when she tells me, "Master got himself a new man."

Her voice was softer than I ever heard it. Something stabbed me, twisted in my gut sharper than a knife. "He nice?" I says.

"Yeah. He nice." There's a smile on her face I never seen before. She kinda glowing, like there's a flame warming her from inside. And right away I feel unsteady, like someone's pulling the ground out from under me.

"You gonna jump the broom with him?"

"Hush your mouth, child!" She flick her apron at my head and go right on with her mashing. But that smile gets bigger. And that night she don't sleep on her side, her arm across my chest, holding me close, whispering stories about Moses and Jesus and Joseph in my ear. She lie on her back, silent, her head turned away so she can look out at the stars.

The very next day Cookie finds that the pan she want to cook dinner in is in need of repair. Well, would you look at that? Them handles is close to coming off! They going to need a rivet through, and she know just the man to do it. That pan's got to be taken to the smithy. And it far too big and serious a job and that pan is way too precious for me to carry over there. She got to do it all by herself.

She leaves me in the cook-house, peeling and chopping and dicing – whistling my head off the whole time because Miss Louellen is between babies and she up and about and acting mean. And you wouldn't believe how long it takes

Cookie to carry that pan to the smithy. That place got to be far off as Grandma Rideau's house the time it takes her. Far off as town, even. I almost got the whole meal cooked by the time I hear her coming back across the yard. And she ain't even carrying the pan! When I ask her what she done with it she say Amos is gonna bring it himself when he's done mending.

One, two, three days pass and he don't show up. It's like Cookie's sat on an ant-hill. She can't keep still. She all fidgety. Restless. Short-tempered and snappish as Miss Louellen.

When Amos finally come he's carrying the pan in one hand and a bunch of flowers he's pulled from the roadside in the other. And he's wearing a big stupid smile on his face, same as Cookie.

Cookie's old! Older than the master even! She got grey in her hair. The skin on her face is wrinkled up like a dried apple. But she giggles like she just a silly girl. Puts them flowers in a jug, handling them so careful, like they more precious than Miss Louellen's diamonds. She look at Amos. Amos look at me. The next thing I know Cookie's telling me to go off to the garden and bring her back some carrots for the master's dinner.

"I done that already! I pulled a whole bunch of them. They right there on the table. How many more you need?"

Cookie don't pay no attention. She just shoos me out the door. "Onions then. And fetch me some peas."

25

Ain't no vegetables ever been picked by someone in a worse temper than I was then. Why, I already picked plenty for the meal! Miss Louellen was gonna think I was thieving! I was gonna find myself on an auction stand. Didn't Cookie care about me no more? I was ripping them onions out of the ground, throwing dirt every which way. I was madder than a whole nest of hornets. But I was hurting too. Felt crushed and bruised like them peas I was picking so rough. My chest was tight, like someone had put a belt around and pulled it hard. And that feeling wasn't going away any time soon.

Next thing, Cookie finds that every pot and every pan in the entire cook-house is in a parlous state of disrepair. She don't know how she managed all this time! Why look here! This one's almost worn through at the bottom. And this one's bent so its lid don't fit. This one's handle needs straightening. They all got to be taken to the smithy to be fixed. One at a time.

Sunday come. They was special days on the plantation, leastways for the field hands. Six days a week they was worked from sunup to sundown, but on Sundays they got to rest. Me and Cookie didn't. We was up before the dawn, same as ever, because the master and his family still got to eat. And Mr Delaney was a sociable kind of man. Liked inviting his neighbours. Sometimes there was fifteen, twenty folks sitting down to dinner. This particular Sunday there was twenty-seven. There was a heap of work to do.

But Cookie got herself a spring in her step. She's whistling like she means it.

By the end of the day, I'm asleep on my feet. When I was tired that bad Cookie used to sling me over her shoulder like a sack of flour, carry me up to the attic and lay me down, curl herself around me like a big old wall, keeping the outside world away, keeping me safe from harm. But tonight she don't even come up the ladder. When we're finally done she tells me to go get some sleep. Then she slip off into the night. The only thing that kept me from following was the fear I might run into Jonas Beecher.

Well, it ain't too long before Amos goes to the overseer, and the overseer goes to the master and the master is feeling in an accommodating mood — maybe on account of the fact that Miss Louellen has took to her bed again and the place is so peaceful — because he give permission for Amos and Cookie to be wed. There can't be no noisy celebration with the mistress sick. But they jump the broom. And that night Amos moves into the attic.

We was all shoulder to shoulder in there night-times before he come, and now we packed so tight you can't stir us with a stick. But come the morning I find I'm lying on my back with my arms stuck straight out like Jesus on the cross. I ain't never had so much room to myself. Cookie and Amos had snuck off someplace — to the woods maybe

– to have themselves some private time. When she come back to fix the master's coffee she smiling fit to bust. Cookie ain't never been so happy. And I ain't never been so miserable.

4.

Well, heck, maybe it didn't matter if I did get sold! Didn't no one seem to care whether I was here or not. The day after Cookie and Amos jumped the broom I was banging and clanging pots around in the cook-house, banging and clanging them so loud it sounded like Jonas Beecher had set me another trap. I stormed across the yard to feed the peelings to the hogs, yelling their names, thumping the pail into the trough. Miss Louellen was sick in bed and I was singing my head off when I come back, singing my lungs out. But the master didn't tell me to git. Mammy didn't come scooting down to whup me. Cookie didn't tell me to hush my mouth. No one even noticed. I was so wrapped up in myself it never occurred to me to wonder why. It's dark by the time I find out.

We all in the attic but ain't no one settling down to sleep. Amos is whispering about how the South don't want to be part of the Union no more; they want to be a country all by themselves – only the North don't want to let them go. Some gentlemen someplace had taken to shooting at each other. I didn't hardly listen to him. I didn't give no thought to what it meant. It was just white folks, a long way away, doing who-cares-what to each other. When Cookie clasp him by the hand and murmur it's the beginning of a war, that don't mean nothing to me neither. I ain't got the faintest notion of what a "war" might be. It didn't make no difference to nothing, as far as I could see.

But I was wrong. Because the first thing that happened was that Mr Beecher packed up and left.

Next day, I'm drawing water when I see a cart piled high up outside the overseer's house.

"Hey, Ham! What's going on?"

The master's valet come over and explain it to me.

Up until now I thought white folks was the same all over. But it seemed there was two kinds: Yankees and Confederates. Mr Beecher was a Yankee. He been born in New York, or Washington or someplace way up north. Mr Delaney was a Confederate. Now the Confederates was rebelling against the Yankees and they'd all started fighting each other, Mr Beecher figured he'd better take himself back home, sign up for the right army.

I didn't understand more than half of what Ham told me. But one thing sure grabbed my attention. "So, they going? Leaving? All three of them?"

"Yep. Every single one."

I been miserable as sin just a moment before. But now my heart's pounding and a wave of joy come crashing over me. They going! Leaving! All three of them! My heart's singing it over and over.

I'm standing there with my mouth wide open watching while Mr Beecher check them trunks is roped down good. When he's done, he climb up on the box and call to his wife to come join him.

She all scrunched up, like a dishcloth that been washed out one time too many and never smoothed flat to dry. But when Mr Beecher flick the reins and the horse move on away her shoulders drop and she sits up taller, holds her head higher. She don't look back, not once. As they go down the drive it's like seeing a weight being lifted off her. I know precisely how she's feeling because I'm feeling the same.

Jonas is sitting at the back, legs dangling down. He's maybe fifteen years old but he's crying. Snuffling and crying like a baby. And he's looking my way.

I'm thinking, I won. I beat you. You didn't get me. You're leaving and I'm still here. I feel like dancing. I can't help myself. I mouth the words at him, "Got ya!"

They nearing the bend in the drive. The last thing I see Jonas do is point at me with one hand. He put the other to the side of his neck and clench it into a fist. Then he jerks it up sudden, cocks his head to the side, lets his tongue loll out like he been hanged. It send a shiver right through me. Just like that, my happy mood is gone.

But can't nothing change the fact that Jonas has left. My heart is pounding it out, over and over.

That same night there was a whole heap more whispering in the attic and this time I paid attention. According to Amos, who heard it from Josiah, who heard it from Ham, who heard it from the Rideaus' Walter outside the post office in town when he been sent to collect the mail, the president of the United States of America – Abraham Lincoln himself – had his heart set against slavery. And most all them fine gentlemen in Washington agreed with him. The whisper was that if the Yankees won the war, we might get ourselves freed.

Well, that confused the hell out of me right off. Mr Beecher was a Yankee. The notion of him heading north to join an army that might free the folks he been whipping the hides off all these years didn't make no sense. The notion Jonas might do the same was even crazier! I figured Amos must have heard things wrong.

But there was this thing: freedom. I didn't know what it meant. Couldn't imagine it. But that word tasted sweet as molasses on my tongue. I rolled it around my mouth, pushed it up against my teeth, stowed it away in my cheek like a wad of tobacco. My lips formed the shape and I breathed it out on the warm night air. Freedom. There was something powerful good in the sound of it.

I made my own picture of what it would be like. Took the notion from the stories Cookie had told me nights before Amos come along, and from the words of songs I'd heard drifting in from the fields on the wind. I figured Freedom was out there, just waiting over the horizon for the right time to show its face. And one day it would arrive in a blaze of dazzling light, trailing clouds of glory and there would be a whole host of angels singing sweet alleluias carrying jugs of lemonade and plates of gingerbread and one of them angels – the one with biggest wings and the brightest halo – would give me a spoon and a whole tin of molasses all to myself. Me and Cookie, we'd sit easy in chairs on the big house porch, rocking slow and steady, watching the sun go down just like the master and Miss Louellen.

To begin with, the fighting was all happening a long way off. News was spread from mouth to mouth in whispers. There was battles and there was Confederate victories and Yankee defeats. Then there was Yankee victories and Confederate defeats but we all remained the property of Mr Delaney. A whole year went by. Then two. Three. Mr Delaney's neighbours was losing sons. Brothers. Husbands. Old Grandma Rideau lost every single man – they all got themselves killed, one after the other. But the only thing that changed on the Delaney place was that the cotton harvests got stacked in the barn instead of being took off to be sold. Seemed them Yankees was stopping everything from coming in or going out of the county. Miss Louellen's dresses was getting faded and worn and fine cloth to make new ones just couldn't be had. She minded about that more than anything. As for the master, he couldn't get no Irish liquor. He took to sending Ham off into the woods to buy corn whisky from the white-trash family lived there. The other thing they had to whistle for was coffee. And ginger. Molasses. Cookie and me couldn't bake no gingerbread no more. The Delaneys had to eat what come off the plantation, same as us. But they didn't have no one measuring out rations of cornmeal for them. So they ate plenty and we ate less than ever. They was doing fine on it. But we was all getting one heck of a lot thinner.

Then, about three and a half years after it started, the war come riding right on into the neighbourhood. The second that happen, Miss Louellen go riding right on out. When word come that General William Tecumseh Sherman is marching the Yankee army through the mountains and heading right on down towards us, she takes her children, along with Mammy and most all the house slaves, and runs off to refugee someplace with her cousins. I was almost as glad to see the back of her as I had been to see the back of Jonas. Suddenly there was no one watching me. No one trying to trip me up, catch me out. So long as I kept out of the master's way when he was

34

having one of his drinking times there was no one even trying to hit me.

I figured General Sherman must be Moses, Jesus and Joseph all rolled into one. He was gonna lead us to the Promised Land. I was expecting them Yankees to bring us a slice of heaven.

But what they bring is more like hell on earth.

5.

Word on the grapevine was the Yankees was attacking someplace fifteen, maybe twenty miles north of us. I was dizzy with excitement. But then they come marching a whole lot closer and my mood turn itself on its head.

We was three miles from town and I never been there but I knew in which direction it lay. And there wasn't no angels hovering in the sky and there wasn't no blinding glorious light. Sure wasn't no heavenly choir. What there was, was smoke rising. The smell of gunpowder carried on the wind. The smell of burning.

I could hear the cannon, feel it pounding through my feet. Set every nerve in my body jangling. Made every tooth in my head rattle. It went on for two, three, four days and it was bad. But it was worse when it stop. Then there was just a silence hanging over everything like the one before a storm. Any moment the clouds would burst. There'd be thunder. Lightning. Rain would fall. Hard. Heavy. We'd all be needing to run for shelter.

I was in the garden, grubbing in the dirt same as always, when I see clouds of thick black smoke coming from beyond the woods. I'm thinking, Hey! Did Grandma Rideau's place catch fire? How'd that happen?

Then there's a speck in the distance. It's moving fast. That speck turns into a man, and the man's running from the woods across the fields towards the foreman. Foreman jumps off his horse. The man grab him by the shoulders. He scream something in his face. And the foreman throws his straw hat in the air and give a whoop of triumph. And then all the field hands start yelling. They grabbing each other, hollering, cheering. Then they calling out. They start piling into carts, young ones first, men and women reaching back over the sides lifting up the children by their arms, taking hands, pulling the old folks in. Then they whipping up the mules, driving away right off the plantation, stirring up clouds of red dust as they go, moving like every demon in hell is chasing after them. Before I know it the field hands is gone. They left! Run off. Just like that. Hadn't none of them thought to wait for me. Or Cookie. Hadn't none of them thought to wait for any house slave.

I'm still standing there when Amos come running from the smithy. He been close enough to hitch a ride but he wasn't going no place without Cookie. He's looking for her right now but as he reaches me there come the sound of hooves thudding on the road. Hundreds of them. And around the bend in the drive come the Yankee army.

I hadn't never seen no soldiers before but I'd spent a heap of time imagining them. I'd pictured smart uniforms, gleaming boots, fine horses. Men with warm eyes and gentle voices who would speak to us kind. I'd imagined heroes. Gentlemen. Angels.

These was worn-out from fighting, I guess. They was shabby, filthy, mean-looking, reeking of blood and sweat. Wasn't a halo in sight. And wasn't none of them remotely like Moses, Jesus or Joseph.

Me and Amos, we couldn't see the front of the big house from the garden but we knew well enough the master was there. He been sitting on the porch for days, rocking in that chair of his, drinking corn whisky, oiling his gun, watching the driveway, cussing all the time and saying that his pa built this place from nothing, and his grandpa before that, and how he wasn't never gonna let no damned Yankee set foot on his land.

Mr Delaney don't give no warning. He fires at the soldier leading the column. Clips him is all. The Yankee don't even fall off his horse. He don't speak neither. Just cocks his gun, fires it back at the master. We hear Mr Delaney hit the porch deck. Then nothing. He don't cry out. But Ham does. He been with the master since he was a boy. Ham starts screaming, "He dead! He dead! Master's dead!"

The air is knocked from my chest. Can't seem to breathe. The master's dead? Lord above, Mr Delaney's dead? I can't feel nothing. Not sorrow. Not joy. Nothing.

Them soldiers come riding right up to the house and they yelling, "Everyone out. We got orders."

Miss Louellen had took most all the house slaves with her when she went off. But Kissy and Rose is here. They pull Ham to his feet and drag him along to where me and Amos is rooted to the spot. Cookie come running over. We huddling together while the Yankees go storming through the house.

They know precisely what they're doing. They was like the locust plague of Egypt, come to strip the whole place bare. Couldn't have been faster or more efficient. Looting don't take them no time at all. They come back out, pockets stuffed with trinkets. One got Miss Louellen's ear-bobs; another, the master's gold watch. When they done with the thieving they start on the burning.

The barn goes up first. Three years of cotton harvests is stacked high in there: them bales catch real good. Don't seem a moment before that fire is raging, the heat enough to singe our hair even from where we standing. Then they smashing the windows of the big house, throwing in blazing torches. The curtains catch, flames running up from floor to ceiling, spreading from the dining room to Miss Louellen's bedroom above. Ain't long before that fire is poking its fingers between the tiles on the roof. Then it take them rafters in its mighty fist and pull the whole house down.

And them Yankees ain't finished yet. Heck, they only just getting started. Overseer's place, stables, stores, cabins, smithy, cook-house – they all go up in flames, along with the master.

The air's thick with smoke, the sound of roaring and crackling. They kill the hogs. The chickens. The cows. Feathers flying. Shit spilling. And animals squawking, squealing and screaming, screaming, screaming. They're butchered where they fall. Loaded up onto a cart. Rivers of red blood on the red dirt. Red flames. The whole damned world turned red. Scarlet.

Next them soldiers come right into the garden. We're all pinned up against the fence while they're riding their horses back and forward, back and forward, them hooves mashing up the earth until all the vegetables in the garden are trampled down into it. Ain't a mouthful left can be eaten.

By the time they're done, Ham is on his knees, arms wrapped around himself, rocking, wailing, "Master's dead! What do I do? Oh Lord, Lord, what do I do?"

In reply, them Yankees tell him he can stay or he can leave. All of us got a choice. Seems we can do whatever we please now. President Abraham Lincoln himself has proclaimed we're free.

I stood in that stinking mess of ruination, too

deep-down shocked to feel a thing, thinking, Free to do what? Free to freeze to death? Free to starve?

They ready to go riding on out, leaving us there, when Kissy starts sobbing. And it's Kissy's sobbing that changes everything.

She's a fine-looking woman. Soon as she starts up one of them Yankees takes pity on her.

"You a field hand?"

"No, sir. I's a maid."

"You can wash clothes, right?"

"Yes, sir."

He points to Cookie. "You?"

"I's the cook." She put a hand on my shoulder. "She a cook too."

He nods, thoughtful. Points at Amos. "You? What can you do?"

When that man finds out Amos is a smith, his eyes light up like a swamp crocodile's. Suddenly he's weighing us up like we're all on the auction stand.

And then – for the first time in my life – I find I'm walking off the Delaney place. For the first time in my life I see what lies around the bend in the driveway.

Because suddenly it's turned out we ain't quite so free after all. We're being taken right along with the Yankee army. We ain't slaves no more. We're confiscated enemy property. We're officially classed as "contraband".

Don't know how we're supposed to tell the difference.

6.

The Yankees ain't told Ham to come but they ain't told him to stay neither and we can't go leaving him standing there all alone. Me and Cookie take a hand each and bring him with us. The army march and we follow, trudging along at its rear end.

To begin with don't none of us say nothing. Ham was crying, gulping sobs that come up from someplace deep inside of him. But as the hours wore on and we walked further and further away from the plantation he fell silent. His palm was cold as ice in mine. I kept glancing at him sideways. He looked the same on the outside but there was an emptiness within: like a fly once a spider done feeding off it. I couldn't understand. Wasn't like he'd loved the master. Hadn't liked him even. I lost count of the times I heard him cussing the day that Mr Delaney been born. But now he was gone there just didn't seem to be anything left of Ham. I was afraid for him. See, me and Cookie, we was useful. So was Amos. Officer's horse tread on a stone, mule go lame, wheel come off a cart, he was running every which way fixing things up. But Ham was a gentleman's valet: he didn't know nothing else. What in the heck was he gonna do in the middle of an army, in the middle of a war?

After a while Cookie starts sucking her teeth and grumbling about Kissy and Rose and, What in the Lord's name had those two girls been thinking of? Kissy had rode off the Delaney place on a Yankee's horse, perched sideways in front of him, his arm tight around her waist. He'd give her Miss Louellen's thieved ear-bobs and they been dangling from her lobes. What she was gonna give him in return didn't take much imagining. Rose been pulled up onto the back of another horse. Cookie was saying over and over that no good would come of it but my head was too full of other things to care. Besides, it wasn't like either of them had any choice.

The master was dead. It banged around in my head with each step I took. The Delaney place was burned and the master was dead.

Something been torn in two. Was like them Yankees had picked up one of them big heavy ledgers Mr Beecher used to write in and split it down the spine. The past been thrown to the wind, the pages blown away. Them old rules was gone. What was left was blank sheets ready to be writ on fresh. There was a whole new world beginning. But I didn't much like the way it was starting out. Someone was writing it all wrong.

I kept thinking, who was gonna tell Miss Louellen? How was she gonna know her husband was dead? How was them children gonna know their pa was gone?

That question snagged in my head and I couldn't shake it. Someone should have wrote her a letter. Sent a telegram. Ridden off with a message. I don't know why I had me such a thing about it. Wasn't like I was especially concerned for her feelings. But there been right ways of doing things. There been order. Now there was none and it wasn't glorious, like I'd imagined. It scared me half to death.

As we walked on I was hoping things would get better. That things would take shape. Come together. Make sense. But they didn't. The further we went, the worse it got.

War is supposed to be armies fighting each other, ain't it? Soldiers against soldiers. Men against men.

But these Yankees wasn't fighting Confederate soldiers. They was doing what they done to the Delaney place over and over again: burning women out of their homes. Old folks. Children. Babies. We kept passing big houses that been razed to the ground, just the chimney stacks left, standing to attention like soldiers on guard duty. And a heap of white folks in carts heading off to Lord-alone-knows-where. Guess they had cousins someplace safe, like Miss Louellen. Families that would take them in.

But their slaves? Heck! Where was we supposed to go?

Where was we all meant to live? What was we gonna eat?

We was trailing along a path of destruction. Looked like Judgement Day. Now, I ain't never seen a railroad so I ain't exactly sure what they supposed to look like. But I'm sure as sure them rails ain't meant to be wrapped around trees like neckties. Sure telegraph wires ain't supposed to run along the ground neither.

"Why the Yankees doing this? Why they smashing everything up?"

Ham don't answer. Neither does Cookie for a long while. It's only when Amos come back from fixing something and start walking by her side that she turn to face me.

"They're ripping their enemies' hearts out, child." There's something in her eyes I ain't seen before. She look about a million years old. "If you take away what somebody cares for most … well, then, they don't have no fight left in them. Ain't no reason to go on struggling."

Amos puts his arm about her and she rests her head on his shoulder. I feel that knife twisting in my gut. She talking about them Confederates? Or she talking about herself? She had something took away? What? When? I don't know what she talking about. How come Amos does?

"But it don't make sense!" I says. "It don't make sense!"

Don't neither of them try explaining.

It don't make sense. It don't make sense.

Them words keep pounding between my ears. By the

45

time we stop walking my head's almost splitting. My feet is all wore-out – they ain't used to this. But I can't go sitting down and resting. One of them Yankees is yelling for Amos. Another is yelling for Cookie. Me and her, we spend most all that night boiling up the master's hogs for them troopers. Then we got to stand there, bellies grumbling, watching white folks eat. Some things don't never change.

By the time they had their fill there's barely a mouthful for me and Cookie. Ain't none at all for Ham.

We was smarter after that. Next time them Yankees gone thieving meat and hand it over to me and Cookie to prepare we hide some. I stuffed the wing of the chicken I been plucking inside my shirt. I keep the neck too. And the heart and the liver. Cookie tuck one foot of the hog we about to start boiling right down her bosom. We waited until all them soldiers had done eating. By then it was dark and they had other things on their minds. We poked what we got into the dying embers of the fire. Wasn't much, but it kept us alive. I figured so long as we was careful, the three of us could eat.

We didn't need to worry about feeding no one else. Kissy and Rose was being taken care of by their gentlemen friends. And Ham was gone. Don't know what happened to him. When we lay down to sleep he been there. Come the morning he wasn't. Must have wandered off. We tried calling him. Yelled ourselves hoarse. Seemed he'd just melted away like butter into a yam. We couldn't go looking for him. As soon as the sun was up, we was on the move again.

It went on and on, one day much the same as the next. Days become weeks. Nights, we slept on the ground in the open, no roof to keep the rain off, not even a blanket between us. Daytimes we walked and we walked and we walked and the number of folks walking along behind the Yankee army gets bigger and bigger. Some been told to come. Some just followed because they didn't know what in the heck else to do with themselves. Seemed to me the men was all right but the women didn't have it so easy. By night most of them was given over to entertaining soldiers. Some was willing. Some wasn't. Their willingness or otherwise didn't seem to concern the soldiers none. If they couldn't persuade or pay a woman to lie down with them they'd carry on regardless. Them soldiers' appetites was nigh unquenchable. Sometimes you couldn't sleep for all the grunting and squealing going on under cover of darkness. Sounded like hogs in a swamp.

Well, whatever Amos had heard from Josiah, and whatever he'd heard from Ham, and whatever he'd heard from the Rideaus' Walter outside the post office in town, I figured they all been hearing plain wrong when it come to the Yankees.

"You sure they want us freed?"

"I'm sure," says Amos.

"Only they don't act no different to the master and Miss Louellen."

"They civil enough to me," says Amos. But he's lying. I hear the way they talk to him: *Boy, do this. Boy, do that. Shift your lazy nigger ass. Get your worthless black hide over here.*

Cookie knows it as well as I do. But he's her husband. She weave her fingers through his and give me a real hard look that tell me to hush my mouth even if she ain't saying the words out loud. "This here's a war," she says. "Guess folks is all kinda crazy right now. They be different when peace come."

"You right," says Amos. "Things be better then. You'll see."

I wanted to believe him. It give me something to hope for. Meantime, we had to pass through a place where there been fighting. There was bodies smashed up, left out in the open so the flies and the rats had got to them. Made me heave my guts up, so I stopped thinking. Stopped trying to make any sense of it. Concentrated hard on getting by. Walking, head down, eyes on the dirt. Seemed we'd wandered right on into hell. Didn't know how it had happened – we must have took a wrong turn someplace. Any day now the Devil was gonna appear and shake us by the hand.

I knew that day had come when we reached the end of the world.

We stopped walking. And, when I lifted up my head and looked around me to find out why, I could see we'd

48

stopped walking because there wasn't no more land to walk on. In the distance there was just water, as far as the eye could see. And a smell. A fresh smell. Kinda pleasing. A tang of salt in the wind.

"Well, look at that!" Cookie put an arm around my waist. She's gotten smaller. Or maybe I got taller. All of a sudden I can rest my chin on the top of her head. "Hey, girl! We walked all the way to the ocean."

Seemed we'd reached the eastern shore of America. Amos got called away to fix something or other, but he listened good while the officers was talking. When he find us later that night he says there a town along the way and the Yankees are hell-bent on taking it. There gonna be a battle some day soon. But right now we're staying put in this big old foul-smelling army camp with a bunch of loose-living Yankees and some truly worn-out women.

But I guess Cookie was right: the heart been ripped out of them Confederates. Don't seem to take more than a few days before the folks in that town give themselves up. They roll over like puppy dogs, show their soft bellies to the Yankees, wag their tails and beg to be treated nice. I'm expecting them soldiers to go storming on through there. To hear more screaming, see more smoke. But they don't.

The army rubs its hands together, tips its hat and says, "Thankee kindly for surrendering so nice. We gonna leave your buildings standing as a reward." Then it sit down on its pimpled white ass and has itself a nice long rest before it march north to start thieving and burning and killing all over again.

But this time we don't follow.

This time, when the army start marching Cookie, Amos and me get up like we been told. But we ain't gone far when Cookie turn her ankle in a rabbit hole or some such thing. She fall down. Her foot start to swell so Amos tear a strip off her skirt, wet it in a stream and start to strap her foot up. By the time he finish the army is along off up the road. They two hundred yards away already. And hadn't no one come back yelling at us to get our butts moving, or to shift our lazy hides.

Cookie look at Amos, Amos look at Cookie, they both look at me. Don't none of us say nothing. But we stay put. Sit tight. And when the army is out of sight, we turn our heads in the other direction and we start walking, fast as Cookie's ankle will allow.

We didn't know where we was going. Away was all. That first day we just headed blind. Hunkered down that night in the burned-out shell of some big house. Hadn't had a bite to eat.

Come the morning Amos went raking through the ashes of the slave quarters. Found the head of a shovel in amongst them. Handle been burned clean away but he had his whittling knife – Amos was never without that. He cut a branch off a tree, fashioned it into a good-enough handle to make that thing just about useable.

It was that shovel saved us from starving. The Yankees had trampled down all that been growing in every garden we come across, but there was some things buried too deep for them horses' hooves to smash entirely. We lived on potatoes. Yams. Raw, because we didn't have no means to light a fire. Not until a few weeks later when we was wandering through a clump of woods and we come across the body of a dead Yankee lying curled between the roots of a tree.

Well, we seen enough by then to know his pockets and his pack would have been rifled through long ago but we looked just the same. And it was good we did. That man can't have been killed in no battle. He must have gone off alone. Deserted, I guess. Or got left behind. Because no one had thieved his belongings. There was strips of jerked beef in there and some hard-tack crackers. And – praise the Lord! – a box of matches.

For a long time we was well and truly lost. Wandering, just wandering. Keeping moving in the hopes of finding someplace better tomorrow than the one we was in today. We avoided people, black and white. We'd take a wide detour around where there was big groups of freed slaves camping out, looking dazed and hungry. There was always a real bad stench hanging over them places. You could tell just by breathing it in that Sickness was standing in the shadows: that it would probably be carrying off them folks long before Hunger did.

Them days was dark and they was desperate. But then come a morning when I woke and the air seemed to smell different. The wind had changed direction. There was something familiar in it. Something that was calling to me.

Amos and Cookie was for going east, but I grab Cookie's hand and start dragging her behind me. "This way. We got to go this way."

I had this feeling, deep down inside, that now I wasn't going away from something, I was going towards it. The closer I got the stronger that feeling become. We walked all that day. By the time the sun was ready to go down, the earth seemed to be humming beneath my feet. I was footsore, half starved, bonetired, but when we come over that last rise, when I look across the fields below me and see that curving river, that hump of hill, that clump of woods, I start running.

We'd come right back to where we started: the Delaney plantation.

The place was deserted, it was bleak, and it was godforsaken. But to see that land: oh my sweet Lord, it was like being small, snuggling under Cookie's arm. I lay down flat, took me handfuls of that red earth and squeezed it through my fingers. I was rolling in it every which way like a hog in muck. Heck, I even hugged the cottonwood! I pressed my face against that bark, smelled that old familiar smell and felt that I'd come home.

There was just one cabin that wasn't entirely burned to the ground. It was the one furthest from where the big house been. Its walls was scorched and its roof was caved in on one corner but it was just about standing. That feeling of being back home was powerful good. When we hunkered down our first night I wrapped myself up in it like it was a blanket.

But you can't live on a feeling. Can't light a fire with it. Can't eat it. Come the morning our bellies was emptier than ever and we didn't have nothing to put in them.

There wasn't a scrap left to eat on the place. Someone had already dug up what been left in the ground. But hey! There's the woods and there's the river. Amos goes off to set some snares, see what he can catch. Things is gonna turn out fine. I'm singing when me and Cookie set off gathering firewood.

I forgot the whole county was already crawling with folks who had nothing. All the fences been torn down, taken away. Was a miracle that cabin been left. Wasn't a stick of timber on the place. We didn't find more than a heap of damp branches. When Amos come back at sunset he had one small fish for the three of us to share, that was all. Seemed there wasn't no possums left in the woods. There wasn't hardly no fish in the river neither.

We survived that winter grubbing around in the dirt like hogs for whatever we could find. I don't care to recall what we ate. Some things is best forgotten.

By the time spring come, our clothes was hanging off us. We was little more than skin and bone but one afternoon Amos come home – empty-handed, but smiling.

Now, we didn't see nobody but ourselves from one week's end to the next – news was months old before we got to hear it. But that particular day Amos had run into a man who been trying to fish down along the river who told him we been declared free.

"I thought we was already," I says.

But no – it turned out there was a difference between President Lincoln proclaiming something and them fine gentlemen in Washington agreeing he could do it. They been arguing back and forward all this time. Amos says now they passed the Thirteenth Amendment. The Constitution been changed. Slavery is dead.

Well, I was way past trying to make sense of what white folks did. I didn't understand any of them big words. Couldn't see what difference it made: we was still starving.

But what Amos said next made my jaw drop wide open. Seemed them Confederates had surrendered. It taken four long years but the war was done. Over with. Finished.

"Ain't no more North and South! No more Yankees and Confederates! No more slaves and masters." Amos is grinning so much his face is split in two. He squeezing Cookie so tight he gonna bust her ribs for sure. "We all one now. We the *United* States of America!"

Well, that *did* make a difference. As a matter of fact, that changed everything. I figured we could take ourselves into town. Find ourselves some work. Start to live like regular folks. How did regular folks live, anyhow? I was itching to find out.

7.

I guess I was around about fourteen, fifteen when we finally went walking into town. I wanted to try that word "freedom" on for size, see how it fit. Amos and Cookie had took some persuading to come along with me. I been on at them for days. They was for keeping their heads down, lying low on the Delaney place. So they wasn't saying much but I was whistling through the gap in my teeth all the way there, telling myself things was gonna be fine and dandy from now on in. We're free! Ain't we reached the Promised Land?

A whole way of life been blown away. Didn't no one know what was coming around the corner now. To me the air seemed full of hope. This was a new start, wasn't it? We could make the world the way we wanted it. I was busting to get going.

What I didn't know was how deep down sore the white

folks was about having the rug pulled out from under them. Guess they was scared too, and it seems scared white folks is mean white folks. Scared is dangerous.

As we walked on into town they was watching the three of us. Men, women, children. Rich gentlemen right the way down to poor trash, all staring as we go on by. After a while that multitude of eyes weigh heavy on my skin. I stop whistling and start worrying. Didn't none of them folks look ready to stroll on up, shake us by the hand and offer a fair day's pay for an honest day's work. Wasn't nothing for us to do but keep right on walking. But it didn't feel like we was the Israelites entering the Land of Milk and Honey no more. It felt like we was the Egyptians who followed Moses into the Red Sea. Like there was walls of water standing high on both sides. And we wasn't gonna make it to land before them walls come tumbling down.

Ain't none of us never looked for work before. Didn't know where to begin. Who to ask. We're walking, wondering, when a voice call, "Hey, brother." He skinny as a rake and his clothes is hanging off him in ribbons, but he seem friendly enough.

"Hey." Amos give him a nod.

"You looking for the bureau?"

"The what?"

"Freedmen's Bureau. It down there on the sidewalk, see? They help you."

Amos give him another nod and we set off towards it.

But we don't never get that far.

We was going along the sidewalk when we see this piece of trash coming towards us. She wearing a new silk dress. Scarlet. It so bright I damn near have to shade my eyes. Her face is painted like she a china doll sitting on a sideboard. The word "whore" is written in the air over her head in letters about a mile high. She's hanging on the arm of some man.

He don't even glance our way. His head is cocked on one side listening to something his lady friend is telling him. They powering along the sidewalk straight at us.

Now we was free. Abraham Lincoln said so, and them fine gentlemen in Washington agreed. It's official. Amos and Cookie been repeating it over and over like a prayer, like they was finding it hard to believe they finally got what they been wishing for all these years. And I guess deep down in their hearts they didn't truly believe it. Soon as Amos and Cookie seen them white folks coming, they step off the sidewalk and into the mud. Keep their eyes lowered, like it the master and Miss Louellen coming at us. Like they still someone's property.

Amos and Cookie. I see the two of them, standing there together, arm in arm. Pressed close, shoulder to shoulder. A wedded couple. Leaving me out of it. Always the third. The extra. The spare. Always in the way.

That knife twists in my belly. It's like I'm a child again. Mad as hell. They're slipping in the mud, but I ain't moving.

I ain't going nowhere! I figure, if I'm free, ain't I got a right to be on that sidewalk? I'm staying put. And I sure ain't lowering my eyes to the floor.

Now that sidewalk was wide enough for all of us. If them white folks had turned a little itty bit, they'd have got past, sure enough. Didn't have to be no problem about nothing. But they walk on like I'm not there. Like I'm made of glass. Like I'm invisible to the naked eye. I stand still. I ain't going nowhere. As they draw level, that man look at me. His eyes meet mine.

Next thing I know, that whore lady has banged her big old hooped skirt into me so hard it's risen right up and the whole town gets an eyeful of her pantalettes.

Well, a woman don't show nothing of what's beneath her skirt but an inch of slipper. Leastways, not in public, not even if she's a whore. What I seen of that woman's legs was downright indecent. Made me gasp loud enough for them both to hear. After that she's clutching her chest, reaching for her smelling salts like she's going to swoon clean away. The man is holding her arm, fanning her, but all the time he's looking just about ready to strangle me with his bare hands. Folks is gathering round us and every single one of them pink and ivory faces look mean as mean can be. I ain't simply been uppity – I done insult a white woman. And I'm just about scared witless at the thought of what might happen next.

But nothing did happen. Not there. Not then. A Yankee

officer come out of the Bureau. He seen a crowd gathering and come to find out what the fuss was. Folks melted away like snow in sunshine. The three of us walks out of town real quick. We head back to the Delaney place, checking over our shoulders the whole way to see we ain't followed.

No one had come after us. Well, not that we could see. Didn't mean we felt safe. Amos and Cookie was too scared even to be mad at me. We sat in that cabin, avoiding each other's eyes, not talking, twitching every time the wind rustle the leaves or a bird fly up sudden. Amos was whittling a piece of wood down to nothing until it got too dark to see. We didn't light no fire.

I was out of my mind with fear, but I still fell asleep. Guess Cookie didn't. In the dead of night she heard the sound of horses coming hard and fast up the drive. I hadn't gone looking for trouble. But she know right away that trouble had come looking for us.

Cookie grab my shoulders and push me down into the yam cellar. One second I'm sound asleep and snoring, the next I'm crammed in a hole in the dirt floor no bigger than a tar barrel and twice as dark. She's hushing me and telling me not to make no sound. She lay the boards over my back. So I hear what happens even though I can't see none of it.

Amos figured the Lord would protect him and Cookie. They ain't done nothing wrong, after all: they stepped down into the street. And Amos always was a praying man.

He starts singing. Couple of verses of "Swing Low, Sweet Chariot" and he figures they'll be safe. His voice rises up and Cookie's joins it, twining around his like honeysuckle. They singing like a pair of angels but down in that cellar I'm wishing they'd turn tail and run.

Because it turned out them white folks was a whole lot scareder and meaner and more dangerous than any of us could have imagined. Didn't care who they lynched. White woman been insulted? Hell, some nigger's got to pay! Wasn't long before they had Amos strung up to a tree. When that was done they turned their attention on Cookie.

While Amos is choking, he's listening to his wife's raping. While they raping Cookie, she's listening to her husband choking. And I'm listening to it all, and I can hear them men whooping and yelling and laughing. Laughing. Laughing. I know their eyes is popping with the thrill, and there ain't nothing I can do about none of it. They having her right there, right there above me. There's animal sounds – grunts, squeals – the stink of men. Mating. Sweat. Whisky.

But that ain't the worst part. That ain't the worst part. The worst part is that I know one of them. I know that voice. I know that whoop, that whistle. I ain't got no idea what he been doing all these years. I ain't got no idea why he come back. But that him all right: that's Jonas. Ain't no mistaking his laugh, his squeal, high-pitched as a hog's. His smell.

It in my nose, down my throat, it choking me. It filling my head and I got my fists in my mouth to stop from sobbing and I'm praying and praying for it to stop. The words of all Amos's songs are whirling round and I'm begging Moses to come, begging for that band of angels and that sweet chariot to carry us all away. But I guess the good Lord ain't listening. Or else he got a strange way of helping folks who ask him for it. Turned out it ain't enough just raping Cookie. When them gentlemen done finish they string her up alongside of Amos. Then they torch the cabin.

Given a choice between staying quiet and burning or getting out and getting raped and lynched I chose to burn. Not that I had any kinda choice. Truth is, I was too much of a goddamned coward to move. I was so deep down terrified I passed out. When that first torch come flying into the cabin – when I hear Jonas cry, "Got ya!" – I fell somewhere so dark I might of been dead.

8.

I lived, which was lucky – or not – depending which way you look at it. The walls and roof of that old cabin were damp. They didn't catch good. Fire had died not long after I passed out. When I woke my back was aching and my head was hurting like hellfire but that was all. Wasn't a scratch on me.

I come out of that yam cellar like a rabbit out of his hole. First thing I saw was Amos and Cookie twisting in the breeze like they was dancing, real slow. Their faces was all wrong. There was this silence. Just the creaking of the tree and the scratching of ropes against the bark.

Well, when you see a sight like that you gonna do one of two things. Either you gonna lay down and die. Or you gonna carry on living. You gonna survive.

Don't get me wrong. I ain't no hero. I tried the laying down and dying option first. I was so scared and sorrowing, so eaten alive with guilt at what I brung to Amos and Cookie's door that I lay me down and hollered till I couldn't make no more noise. I yelled for the Almighty to strike me dead. I prayed for the good Lord to fetch back that band of angels and that sweet chariot and carry me away from there like He done Cookie and Amos. I wanted to go right along with them. But He didn't send me nothing. Seemed I didn't have no choice but go on living. After a while I stood up again, sucked in a deep breath, and wondered what in the hell I was gonna do next.

Amos's whittling knife was still in his belt. They'd grabbed him so quick he'd never had time to fetch it out. Besides, what use would a blade that size be against a gang of men fired up on whisky?

I cut them both down. Took a while. Ain't ashamed to say I couldn't see sometimes for crying. Was hoping all them things Amos said about heaven was right. Hoped they was together someplace a whole lot better than this. Singing, right along with the angels.

I picked up the shovel. Couldn't dig more than a shallow grave in the plot behind the cabin but I done it. I rolled Cookie in. Covered her over. But before I done the same for Amos I took off his shirt and britches.

What kind of a girl steals the clothes off a dead man's back? A desperate one, that's who. Them things covered me good. I figured if a mob come looking, I'd get lynched. But if I was wearing these then maybe, just maybe, they'd skip the raping part. By the time I walked off of that godforsaken plantation, I'd become a man.

I took Amos's knife too. Wasn't much of a weapon but I wanted to have something sharp in my hand. Felt safer that way. I turned my back to home. Was bent on getting about as far from it as my two feet would carry me.

I don't rightly know exactly what happened after that. Was just a whole heap of empty days and lonesome nights. I was hurting real bad inside. The only thing that stopped the sorrow swallowing me whole was that I was mad too. I was burning mad with Cookie. Flaming mad with Amos. Raging mad with the both of them for standing there singing when they should have been running; for thinking the Lord would protect them; for going off to heaven together and leaving me down here all alone. I was raving at the two of them, and I was raving at Jonas and every white man had ever walked the earth, but mostly I was raving at myself. And so long as I was doing that I was staying alive.

I didn't pay attention to no one. Walked along with anyone travelling in the same direction. There was a whole bunch of freed slaves who was off their plantations. Most of them was field hands who didn't know nothing but planting and picking. After a few weeks of wandering they was heading back to where they come from because there wasn't no work to be had nowhere else. Was a stream of faces I can't recall. They was shadows in a bad dream.

Remember one thing though: they all looked at me kindly. They shared what food they had – if they had any – and talked nice. But after they'd spent a night by the roadside in my company they was glad to see the back of me.

See, I'd drift off to sleep, then straight away I'd start dreaming I'm back in that yam cellar. Only this time I ain't passed out. This time I don't stay hid. I'm curled there and someone's pulling back the planks, real slow, and I'm so scared I shit myself. He's holding a flaming torch in my face. The heat's crackling my skin like pork. I can't see no more than his outline. A halo of golden curls dancing in the firelight. But I can hear his voice. And I can feel the rope around my neck. Rough against my skin. Tightening.

Every night I woke up screaming. Drifted off again, dreamed the same dream again, screamed again. Over and over. Kept it up until sunrise. Wasn't no getting away from it. Each and every time I dreamed that dream it ended with my feet dangling, kicking against the empty air while Jonas Beecher stood watching. Laughing.

9.

They tangled themselves together – dream and memory – until I didn't hardly know which was which. I couldn't tell whether I was alive or dead. Seemed most likely I was a ghost, that I'd be wandering for all eternity.

There was times I'd try telling myself that I hadn't seen Jonas. Hadn't seen any of that lynch mob. I'd been face down in that cellar, eyes tight shut. I'd tell myself it couldn't have been him. His pa went away. Whole family was gone soon as the war begun. He just couldn't have come back. Cookie would have yelled out his name. Pleaded with him. Said something. Besides, he wouldn't have done that to her. Not to her! He grown up right there on the Delaney place. He couldn't have done something like that. He just couldn't have been with them men: my mind been playing tricks on me!

But I kept walking.

One time I fell in with a family with a broke-down wagon and an even more broke-down mule. Never did know their names – never asked them – but they was good to me. They heard on the grapevine there was pay and lodgings to be had working in the mines. And if there wasn't, there was factories in the North. So I went along with them.

Didn't occur to me till I saw them mines that they was underground. Since them men come calling I'd gotten real scared of the dark. The notion of being underground all day give me the shakes. And I ain't never seen nothing so bad as them miners' cabins. Slave quarters was bad back on the plantation but at least the air been clean. At least there been woods to snare possum and rivers to catch fish. If I had me a choice I'd prefer to be a field hand. Cotton picking was real hard labour but it was out in the open.

I looked about me and figured that if that mine was bad then maybe them factories was even worse. That family was looking at me sideways. And all of a sudden I was tired of being a burden. Tired of weighing heavy on other folks. I'd gone and got Amos and Cookie killed. Maybe I was better alone.

So I took myself off, walking westwards again. Don't know how long I done that. Days? Weeks? Months? I plain don't know. Don't know how far I went neither. Could have been ten miles, could have been one hundred, could have been one thousand. I just kept setting one foot down and then the other followed right along.

I thought the Lord didn't care none if I lived or died but I guess I was wrong. Because all the while I was roaming the country no harm come to me, though I seen sights that would make the Devil weep. Seemed there wasn't nothing some folks liked more than the sight of thick white rope around a thin black neck. One morning I seen a whole family dangling heavy from sagging trees like they was ripe fruit ready for picking. Not just the grown ones neither. There was children. All sizes, right down to a tiny baby. What manner of a creature would do that to an itty-bitty baby? Felt like I'd walked straight into the heart of hell this time. And this time there didn't seem no way out.

But one fine day a cart come rumbling up behind me. Wasn't no sweet chariot, and the driver wasn't no angel, but it sure carried me home. Leastways, it carried me to the closest thing I could call a home. Sitting on that cart was a bent old man who give me a good looking-over before he says, "Where are you heading, son?"

Son. He takes me for a man, same as everyone else done. "No place special."

"Can give you a ride to the next town," he says.

"There work there?" says I.

"Some. Climb on up."

And that's what I done.

He was carrying a load of lumber and I was glad to go along with him. Was so darned tired I was finding it hard to keep dragging one foot along after the other. But if I needed a ride, he needed company just as bad. That man was a talker. Charley was his name and he had a heap of things he wanted to get off his chest. Didn't none of them make me feel no better. He seen whippings and burnings and killings just about every place he passed through. He seen folks starving, dying by the side of the road. Didn't seem to be nowhere in the whole damned country I could live safe.

I didn't do more than grunt each time he paused for breath. I didn't feel much like talking. Couldn't speak about what I'd seen. Couldn't tell what I'd done. Couldn't say what, in God's name, I was going to do next. Wanted to sit, just sit, put my fingers in my ears, empty my head, not even think. Didn't like what ran through my mind when I was thinking.

Most of what Charley said flowed clean over me. But then I hear, "… President Johnson pushed it through Congress. The army taking on coloureds now."

Something snag in my head. "Johnson?" I say. "What happened to Abraham Lincoln?"

Suddenly he looking at me like I'm plumb crazy. "Hell! Where you been all this time, son? He dead."

"Dead?"

"Yep. Long time back. Got himself killed. Wild, crazy Confederate sonofabitch shot him."

It takes a while for that to sink in. I got no idea of

whether it happened before Cookie and Amos been killed or after. Before – news been hard to come by. And after? Well, after, I wasn't in no state to take anything in. Folks could have been screaming it in my face and I'd never have heard nothing.

Yet now I had. Guess I was waking up some. Coming back to life. But I figured that if the white folks been scared and mean enough to kill their own president, what in the heck chance did I have of surviving? If it wasn't Jonas, it would be some other man. Yankee, Confederate: as far as I could see they was both the same. I might as well give up right here and now.

A silence fall. For a while there's just the creaking of the cart and the horse's hooves on the dirt road. Then Charley start up again.

"You know, son, from what I hear the army be happy to take on a young buck like you."

A young buck like me? I look at my shirt. My britches. They in a parlous state. I might look like a man. I sure got him fooled. But do I look like a soldier? Is he messing with me? I mean, the army? The army?

I says, "They pay anything?"

"Thirteen dollars a month."

"Is that good?"

"Enough to live on, I guess."

The cartwheels keep rolling. I don't say nothing.

"They giving food too. Lodgings. From what I hear."

Food in my belly? A roof over my head? Money in my hand? All three at the same time? Sounded too good to be believed. Sounded like the Promised Land. Still, the army? I seen what them soldiers done. I couldn't go acting like that. But maybe I wouldn't need to.

I says, "War's over, ain't it?"

"Surely is."

"What they need men for, then?"

"Keep the peace, I guess."

Keep the peace. I liked the sound of that. "I'll get me a weapon, won't I?"

"'Spec' so."

Them words filled my head with something other than darkness. They warmed my belly with a kinda fire. My mind was racing.

I'd grown a whole head taller than Cookie. Been as strong as Amos almost, before he died. Hadn't no one took me for anything other than a man the whole time I been wearing his clothes. If I signed up, well, there'd be some practical difficulties. But I was on the flat-chested side. A thick army jacket would cover up what I got growing on there. And, from what I seen, soldiers slept in their clothes same as slaves: I wouldn't never need to go stripping in front of nobody.

Of course, I couldn't piss standing up. But I'd already solved that problem by making out I needed to shit every time my bladder was busting. I'd squat down behind a bush.

Didn't no one ever come looking to check my leavings.

As for them monthlies, I was lucky: they didn't come regular and they wasn't never heavy. A pocket full of rags and an imaginary shit sorted that problem out too.

There was the question of shaving to consider. Right now I was young enough to pass for someone whose whiskers hadn't started to push through. But when I got older? I figured as long as I lathered up, shaved like every other man then wouldn't no one look too close at my baby-smooth chin.

I glanced sideways at that cart driver.

Folks see what they expect to see. Charley thought I could do it. And if he figured I was man enough for this, why wouldn't they?

By the time we drove into town my mind was made up. I surely didn't have nothing to lose. I was for the army if they'd have me.

Charley drops me by the recruiting office doors.

Wishes me luck.

Drives off.

And I take a real deep breath and walk on in.

10.

I stand there, in front of that desk.

"Name?" says the recruiting officer.

"Name?" says I.

He looks at me. "Name," he says again. "What do people call you?"

Heck! What do I tell him? Cookie called me child. Girl. Honey, sometimes, when the mood took her. The things other folks called me ain't fit to repeat and I can't tell him the name my Ma give me. Charlotte was a fool, fancy thing for a slave. Was a downright crazy one for a soldier!

But hey, guess I can pick my own now. I can be anyone I damn well please!

Only I can't come up with nothing. He's staring at me, tapping the end of his pen against his teeth. So I say the first thing that come into my head: "Charley." Figure that cart driver won't mind me borrowing his name. I'd mumbled it, though. Sound like I'm ashamed of my very existence so I try again. Louder, deeper. "Charley, sir." I even try giving him some kinda salute.

He writes *Charley* down in his big old book and then says, "What's your surname, Charley?"

"Surname?" I says.

He's looking at me like I'm soft in the head. "Surname … your second name. You do have another name, I take it?"

"Yes, sir," I says, real slow. My heart's thumping and my palms is getting damp. I ain't never needed no second name before. Only time we was ever called by one of them was when we was off the plantation. When Ham went for the mail folks called him Delaney's Ham to tell him apart from the Rideaus' one. I was never off the place until the Yankees come and I ain't needed no second name then, neither. I guess I could have picked just about anything. My head was spinning trying to think but all that I come up with is another big fat nothing. I look out of the window and there on the side of the building across the street is painted the words *O'Hara's Ready Remedy: A Cure for All Ills*. So I says, "O'Hara." Then – finally – I have an idea so I add, "That's Charley T. O'Hara, sir."

"What's the T stand for?" says the officer.

"Tecumseh," I says, thrusting my jaw out. I figured I'd take one from General William Tecumseh Sherman.

"Age?" says the recruiting officer.

"Eighteen, sir."

He give a sniff like he ain't fooled but he don't say nothing, excepting, "Sign here." He turns the book around. Points where I'm supposed to write.

Sign? I think. Now, what in the hell am I supposed to do? I look at him, trying to figure it out and he's staring at me like I'm a flea-ridden cat or a lousy dog. His nose is puckered up too, like he can smell something real bad and I know it's me.

I done learn all kinds of new things since Amos and Cookie died. One of them was that when a man gets strung up he soils himself. I'd washed out Amos's britches since then but I guess I hadn't done too good a job on it. Hadn't cared much on the road but in the warmth of that office I was aware of the stench rising from my rear end.

"Are you literate?" he says again. "Can you read and write?"

Well, I ain't never held a pen in my life but I can read well enough. Mr Beecher had sat under the cottonwood tree teaching Jonas his letters the evenings Mrs Beecher was out at her sewing circle. The overseer had always yelled for me to come and fan them, keep them cool.

Truth be told, Jonas wasn't none too smart. His pa was patient but it took a whole heap of time for his son to learn. There wasn't nothing for me to do but stand and listen and watch. Mr Beecher draws out the letters in the dirt for

76

Jonas to say out loud over and over. Before I know it, the alphabet's drummed into my head like the words of one of Cookie's stories.

One evening Mr Beecher come with a book. I'm looking over his shoulder and his finger's moving along the line of black shapes. And suddenly them squirming little things on the page form themselves into something that make sense. Jonas was stumbling to spell it out but I saw "cat" long before he did. Saw the whole darned sentence. I almost said it out loud. Was so shocked I dropped the fan. It hit Jonas on the head and I was sent back to the cookhouse. Mr Beecher didn't never go calling on me to fan them again.

I didn't tell Cookie. Didn't tell no one. I recalled too clearly what happened when the master found out Ezekiel could read. Had the book-learning beat clean out of him. I breathed me a big sigh of relief that Jonas never figured out what I could do.

But maybe Mr Beecher did. Because once in a while I'd catch him looking at me. Watching. Just watching. Wondering, maybe, if I was gonna give myself away.

I look at that recruiting officer. Telling the truth ain't worth the risk. I shake my head and he sighs and I can see him thinking, "Ignorant darkie!" so plain he might as well have writ it in big black letters right across that page.

"Make your mark, then," he says. "There."

I take up the pen in my fist and scratch an X. Before

the ink's even dry he slams the book shut.

And, for better or for worse, I signed away my life to the United States Army.

That very same day me and a whole heap of other raw recruits was shipped on out. We was all freed slaves, far as I could tell. Must have been a hundred or more of us. I wasn't worried about where we was headed. West, was all. Further away from the Delaney place. Further away from home. Further away from Jonas.

It felt good to be surrounded by a crowd. A big crowd, heading the same way. Felt good being told what to do. Where to go.

Then we set foot on that paddle steamer and for a long while nothing felt good at all.

I ain't never been on a boat and I sure didn't like the way that thing rocked and rolled. Sight of that brown water boiling either side made me sick to the stomach. I started retching and soon my head was spinning so bad I had to cling onto the rails to stop myself falling in.

Everyone was keeping just about as far away from me as they possibly could and I can't say I blamed them. The only recruit come near was a fella by the name of Henry. He was a great bull of a man – nothing but muscle. Me retching and spewing my guts up didn't seem to bother him none. He was like a dog that'll come and rest its head in your lap when you're feeling blue. He stuck close to me the whole time. Didn't say nothing. Didn't do nothing. Just stood there, staring out along that horizon, solid as a rock.

In between them retching bouts I come up for long enough to see there's a big old dent in the front of his head.

"What happened there?"

"Where?"

"There. Right there. On your head."

He run his finger around the edge, then give it a poke in the middle. It go in halfway up to the first joint. He looks kinda surprised, like he only just noticed it. He shrug. "Don't know. Fell, I guess."

Maybe the reason wasn't worth remembering. But it looked to me like he been hit hard enough one time to near cave in his whole skull. It had healed on the outside, but something been knocked loose in there and his thoughts didn't hang together the way they should. Guess we was two of a kind.

I was thankful for him being there, and I was a whole lot more thankful when the riverboat stop and we get to marching to some fort. Truth be told it wasn't far but my legs was hell-bent on giving up on me. Henry took hold of the back of my britches and swung me along like a rag doll every time I stumbled.

By the time we arrived the sun was going down, streaking the sky with scarlet and turning the river that was winding in big, easy curves behind us red as blood. Ahead and to either side there was rolling hills, some wooded, some not. The fort we fetched up in was four lines of long, low buildings set around a square of open land. There was plenty of soldiers there already. One, maybe two hundred white faces glowing like ghosts in the twilight all staring in our direction.

We get fed. Hot food. Beans and salt pork. Plenty of it. Coffee. Then we get given bedding and we get told to settle ourselves down in the tents that are grouped maybe half a mile down along from the buildings where the white soldiers sleep. And maybe the ground underfoot is on the marshy side and maybe the tent canvas has got some holes in it and maybe the seams are split in places, but I ain't had even that much over my head in a long, long while. For the first time in my entire life I got me a full belly. I got a good, thick blanket all to myself to roll up in. The men in that tent are talking and laughing with each other. But I'm so tired I go right off to sleep.

I didn't dream. Didn't even stir until the bugle sounded next morning and we was called to get up. That was the first night since Amos and Cookie was lynched that I hadn't woke up screaming.

11.

The first thing they done was hand out uniforms.

Back on the Delaney place we been given clothes once a year. Shirt if you was small. Just one. If it wore out before next ration day you'd be walking around stark naked. Them shirts was wove from flax so scratchy on the skin it was worse than rolling on an ant-hill. Cookie worked on it night-times, kneading it between her hands until it was soft enough for me to wear without driving me plumb crazy. When I got bigger the master give me a skirt too. But I ain't never had no shoes.

And now here I am, being handed a pair of army boots. Leather. Up to the knee. And more clothes, almost, than I can carry.

They was clean enough but they sure had seen some action. The pants was close to being worn through at the knees but they was one hell of a lot better than Amos's britches. I was mighty glad to ditch those. I kept his shirt though. Pulled the army one right on over it. Then come the jacket. Blue, trimmed with yellow. Close-fitting, down to the hip. Bright, shining metal buttons. Cloth was good and heavy, but when I pull it on I see mine has got a hole over the heart. It been patched but looked to me like a bullet been put through it sometime. I guess I was in a dead man's clothes again. But I wasn't complaining.

Got me a cap, to keep my head warm, with a leather peak to keep the sun and the rain from going in my eyes. On top of all that I was given a long coat. Mine was so big on me, it started a fella by the name of Reuben laughing. He offered me his, standing there bare-chested while he said, "This here's smaller."

I shook my head. "I'm good." It hung almost down to my ankles. Covered my chest, my ass, covered my privates. That was all I cared about. That, and the fact that it would keep the wind out. I hadn't never had nothing so fine.

We was given our weapons next. Got me a sabre fixed to a belt that go around my middle, but no rifle. We'd be getting them later, we was told. I found that disappointing.

Now I didn't know nothing about how the United States Army was organized. Soldiers was soldiers, as far as I was concerned. Yankees rode horses. Confederates marched barefoot. That's what I learned in the war.

If I'd known anything at all I'd have signed up for the infantry. But I'd walked into a cavalry recruiting office. I knew that was a big mistake the moment we was told to take a horse each and saddle up.

I didn't know nothing about the army but I knew even less about horses. The closest I'd come to handling anything with hooves was before the Yankees burned the plantation. There was a man come from the mill sometimes with a mule named Yeller, piled high with sacks of flour for Cookie. Yeller might have been called a mule, but I knew that creature was the Devil in disguise. Every time he come the man told me to hold Yeller's head while he unpacked his load. Guess it made him smile to see me struggling so bad. That creature would jerk his head up, lift me clean off my feet. Drop it down, dump me in the dirt, take a bite out of my belly. I never did find me a way of dealing with Yeller without getting hurt.

Standing there thinking on Yeller and Cookie and looking at that army horse I was suddenly hit with grief so bad it near bent me in two.

Then Henry sticks his head under the neck of my horse. He's working himself into a muck sweat. "You know what to do, Charley?"

"No."

"Me neither."

I mean, I got the saddle on, but fixing the straps to the buckles in the right places was another matter altogether. Henry was perplexed as me by it. Lucky for us a recruit by the name of Elijah knew what he was doing. Turns out he been a smith before the war so he can tell one end of a horse from the other. He give me his animal to hold while he buckles all the straps up right. I watch real careful so as I can do it next time.

Seemed I wasn't the only dumb recruit in that place. The troopers on guard duty – their shiny white faces sticking out of new-made uniforms – was damned near splitting their seams laughing at us. None of us knew how to get a saddle and bridle on a horse. Elijah was real busy. And all the time them horses was getting twitchier and twitchier.

When Elijah was done helping out, he come back and takes his own horse from me.

"You know how to ride?" I says.

"Nope." Elijah smile. "You think my master gonna let a worthless heap like me on top of his horses? I ain't never sat in no saddle in my life."

The man who's giving out the orders is called Captain Smith. He looking a little perplexed by now but he finally give the command to mount. We does our level best but what follows is enough to make his eyes pop.

We're strapped up with sabres at our hips and water canteens across our chests. Was just as well we ain't got no rifles because them sabres was enough to get in the way. Add rifles in and we was likely to have all been killed stone dead. I couldn't see for the life of me how to get all the way from the ground up onto that critter's back. As soon as I get one foot in the stirrup the animal starts walking forward. I have to hop along to keep up. Can't get my foot out but can't jump up neither. I hop clean across the parade ground like that. Animal only stops when it reaches the water trough and lowers its head for a drink. That's when I make my move. I grab the front of the saddle and give a great heave. My leg gets tangled with my sabre, but I manage to throw it across his back before we're off again.

I ain't got no notion how to steer the thing. But if I'm faring badly them other recruits is faring worse. All about me horses is snorting and squealing and men is cussing fit to make a preacher's ears bleed. I see Henry's horse kick its heels up. It come back down, then stands right up on its hind legs, pawing the air like a lady's lapdog, begging for a treat. Henry comes flying off, crashing into the muck heap. A man by the name of Isaiah is flat on his back in the dirt. One by the name of George is yelling his head off because his horse is treading on his foot and he can't shift it.

Elijah's critter is running in circles around the parade ground and he's begging it, "Hey! Hey, horse! Horse! Don't do that! Whoa! Stop!" But that animal don't pay the blindest bit of attention. It gallops clean out of the fort, starting a regular stampede. Mine follows along with the rest of the herd and I find myself begging and pleading like Elijah.

"Mind the fence! Horse, stop! Stop! Hey, stop!"

Guess I was lucky. Luckier than Elijah, anyhow. My

mount proved to be plain greedy. Soon as he feels good grass underfoot he slows down to a trot, then stops dead. I get thrown onto his mane and before I can set myself right he lowers his head to snatch a mouthful of grass. I slide down the length of his neck real slow, reach the ground and roll sideways onto the turf. Wasn't a dignified ending to our glorious cavalry charge, but at least I ain't landed in the muck heap like Henry. Least I ain't disappeared over the distant horizon like Elijah.

I lie flat on my back for a while, waiting for my heart to stop thumping. Feel like all the breath been knocked out of me. Was half hoping the horse would run off again so I don't have to do nothing more with it. But it don't. It just stands there, chomping. So finally I have to get back on my feet and figure out what to do next.

I can see a few soldiers coming back. Some was leading their horses, scared to get up in the saddle in case they took off again. Most had lost their horses altogether and was walking on their own. A few must have taken a bang to the head because they was weaving from side to side like the master did when he was drunk. All of them done lost their caps.

I look at that horse of mine and he looks right back and I decide there ain't no devilment there, not like there been with Yeller.

"Look here," I says. "I don't know you and you don't know me, but we in this together. If you don't go running away with me, I won't go kicking and whipping you. You got that? We got ourselves a deal?"

He lowers his head and goes back to cropping the grass. I cram my cap down hard on my head. I been licked by a mule but I was damned if I was gonna be beat by a horse too.

I take them reins real gentle. Don't pull his head up. Figure I'll let him eat while I work out how to get back on. Get my left foot in the stirrup, my left hand on the front of the saddle. Then I give a little jump like I seen white folks do and haul myself up there. Don't seem so hard doing it the second time.

My horse was mighty easy-going, truth be told. When I give a tug on the reins he lifts his head and starts strolling towards the fort. I don't have to do nothing but sit there. But I'm the only recruit from Company W who come back into that fort on horseback. Got me a nod from the Captain. Got me a clap on the back from Henry. Was so darned proud of myself I couldn't keep this big old smile from breaking out across my face.

One by one the rest of the recruits trickled back in. The Quartermaster and one of the other officers rode off in search of the horses. They brought all of them back, excepting Elijah's brown and white one. And after an hour or two there still ain't no sign of them.

"Thought he been a smith," says Reuben. "How come he don't know what to do with a horse?"

When he hadn't shown after three long hours of watching and waiting Captain Smith took a party off looking for him. And because I come back riding I had the dubious privilege of going along too.

We didn't find Elijah's horse till nearly sundown. It was grazing quietly near the river, about six yards from a stunted tree. Couldn't see no sign of Elijah.

"Must have come off somewhere else," says the Captain. "Lord, he could be anywhere. I hope to God he's not injured."

My mouth fall open. Can't help it. That's the very first time I ever heard a white man sound concerned for a black one. Does he mean it? Or is he fooling?

Just then we hear a rustling, and Elijah's face pops out of the leaves halfway up the tree. He been thrown there by his horse and his canteen strap was caught on a branch. He was held so tight he couldn't get back down and it took me and the Captain a while to get him freed.

We didn't ride back into the fort till after dark. Me and Elijah was ordered to take the horses and bed them down while Captain Smith reported to the General. Their voices drifted out of the officers' quarters on the cold night air.

General Michaels is just about laughing his head off at the mess we made of things. But the Captain ain't joining in. He saying how he been too hasty with us, how he been expecting too much, that it was him was at fault, not us. He needed to go more slow, he said, teach more careful. While

Elijah show me how to give my horse a good rub-down we can hear the Captain promising his superior officer that, come what may, he gonna lick us all into shape.

12.

Next day, Captain Smith has us all stand shoulder to shoulder. As he marches up and down the line he tells us we're part of a new-formed regiment. Ain't that something to be proud of? We're Company W. And we got ourselves a fine and noble job to do. Folks is flooding in from Europe, coming to settle in America, Land of the Free. Every single day hundreds, maybe thousands of them are setting out in wagon trains, heading west, taking hold of the empty wilderness and turning it civilized. They're carving ranches out of nothing, building homesteads, churches, towns. And them brave, upstanding folks are in need of our protection. He starts talking about honour and patriotism and nation building and a whole lot more besides.

Well, I didn't go joining the army to defend nobody. I wasn't interested in upholding the nation's honour. Only person I was interested in protecting was myself. Only honour I wanted to preserve was my own. But hearing Captain Smith talk gets something stirring deep inside of me. I start wondering if maybe I can't be part of something. Something big. Something fine.

When he finish he come to a halt right in front of me. I can feel him look me up and down, real slow. His eyes are sliding over every inch of me and I'm feeling hot and cold all over. Can he see through this uniform? Damn! Has he found me out? Am I gonna get kicked out on my ass already?

Whatever he's thinking, I learned my lesson. I ain't never looking no white man in the face again. This time I'm keeping my eyes fixed firm on the ground.

"Chin up, O'Hara."

"Sir?"

"Chin up. Shoulders back. Eyes ahead."

"Sir?"

"Come on. Like this. Look up. Look at me. I won't bite."

I can feel the sweat coming. Is he messing with me? What's he planning to do? There's a whip in his hand. He's gonna flick me across the face with it the second my head come up. Punish me for sassing him; punish me for impersonating a soldier. Hell! I ain't got no choice. I lift my head.

He don't hit me. He look me in the eye. Simple. Straightforward. Like it's a natural thing to do.

He got eyes the same colour as Jonas.

And all of a sudden I'm small again and I'm being swung through the air. Someone's got their arms under mine, their hands clenched tight across my chest, and they whirling me in circles under the cottonwood tree and I'm laughing so hard my face is aching. And whoever is swinging me is laughing too. Squealing, almost. High-pitched. Like a hog.

That's all there is. Just that one little flash. Then I'm back in the here and now, looking my commanding officer square in the face. He's smiling at me.

He slap me on the shoulder. "Good man."

Relief come washing over me. I'm safe. But I'm mighty puzzled. Why's he being so kind? All I can think is that he must be sick in the head. He got to be the craziest captain in the entire army.

Well, crazy he may be, but he sure knows his job. For the next few days he has us up on them horses and he's teaching us to ride and we're at it until our rear ends is so sore can't none of us hardly sit down. Nights we was laid flat out in them tents complaining.

"I never knew I *had* bones in my ass!" Reuben's a fine-looking man. Only he don't look so fine lying on his belly with his legs spread, trying to fan his behind with his cap.

"My bones is cutting clean through my skin." George's hands is cupped over his butt cheeks like he's trying to push them back in.

"My knees ain't never gonna hold me up again," says Isaiah.

"Your knees is bad? My legs just about ready to snap off at the hips!" Elijah's on his back, rubbing his privates. "And I just about worn these balls of mine off."

"Your wife gonna have something to say about that, Elijah!" says Reuben.

Isaiah tells him, "She gonna have to go someplace else she want to get more babies."

Well, I didn't join in but neither did Henry. I was keeping myself to myself and Henry just wasn't quick enough to keep up when they got to messing with each other. He sat there, smiling and nodding, but the sense of what they was saying mostly passed him by. But so long as we both laughed along didn't nobody mind how quiet the two of us was.

The Captain could train us all he liked, none of them other officers believed we was ever gonna shape up. They'd sit around on the porch outside their quarters evenings and damn near split their sides over what happened when we was first given the order to mount. They tired of that particular source of hilarity after two, maybe three weeks, because by then we could all of us ride well enough to keep a tight column and do a passable charge.

Instead they started remarking on our level of general competence and wondering aloud about the wisdom of allowing men of colour to sign up for the army in the first place. "What in God's name were they thinking of in Washington?"

It didn't surprise none of us excepting Henry. Whenever he heard them his eyes would go wide and he'd have the look of a puppy dog that been kicked. "Don't they want us here, Charley?"

"Guess not."

"Why'd they let us sign up, then?"

"I don't know."

Henry wasn't the only one puzzling things out. The last few weeks I hadn't heard a voice that sounded like the master's, not once.

"They all Yankees, ain't they?" I asked the others.

"Sure are," says George. "Ain't no Confederates allowed in the army."

I recalled what Amos said. "I thought we was the *United* States now."

"Yep. But they started the war. Them Yankees don't want to put no guns in no rebels' hands."

"Why'd they fight for our freedom? Can't none of them stand the sight of us."

Elijah spoke up. "Yankees wasn't fighting about us. We was a sideshow is all. It was a white man's war. About who's in charge. Who's the biggest rooster in the yard. Who's sitting at the top of the woodpile."

Henry asked again, "But why'd they let us sign up?'

Couldn't none of us answer him.

Henry was on the simple-minded side. I figured his question didn't much matter. But maybe I should have been asking that same thing myself. Maybe we all should.

I put it to the back of my mind. I was more occupied with trying to figure out Captain Smith. Any time he heard them whitey troopers shooting their mouths off about us he'd speak right on out. He'd take on the officers too. One time he even done it to the General.

General Michaels was sitting there, saying loud and clear, "Allowing volunteer regiments in wartime was one thing. But I see no reason to have coloureds in the Regular Army now. They're simply not up to the task."

Captain Smith didn't sass his superior but he wasn't going along with him neither. "They lack training," he says real calm and reasonable, "but they've been in the army less than a month. Give them time."

The General come right back. "It's a question of raw material, Captain. If that's inferior, the finished product will never make the grade." His eyes fall on Henry. "Some of your men don't seem to have the sense of children!"

Captain Smith give him a smile. "Children, you say. And yet children grow, sir, and are nurtured and educated as they do so. With the right encouragement I see no reason why my men shouldn't make fine soldiers."

"Care to make a wager of it?" says the General. "Ten dollars says your coloureds will never match the standard of my troopers."

Me and Henry watched them shaking hands on it. He told Isaiah and George; I told Reuben and Elijah. By the time we bedded down for the night word of that wager had spread through Company W's tents like a fire through cotton bales. Before it was even dark we was all bragging, talking big and swearing solemn that each and every one of us was gonna prove General Michaels wrong.

13.

Day followed day and we was being drilled most all the time, on our horses or off of them. We was issued rifles – Spencer repeating carbines – that felt good and heavy in the hand. Them things had the bullets lined up in a magazine in the butt; could fire off seven shots, one after the other, in as many heartbeats. Leastways, they was supposed to. Mine had a habit of getting itself jammed no matter how often I cleaned and oiled it. Was the same with my pistol: Colt .44 single shooter with a hammer that was prone to sticking. Seemed my weapons was as independent-minded as my horse.

We practised shooting until our trigger fingers was just about dropping off. I soon figured out that so long as I aimed a little to the left with my rifle, a little to the right with my pistol, I could hit the centre of my target every time.

After that come the inspections which covered everything from the cleanliness of our sleeping quarters to the cleanliness of our socks. Heck, we weren't even allowed to gather no fluff between our toes.

Didn't none of us mind. The war had turned the world on its head, but it was over now. Company W was settling down into place, like the dust after a storm. We been slaves: we was used to doing what we was told. But there was something different about being in the army. Something new. For the first time I was following the orders of a man I could respect. A man who might be plumb crazy but who seemed to respect us, who looked us in the eye, who wanted to see us do well. Not just to please him. To please ourselves.

We all of us picked up army routine quick enough, excepting Henry, who was on the clumsy side. He was always dropping his sabre or falling off his horse, climbing back up again with that big, empty grin spread across his face. The Captain never got mad though – I never once saw that man yell at him. I did my best to help Henry along, shining up his boots, fastening his buttons, tightening his belt, so he'd be ready on time. I even took to running him through the manual of arms when we was off duty and Henry improved some, but he always stayed one beat behind the rest of us.

Yet when it come to it, it wasn't Henry let the Captain down. It was me.

★ ★ ★

Now the way things worked was this. Guard mount happened in the morning, and most all the officers and their wives and families turned out to see it, there being so little else to do in that place. While we was training we didn't take part, us being such a goddamned shambles to begin with.

But then the day come when the Captain decides we're ready to be drilled along with the whiteys.

I hadn't paid much attention to them. Their quarters was a building along one side of the square parade ground. We was kept separate down in them tents. We didn't have no reason to mix. It's only when we're all lined up there together that first time that I catch a glimpse of golden curls out the corner of my eye.

And then my heart's pounding; my throat's dry; I can't breathe. Feels like I'm having a seizure.

I'm supposed to be eyes front, like the rest of them. But I can't help myself. I got to take a look.

I turn my head, and when I do I'm so relieved my knees give way just for a second. It ain't him. Thank the Lord! It ain't Jonas.

"You all right, Charley?" Reuben's right next to me.

"Yeah."

"You know him?"

"Who?"

"That man you was looking at. Angel Face."

"Nope."

The relief's so strong it's turned my insides to water. I have to run for the latrines. Get there just in time. I was one second short of soiling myself.

I caused one hell of a ruckus on the parade ground, doing what I done. I can hear the whiteys' laughter rising up while I'm sitting there, my pants around my ankles. I figure I'll be lucky if I don't get thrown out of the army. Gonna get me a beating at the very least.

But I don't get whipped. I don't get kicked. I don't get yelled at. Don't get no punishment from the Captain at all. He just tell me to get back in line. He give me a wink and advise me to visit the latrines before guard mount next time, not in the middle of it. I feel the shame of what happened, but he don't seem to.

We went to guard mount every morning after that. And every morning the cleanest and best-drilled soldier got chose to serve as orderly for the commanding officer. It was an honour. A reward for doing your soldierly best. Those was army rules and regulations.

The name Reuben give that golden-haired trooper stuck. Them first few weeks you could lay money on the fact that if Angel Face was on duty, he'd get himself chose, him being something of a dandy and a kiss-ass who was forever sucking up to General Michaels. If Angel Face wasn't around, one of them other whiteys would get lucky.

But bit by bit we got better. Sharper, tighter, more soldierly. Captain Smith was proud of us, and we started to take pride in ourselves. Started to feel we was a unit; we was a team. Even Henry was just about getting by.

I was planning on keeping my head down, and my mouth shut. On being a good soldier. Not too good. Just good enough. Passable. I was aiming on drifting along somewhere around the middle where I wouldn't get noticed.

Problem was, Cookie done train me too well. After Miss Louellen gone running off there was times I been put to helping Rose and Kissy with scrubbing and polishing the big house. Cleaning and shining come so natural to me I didn't even think about it. And that's what landed me in more trouble.

This one particular guard mount Captain Smith is in charge so he goes up and down the line once we been drilled. He's real careful with his inspection, and he lingers a long time, going over every inch of my horse. I'd got attached to that animal by then. He was funny-looking but he had a kind eye and a big heart. I'd named him Abe and I took pride in caring for him good.

Captain Smith gives me a nod and then looks over Reuben's horse. Elijah's. Henry's. He goes back along the white troopers. Eventually he reaches Angel Face. Takes a real close look then comes back to me again. And all of a sudden the air's thick with unease. Everyone's wondering what's going through the Captain's mind. Some of them officers is shifting like they got ants crawling up their butts and their wives is whispering behind their hands.

Captain Smith points to Angel Face, pulls him out to the front. Well, there ain't no surprises there. The officers' wives breathe a big sigh of relief.

But then he points to me and Abe. And we gotta step forward too.

Well, if this was a beauty contest, there wouldn't be no trouble deciding it. Angel Face and his prancing pony beat me and Abe hands down. But this ain't about beauty. It's about cleanliness. And it's about drill.

So he puts us through our paces and I'm squirming at being the object of all this attention and I'm wondering if I should make a mistake. Drop my rifle. Miss a move. But I can't; I just can't let Company W down.

He has us off our horses, and we marches left and right and front and rear. We goes through the manual of arms from beginning to end and we was neck and neck in perfect time – you couldn't have squeezed a dime between us.

By now there's a murmuring from the officers and some of them ladies is looking a little faint, but Captain Smith ain't even aware of the concern he's giving them. He still can't choose between us so he marches us both off to the guardhouse and there – in a side room – he tells us to pull off our boots.

Well, by now I'm getting mighty anxious about how

far this inspection is gonna go. If I got to take my coat off, if I got to remove my shirt ... goddammit, there are two itty-bitty things he's gonna notice! There's a hand clutching at my guts at the notion of me getting exposed, but, truth be told, Angel Face is looking mighty anxious too – though I doubt his reasons are the same as mine.

Our socks is clean as each other's so then – Lord alive, save me! – we has to drop our britches! We standing there in our long woollen underwear.

Well, mine was clean on that morning but it looked like Angel Face hadn't changed his for more than a week. Some of them stains was ugly. And stinking.

So I get to report to the commanding officer as his orderly and straight away he send me off to fetch Captain Smith. The General asks him if Angel Face was on duty and when Captain Smith nods he says, "Then why did you send this man?"

"Because he was the cleanest and best-drilled soldier, sir," says Captain Smith.

Well, General Michaels don't even look at me. Captain Smith is speaking truthful but it don't make no difference. The General says I'm allowed to stay that day but in future he wants Angel Face.

Captain Smith's expression don't show nothing. He says slowly – like he's just trying to get things clear – "That's your direct order, sir? Despite regulations?"

The General says, "yep", and leaves it at that. Captain

Smith has made his point and I pass a long day running errands for a commanding officer who can't stand the sight of me.

But the General never did get to have Angel Face as his orderly again. That pretty boy was mocked so bad by them other whiteys, they made him feel so shamed to be beat by a nigger, he done desert during the night.

When I get back to Company W that evening they're so happy to see me they whooping and calling and patting me on the back. They raising me right up on their shoulders and carrying me all around in between the tents. I can't keep my head down no more, nor keep my mouth shut. They won't let me. I'm kinda mad at myself, but mostly I'm feeling good. Real good.

"You beat that cuss!" says Reuben and he slap me so hard he almost knock the teeth clean out of my head. "Captain Smith gonna win that wager for sure."

But it seemed the General wasn't handing his ten dollars over any time soon. Next day we hear him tell the Captain that all them drills don't mean nothing. We got to prove ourselves in the field before he'll believe any one of us will make the grade. And we gonna get a chance to do it real soon. Orders has come in.

We being sent out to fight Indians.

14.

I knew about Indians.

After Miss Louellen gone I been put to waiting at the master's table, working the fan mealtimes – pulling that string, stirring up the air, keeping the flies from settling. One time old Grandma Rideau and a bunch of other folks come over to eat with him and they got to talking. I recall the master saying Indians been on Delaney land before they give it over to white folks. They just been squatting – they ain't hardly done nothing with it. His grandpa been years getting the trees cut down, the stumps hauled out, the weeds and the vermin cleared off. It taken three generations of slaves to get the place properly civilized.

Old Grandma Rideau been picking at her teeth, staring into space, not looking like she was listening at all. But when Mr Delaney stop to draw breath she start talking, soft and quiet, as if she all alone in the room. She saying how her whole family been murdered by Indians when she was no more than an itty-bitty girl. How she lain in the long grass and watched her ma and pa, her two sisters, her brother, getting their throats slit like hogs at killing time.

It been enough to make my blood run cold back then. Give me bad dreams. But now? Well, I figured Grandma Rideau got to be ninety years old or more! It happened a long time ago. Them months I been walking all over the country I ain't never come across no Indians. Not one. Wasn't none left as far as I could see.

But here's Captain Smith saying that the next day we gonna be met by scouts who gonna lead the whole of Company W out across the hills, over the horizon, towards a different river to the one we come down on that paddle steamer. When we reach it we got to ride along the bank until we come to the crossing place. A man by the name of General Sullivan is gonna wait there for us to join him on the other side. Then we going off to a different fort. We got to be up, fed and ready to ride by four o'clock in the morning.

The names of places and marks on maps didn't mean nothing to me. If the Captain told us precisely where we was going it went in one ear and straight out the other. All that fixed in my head was that we was gonna be crossing through Indian territory.

Indian territory? What in the heck was that?

Guess we all must have looked kinda troubled because

Captain Smith tells us not to be alarmed, and that the tribes living there are perfectly civilized. It's the ones beyond we gonna be dealing with: them are the ones we got to subdue so the good citizens of America can settle on their land peaceable.

I didn't know what none of it meant. All I knew was that up until now the army been about drilling. Training. More drilling. Not much else besides. The prospect of doing something for real turned my insides the wrong way out. I could act like a man. Didn't mean I could go fighting like one. If it come to combat, I plain didn't know if I had what it took. Hell, I'd seen the bloody mess men was capable of making of each other!

I wasn't the only one who seen some sights during that old war. To tell the truth, we was all scared witless. But when you scared witless, you can't let it show. You got to cover it up by talking big. Started as soon as we was dismissed.

"Them Indians is cutting up rough," says George. "They killing innocent folks. Running off cattle, violating women, murdering babies. We gonna end their thieving ways."

Reuben got his eyebrows raised. "How we gonna do that, George?"

"We the United States Army, ain't we? We're Company W. We gonna strike fear into their hearts. We gonna show them we so damned powerful there ain't no point them fighting. We gonna kick their butts so hard they be breathing through their assholes by the time we done finish with them."

"We gonna fight?" says Henry. He's at my elbow, smiling like he about to get his Christmas gift from the master.

"Yeah, we gonna fight," I tell him. "We gonna fight real good. You feeling brave, Henry?"

"Yeah, I'm brave. Ain't I?"

"Sure you is."

"You'll look out for me, won't you, Charley?"

"You know I will. No harm ain't gonna come your way. We all be watching your back."

That night I dreamed I was on the plantation. Standing there in the dining room of the big house, pulling that string while Grandma Rideau was telling how them Indians come creeping along on their bellies like snakes. Then the dream changed and I was lying in the grass. Someone was slithering towards me, moonlight glinting on the knife in his hand. Only it wasn't no Indian, it was Jonas.

It come as something of a relief when the call come for us to get ourselves moving. By four in the morning the hundred or so men of Company W was all saddled up and in line, the equipment we been issued by the Quartermaster loaded nice and neat in the wagons. The sky was only just beginning to turn from black to grey when them scouts arrive. We move on out after them and they was way ahead and it was still so dark I couldn't see nothing – they was just shapes in the distance is all. It's only when the sun come up and bring colour back to the world that I notice their skin.

They're dressed like white men. But they're dark as me. Some of them darker. Yet their hair hang smooth and straight.

"Who in the heck are they?"

Captain Smith is coming down the column checking his men. The question slip out of my mouth as he draw level with me.

"Indians," he says.

"Indians? Ain't we supposed to be fighting them?"

"Not this tribe, trooper. They're the civilized kind."

"But they working for the army? Helping us go fight other Indians?"

"That's right. Sounds complicated, doesn't it? Guess it is." He crack open a smile and ride on down the line.

Well, that has me puzzling real bad for a moment. I didn't know there was different kinds, and Indians against Indians didn't seem to make no sense. But hadn't the Yankees and the Confederates both been white? Didn't stop them tearing each other apart. Wasn't no point trying to figure folks out. They was all mystifying.

We follow them scouts for around three, four hours and we're heading more or less westward all the time, so I'm happy. When we come to the river we turn north and ride along the bank until we reach the crossing. The ferryman's supposed to be expecting us but his boat's way over on the other side.

Captain Smith asks one of them Indians, "Where is he?"

The Indian points. "He lives in that house."

"Call him up, would you? Find out why he isn't here."

That ferryman ain't in no hurry to help nobody. The Indian just about hollers his head off but it's a long time before the door open and the ferryman come out yawning and scratching his ass and whining that he ain't had no breakfast. He says he ain't doing nothing till he's eaten his fill because working on an empty stomach is inclined to give a fella indigestion and he's damned if he's gonna give himself bellyache on account of the army.

Time's marching on but we surely ain't. Captain Smith turns to that Indian.

"Can your men steer the boat?" he says.

The Indian nods his head. So there's a heap more shouting and the ferryman agrees to bring that boat over just so long as them Indians take him straight back so he can fill his fat belly with whatever manner of breakfast he desires while they fetch the whole company from one side to the other.

That trashy white man pushes that ferry over with a long pole. Looks mighty unstable to me and I guess Abe's thinking the same because he starts snorting and running backwards like he don't want to set a foot on them planks. Soon as it bangs into the bank them Indians start work loading it up. Can't take more than a few horses at a time so getting us across is gonna take a while. Especially as me and Abe is still going backwards and by now we're almost at the rear of the column and there ain't nothing I can do about it.

Before the ferryboat's even got the first load across General Sullivan and his men show up on the far bank – about a hundred white faces staring across at us, none of them looking remotely friendly.

General Sullivan is mad that we ain't ready and waiting like we're supposed to be and he gives me and Abe a particular hard look because by now Abe's going in circles.

I'm cussing under my breath and praying that Abe would just stand still but he don't. He's jumping now. Little rabbit hops. Going up then coming down four-square. Damned nearly breaking my neck each time he does it.

There's another load of shouting, yelling back and forth across the river, while Captain Smith explains the reason for the delay to the General, but he ain't prepared to wait. Soon as the ferry hit the far bank General Sullivan takes one of them Indians as a guide and then sets off, leaving us to follow as soon as we're able.

That ferry boat come and go and come and go and finally most all of Company W is across; but me and Abe still ain't going nowhere. I'm just about in despair because I can't do nothing to control my horse and I'm feeling mighty foolish when one of them Indians comes and takes Abe's reins and whispers something in his ear. All of a sudden my horse stops the running backwards and turning circles and jumping like a jackrabbit. He stands still, ears pricked forward, and then he lets that man lead him straight onto that ferry and all the time I'm sitting there on his back like a big baby and I feel so mad that I want to spit in that Indian's face.

The sun's high in the sky by the time all the wagons and the horses has got from one side to the other. That good-for-nothing ferryman is just sitting down to another meal when we're finally ready to follow the General's trail.

We're assembled on that bank and ready to move but Captain Smith gives a yell. For a moment I think one of them Indians has stuck a knife in him. But no, he's leaping off his horse, throwing the reins at me and running into the bushes. Thinking his bowels must have given up sudden I turn my head away.

But two seconds later a turkey flies up, startled. Captain Smith shoots the thing stone dead and then he's back, bird in one hand and a pair of eggs in the other. He slings the turkey in the cart but he wraps them eggs up real careful and tucks them inside his coat to keep them warm. We're all kinda surprised but don't nobody say nothing and off we move again.

The further we go, the flatter and the scrubbier the land

gets. It has a godforsaken feel to it but the Captain don't seem to notice. He keeps asking them Indians questions. Questions about the plants and the animals we're passing by. Questions about them and their folks.

As a general rule men – black or white – is mighty fond of the sound of their own voices. They don't truly hear nothing from nobody else unless it happens to coincide with their own opinion. Captain Smith was the first man I knew that really listened to what a person was telling him. He paid close attention when them Indians talked and I did too and the more they talked the more puzzled I become.

See, I figure folks got to have someone to love. Someone to look up to. But they got to have someone to hate just as bad. Someone to look down on, to peck at, just like chickens in a yard.

With the white folks, the big plantation owners pecked at the smaller farmers, and the smaller farmers pecked at the crackers, who was poor but respectable. The crackers pecked at the white trash, who lived on handouts, wallowing shameless in poverty like hogs in a swamp.

Guess we had ourselves a pecking order too. Mammy and Ham at the top, then the house slaves. Amos and Cookie was in the middle. Field hands was down at the bottom.

About a million miles lower than the lowest field hand was them Indians. Everyone pecked at them. I'd heard Mr

Delaney say they was just animals in human form. They didn't have no souls. They was nothing. Less than nothing.

Yet there was this Indian talking to Captain Smith about his schooling. That man had book-learning? He done say it been arranged by the tribal government, whatever the hell that was.

"You a Choctaw?" says Captain Smith.

"No," says the Indian. "Cherokee."

When I hear the word "Cherokee" I damn nearly fall off Abe. I'd heard of them. It was Cherokee land the Delaney place been built on.

Hell, Cherokees got to be the biggest dumbass fools in the whole of creation! The plantation been good farming land. Yet they'd signed it over to the Delaneys and chose to come out to this scrubby patch of dirt? What the devil was wrong with them?

I figured you can dress an Indian in white man's clothes, get him to read even, but it don't make him smart. You can teach a bird to talk, don't mean it understands nothing. Cherokees? Why, they all got to be as soft in the head as Henry!

15.

We finally catch up with the General about an hour before sundown. He'd stopped where the ground was more or less level and there was patches of yellowing grass for the horses. I unsaddled Abe, give him a rub-down and, once I fed him the corn in his nosebag, I led him out on a rope so he could fill his belly some more. It was starting to get dark by the time the supply train come rolling in. Reuben and Elijah made a makeshift corral by stringing lariat ropes between them wagons so I tugged Abe away from the grass – was hard work; Abe never did like to stop eating – and put him in with the others.

Them Indian ponies was kept separate. Their front legs was hobbled – tied together – so them animals couldn't wander far but they could graze all night, which was more than Abe could do. Made me feel sorry for my horse.

General Sullivan and his men was hunkered down in

tents but it seemed Company W hadn't been issued with them. I don't know if the Quartermaster back at the fort had fouled up or if supplies just couldn't be had. We was finding out that if ever equipment was running short it was Company W who had to go without.

We slept beneath the stars, great coats rolled up, tucked under our heads. Might have been all right if the air hadn't been filled with mosquitoes. Every time I dozed off I'd get one buzzing in my ear. Spent most of the time awake and whacking at them. We all did. You could hear it regular – a chorus of *slip-slapping* the whole night through. And in the morning we was covered with bumps. Looked like we'd been afflicted by plague like them Egyptians in the Bible.

We spent the next day itching and scratching. It was punishing hot, and soon them mosquitoes was joined by a host of swarming flies. Couldn't hardly see through them. If you opened your mouth to talk they'd fly right on in. They was in our ears, up our noses. Made us real twitchy. Made the horses even twitchier. Henry's set to bucking and he never could sit through one of them equine explosions. He come off more than once. I would have helped him if Abe wasn't doing much the same thing. Most all my attention was on staying in that saddle.

But I noticed the herds of cows we was riding by. They was being tended by more Indians and I guess these was Cherokees too because the scouts seemed to know them. The flies was so bad they'd lit smoky fires to try driving them away. Wasn't working. One of them scouts told Captain Smith that some days the cows was driven plumb wild and ran off into the swamps where they was drowned. Hearing that made me even more sure of my opinion: them Cherokees didn't have the sense they was born with.

We didn't stop riding until it was real late. We was tuckered out by the time we made camp. We been in the saddle from before sunup to nigh on sundown, just a few stops along the way to water the horses, let them graze some. When I got down off Abe my legs near give out – didn't seem to be no bones left in them. All I wanted to do was get my head down and sleep. The scouts hobbled their horses and tucked right into some food. But the rest of us wasn't allowed to because General Sullivan start giving out new orders.

If Captain Smith was a listener, General Sullivan was the opposite. Them horses been fine last night in Elijah's makeshift corral. But now General Sullivan looks at Elijah. Then he says to Captain Smith, "Ever seen a stampede?"

"No, sir," he replies. "I can't say I have."

"A stampede's a dangerous thing, Captain. I've seen a herd of horses tearing through tents, destroying everything in their path. Do you know, one occasion I witnessed a whole company of cavalry crushed to death? Men, pulped beneath their horses' hooves. It wasn't a pretty sight."

The General knew we was all listening. Could tell he wouldn't have minded seeing Company W going the same way. He didn't let up, neither. He go on and on, till he got us all staring sideways at our horses like they planning to trample us to death soon as we fall asleep.

The General says the horses ought to be tied to picket pins – nice and far apart so their lines don't get tangled. He give the order. Only it turns out we wasn't issued pins neither – Elijah can't find none on the wagons, which is why he'd made the corral the way he did the night before. But the General's got his mind made up. He wants them horses tied to picket pins and so that's what has to be done. Any second he's gonna stamp his foot and sulk like Miss Louellen done when she wanted to get her own way.

Well, we didn't have no picket pins so we got to make them. Instead of eating our beans and salt pork and settling down to sleep we got to spend the next hour or so splitting wood. Isaiah done most of it on account of him being a carpenter back in the old days. Once them pins was made they had to be driven into the ground, which wasn't no easy task. All the time we was at it the General was passing remarks about the goddamned foolishness of letting the likes of us join the army.

We heard it all before. Didn't none of us pay much attention, not even Henry.

It was dark when them horses was tied up according

to the General's satisfaction. I was so darn tired by then I didn't bother eating, I just lay me down and shut my eyes.

I was sound asleep when the ground under me started shaking. There's something so deep down wrong about the feel of solid earth trembling that it jerks you right awake.

Now what startled them I never did find out. Could have been anything. There was plenty of snakes about. Horse sees one and it darn nearly jumps clean out of its skin. Or it might have been them flies biting in a tender place. The General said later it was us caused that stampede: someone had to be blamed and couldn't none of Company W go answering back. Seemed more likely to be one of them whitey troopers' idea of a joke. Whatever the cause, truth is, it only takes one horse to spook, and panic spread through a herd like wildfire.

Every single one of our horses had ripped out his picket pin. They was charging about the camp, dragging them pins along the ground, screaming and setting each other off until they was all worked up into a lather. Now just one horse seems like a mighty big creature when it's running straight at you. Just one would have been enough to scare the pants off of me. A hundred of them heading in my direction plain froze me where I stood.

I guess the good Lord was protecting me again. I been sleeping with my back to a tree. When I stood up

I was right there next to it. I felt them tails swishing, felt the thudding of their hooves, felt the air rushing as they galloped past, but not a hair of my head was harmed. I was lucky. Reuben got a kick to the leg, Henry done got his head near split open. Elijah got a foot stamped on. No one died, though, which I guess must have disappointed General Sullivan some.

The bugler started blasting away. Army horses is trained, see? Every time they get fed, the bugler sounds a call. Was kinda like whistling for a dog – they hear that sound and they know they're in for something good. And Abe was plain greedy. When the herd come running back he was in the lead, looking for his corn.

Captain Smith arranged a guard on the horses after that, changed every two hours through the night so as we could keep an eye on them picket pins.

The next day was much the same as the one before. So was the one after that, and the one after that. We rode on and we rode on and we rode on.

I thought that the heat and the flies been near enough to kill a person, then come a night things got even worse. I was woke again by more crashing, only this time it wasn't stampeding horses that was causing the noise, it was thunder. I never seen the sky as big as it was there. Seemed to weigh you down, crush you, smother you like a big, black blanket. Seeing it tore apart with lightning was like seeing God Almighty summoning up folks on the Day of Judgement.

The officers had big tents to shelter under. The white troopers had smaller ones. We didn't have nothing but rubber ponchos, which we soon found out wasn't much protection against rain when it coming down like it being poured from the sky in pails.

Well, the way that night was going I figured I could do one of two things: I could lay down and cry or I could start laughing. In a flash of lightning I seen Henry's face: running with water, his eyes near popping out of his head with fright. He looked so darned scared and so darned funny I couldn't help myself. I started to chuckle. Reuben see where I'm looking and he start on too. He slap Henry hard on the back and says, "Ain't you glad you joined the army?!" Then he turn to Elijah. "Ain't you?"

"Too right, brother," says Elijah. Then Isaiah chips in, "Rich folks would pay a lot of dollars to experience something as pleasurable as this."

Reuben says, "Why do they go off to foreign lands when they can experience all this right here in America?"

It was damned fool stuff, but we got to laughing so hard we was crying. Elijah joined in, his deep low rumble of a chuckle, slow in coming as distant thunder and as loud when it finally arrive. Henry was clutching his bandaged head and smiling right on through the pain. Isaiah and George was either side of him and we was all sitting there chortling in the mud and rain, as wet as if we'd been dropped straight into the river. Might sound kinda crazy, but it was the first time in my life I'd ever felt close to being truly happy.

16.

It took us one hell of a long time to get to the place we was being posted. Along the way them eggs Captain Smith got stowed in his pocket hatched. Before we know it he got a pair of tame turkey chicks following along after him like he their mother. I kept hoping they'd head off into the scrub by themselves. I even tried shooing them away one time when no one was looking. But they come right on back. Guess they never heard of Thanksgiving.

After about eight, nine, maybe ten days them Cherokee scouts give us over to some other ones and head on home. The new ones was white men although their skin was burned so dark in the sun and covered in so much dirt it was hard to tell. Captain Smith said they was frontiersmen who knew the territory like the back of their hands. They was hard, rough-looking. Like they'd seen everything there was to see under the sun and didn't nothing surprise nor scare them. Didn't none of them say much, so neither did we. We set off, always heading towards the sunset. And the trees get fewer and the land gets flatter and emptier and the sky gets bigger and heavier until it seems there ain't nothing but a great mass of blue pressing down on this thin line of dusty yellow grass drawn under it.

Once in a while we come to a town. I say "town". Most of them places wasn't no more than a few buildings scratched together out of nothing, sagging in the heat. The few white folks living there all stood and stared as Company W ride on through like we're something out of a freak show.

The fort was right on the edge of the wilderness. Felt like it was right on the edge of the world. At the back of it there was a shallow river and a few trees lining the banks. Out ahead was nothing but empty prairie. Was like looking out on an ocean made of grass. It scared me half to death, all that empty space. If that was what them settlers was after – if that was where they wanted to go live – if that was the land they was planning to civilize, why then I figured the whole damned lot of them must be totally plumb crazy! Guess that made me plumb crazy too, for signing up and being sent out here to protect them.

Not that they was gonna need much protecting. When Company W finally come riding into the fort we come past a few shabby-looking tepees grouped near the post store. The Indians sitting outside them was busy drinking themselves senseless. Wasn't none of them gonna be giving us no trouble.

General Sullivan and his men get given the new-built quarters on one side of the parade ground; we get the tumbling-down ones on the other. But we ain't complaining. God above, there are beds in there! One each. With woven wire springs and a mattress and a pillow. And oh my Lord! Not just one blanket. There are two, three, four of the things! I'd slept on the hard floor every night of my life. That bed was so soft, I thought it was gonna swallow me up. Took some getting used to.

Well, there we were in the wilderness, black and white troopers facing each other across that square of ground. They stare at us and we stare at them and the feeling inside the fort is kinda hostile.

Wouldn't none of them soldiers never speak to us direct, man to man. But they'd talk to each other plenty loud enough for us to hear. We ain't been there more than a few days when the whole place starts running wild with rumours of Indians on the rampage. The way General Sullivan's men talked would have you believe there was dangerous warriors hiding behind every blade of grass on the prairie just waiting to leap out and cut your throat. And worse. They said how them savages would take a knife to your head, cut off your hair, wear it on their belts as a trophy. They was laying bets on how long it would be before the whole of Company W was rubbed out by savages.

They got Henry all shook up. He couldn't sleep night-times. Couldn't keep still in the day. I kept telling him it was talk, was all. He shouldn't believe none of them rumours. I mean, we'd seen Indians with our own eyes now. Them Cherokees was tame as Captain Smith's turkey chicks. They was farmers, not fighters, wasn't they? And out here, well – look at all them Indians hanging around outside the fort, blankets around their shoulders, bellies full of whisky. Captain Smith said they was Comanches or Cheyennes or some such thing but they was harmless as them Cherokees. Most of them couldn't stand up straight let alone hold a weapon. If they cut up rough we'd beat the likes of them easy, wouldn't we? Them whiteys was just trying to scare us, make us feel bad. I told Henry he shouldn't go listening to them. We was gonna be just fine.

Pay day come.

We'd had one of them before but we all been too dog-tired to do anything except rest and soothe our aching butts.

Them dollars sure felt good in my hand. I was happy just to hold onto them. To feel their weight. To know I'd earned them.

It was Reuben decided it was high time we got to spending some. And he was the persuading kind. There was no shifting Elijah: he had himself a wife and a baby boy back east and he was bent on sending every cent home.

But before too long Reuben had a whole bunch of us agreeing to go along to the Captain and see if we couldn't get ourselves a pass.

A few days later me, Reuben, Henry and maybe half a dozen more found ourselves out alone walking to the nearest town. It wasn't no more than a couple of hours strolling along on the bank of the river, the trees giving us some protection from the sun. The day was fine and bright and there was a gentle breeze blowing. We was all feeling real good. We done our training and now here we was: fine, upstanding soldiers of the US Army. Didn't occur to none of us we might encounter hostile Indians. That we'd be easy pickings if we did. We was fresh out from the east. We didn't know what we was getting ourselves into. But it seemed the Good Lord was looking down, keeping us safe. The only living things we encountered on that walk was bugs and lizards.

Henry was skipping along like a puppy dog. He was looking to spend his money on candy.

"All of it?" I says. "You ain't gonna buy nothing else?"

And he stops. His forehead creases up and he looks real worried. "What else is there?"

I laugh and says, "Nothing. If that's what you want, you go right ahead and get it. Maybe you can buy enough to last you until next pay day. You gonna be able to carry it all?"

"You'll help me, won't you, Charley?"

"Sure I will. Reuben will too, won't you?"

Reuben didn't answer. He wasn't fixing on buying no candy. Neither was George. Nor Isaiah. They was bent on getting as much whisky down their necks as their stomachs would hold.

Now I sure didn't want to go drinking no whisky. I seen the effect it had on the master and I didn't like it. When he was in a drinking mood he was harmless enough to begin with. His eyes would mist over and he'd get real sad. Soon he'd be singing the songs his daddy taught him about the old country. When he got to "Danny Boy" Ham would try and get the bottle away from him. If he didn't manage it, and Mr Delaney went on drinking, then pretty soon all that misty-eyed feeling would turn ugly. He'd get mad and it didn't matter much who crossed him or why. There didn't even have to be a reason. When he was like that he'd lash out at the first person he come across. One time he whipped a stable hand so bad the boy never walked right again. When the master's temper was spent, Ham would have to call for Amos to lend a hand getting him to bed.

So I didn't like what drink unleashed in a man. Hated to think what it might unleash in me. All that fear of Jonas, all that grief over Cookie, all that rage: I was doing a fine job keeping a lid on it. Didn't dare go prising it off. And I was doing a fine job passing as a soldier. But to keep on doing it I needed to keep me a clear head. I couldn't take no risks.

Of course, I didn't want to stand out none either. I had to blend in with the rest of Company W. So I went along with Reuben's plan. I figured maybe I could sup some whisky. I didn't need to go swallowing it. I could spit it out or maybe pour it away when they wasn't looking. I had me all kinds of thoughts running through my head.

When it come to it, I didn't need to do nothing.

We walked into that town, keeping our eyes fixed ahead. We was soldiers now, didn't none of us need to look down on the ground. A wagon train was being loaded up. There was a crowd of settlers ready to head on out to God-alone-knows-where, and the whole place was bustling with folks. Each and every one of them turned and stared when we come through.

But Reuben don't pay none of them no heed. He's powering along towards the saloon with a big, easy smile on his face, like there ain't nothing at all on his mind. Like there ain't nothing simpler or more straightforward than us buying ourselves a drink. But Henry's tugging at my arm.

"We going to the store, Charley? I'll get me some candy there, won't I?" He's pointing along the sidewalk but Reuben ain't stopping and I don't want me and Henry to get split from the rest of the bunch. There's a feeling about this place I don't like. Reminds me too much of the time me and Cookie and Amos walked into town. I feel safer if we all stick together. So I says to Henry, "We'll get your candy later. Let Reuben have his drink first. He got a thirst on him after all that walking. Ain't you thirsty too?"

We tag along at the rear and there ain't no ignoring the fact that the air's gotten thick with something. Fear, maybe. Or hate. Even Henry's noticed. His eyes are getting wider and wider and he's tugging at me.

"Later," I snap. "We'll get your candy later."

We step over one of them Indians who's drunk himself senseless on the sidewalk and we go into that saloon and it's empty save for three men sitting in the corner. One with hair the colour of old horse shit, one with ginger, one with black curls and blue eyes. Their milky-white skin been burned scarlet in the sun. Or maybe it was the whisky made them so red-faced. I took one look at them and knew they was long past the misty-sad stage. They was well on their way to being ugly, mean drunk.

Now maybe that bartender would have served us, maybe he wouldn't. We didn't get a chance to find out.

The redhead looks our way and says, "Well, lookee here. Is this Mardi Gras, or what?" He got a voice like the master's. Guess he's Confederate. When he gets up he ain't walking especially straight but he come on over. Looking Henry right in the eyes, he takes hold of the front of his jacket. "What kinda costume do you call this?"

Henry's brow goes into a mess of lines. "I'm in the army," he says, like he's explaining something to a child. "I'm a soldier, see? This here's my uniform."

Blue Eyes joins his friend. "You can put a monkey in a

matching suit. Don't make it a man."

They're both looking at Henry and Henry don't know precisely what's happening but he's scared. There's fear in his eyes and he's backing away, backing into me, which makes them fellas come on even harder. The man with horse shit hair pushes his chair back and stands up. He sticks one arm in the air and scratches his armpit. Then he starts on the monkey noises.

Reuben don't say nothing. But from the way he's standing you can see he's squaring up for a fight.

The bartender says, "C'mon, fellas. I don't want no trouble." But them men don't pay him no heed. And now they done messing with Henry. There ain't no fun to be had from someone who's too dumb to know what's going on. They turn on Reuben instead.

"Ain't you a fine-looking specimen? What precisely are you? Baboon or gibbon?"

Reuben bunches his hand into a fist but the redhead catches it before he can throw a punch. And suddenly that man seems stone-cold sober.

"Go right ahead, boy. Start something." His face is so close that flecks of his spit hit Reuben on the lips. "You wanna get kicked out on that chimpanzee ass of yours? Wouldn't nothing I'd like better than to see that."

We didn't none of us have no choice. We left. Was all we could do. We walked out of that saloon and back down that street with the jeers of them men ringing in our ears.

131

Reuben had his chin up and his jaw clenched. He was more running than walking and the rest of us was hurrying to keep up. But Henry was crying. There was big old tears coming down his face as I dragged him back past the store.

"Candy!" he hollered. But I wouldn't let him stop. I knew too well what might happen if we fell behind. I couldn't explain nothing to him. My throat was too tight. Like someone had fixed a rope around it and was starting to pull.

17.

We headed back to the fort because there wasn't no place else to go. Tears was running down Henry's face and Reuben was so mad his hands was still bunched into fists. He was dying to hit someone. Every time Henry sniffed, the sinews in Reuben's neck stood up tighter. Maybe he'd have turned on him. But when we get within a mile of the fort we see a man stumbling over the grass towards it.

He's a long way off but it's plain from the way he's moving that he's hurt bad. Bent almost double, dragging a leg. While we're watching he falls down. He don't get back up.

Well, there ain't nothing we can do but go see what's ailing him.

He's a small man, bleeding bad. He's damned near torn in half across the middle. His eyes are shut and he ain't moving so we figure he's dead. Don't none of us know what to do next so we just stand there, looking at him.

He's the strangest fella I ever seen. His head is shiny bald all over excepting a long thin rope of hair right in the middle. His face is round and kinda flat, like it been pressed down by an iron.

George says, "That's a Chinaman. What's he doing all the way out here?"

"What do we do with him?" says Reuben.

"Take him back to the fort, I guess."

We got a hand on a limb each and we're about to heft him up when his eyes snap open. Scares the hell out of us. Henry give a shriek. Then that Chinaman start screaming. "Indians! Attack camp!"

We ain't waiting to hear more. We pick him up and run like our feet have grown wings. He don't say nothing. Don't cry out. Don't make no more sound at all. By the time we deliver him to the doctor we don't know if he's in a dead faint or just plain dead. Ain't no time to find out.

Seems there's a whole bunch of Chinamen building a railroad out across the prairie so the place can be civilized. They're under attack and we gonna rescue them. The Captain's orders is to take fifty of Company W's finest to go teach them Indians a lesson.

After what happened in town we're itching to prove we're fit to wear them uniforms. Guess the Captain saw we was busting for a fight because he pick the whole bunch of us. We ain't off duty no more. We're needed. Feels good.

And we know it's gonna be easy as eating cherry pie. We'd lick them Indians good. Hell, we wouldn't even break a sweat!

We was saddled up and mounted in about five seconds flat. Soon as the bugle sound for us to move on out we're off. My blood was pumping and to begin with I was thinking, This is it. Hell, I can do this! We gonna show them. We gonna show them all.

That thought stays with me. It carries me along for maybe the first two, three miles of that ride. Then I start to feel the sun beating down on my back, and how darned thick my uniform is. Dirt is being kicked up in my face from the horse in front and it's getting in my nose and sticking in my throat. The sweat is pouring off of me, running in my eyes so I can't see. After a while there ain't much left in my head but the knowledge that I'm mighty hot and mighty uncomfortable.

There was something real impressive about the sight of that railroad. Tracks, snaking on out over that open prairie, taming it, breaking it, making it useful – like putting a saddle on a wild horse. I thought it was astounding what folks could build when they had a mind to. But I guess them Indians wasn't of the same opinion. They'd come riding over the horizon screaming and cussing in their heathen tongue and hit those Chinamen hard and fast.

By the time we got there them warriors was long gone. What they left behind them wasn't a pleasing sight. Wasn't a pleasing smell neither. There was blood and shit and guts spilled over the grass and the sun been baking it till it stank to high heaven. There was sixteen dead but it seemed like more. Bodies and bits of bodies was strewn every which way. Their fingers been cut off. Some been stuck in them fellas' mouths. And they all been scalped.

I couldn't get over the savagery of that. I mean, killing an enemy's one thing. But cutting off a piece of him? Keeping it as a trophy? The master been right: they was animals. Worse than animals.

Looking at them hacked-up bodies made me finally figure out there was two sorts of Indians – tame ones and wild ones. Them whiteys hadn't been telling tales to scare the wits out of us; they'd been speaking God's honest truth. Up until now we only seen the tame sort. But now – flaming hellfire! – we was going after the wild kind.

We trailed that war party until sundown. I'd gotten good at stopping myself thinking by then. I'd had plenty of practice, shutting out thoughts that was unwelcome. Guess I'd have been driven crazy otherwise. But I couldn't shake the fear that was building up inside of me.

When it started to get dark Captain Smith said we couldn't do no more that day. We made camp and tried our level best to get some shut-eye. Soon as it was sunup we followed on after them Indians.

We'd been going along for a few miles when the trail ran out. It seemed to stop dead on the banks of a river.

Looked like they'd ridden right into the water but there wasn't no sign of where they'd ridden out. Captain Smith was off his horse taking a look when about a hundred Indians come bursting from the scrub around us. We done ride into an ambush. And these ain't blanket Indians who can't walk straight. These ain't tame Cherokees. These are wild as coyotes, painted warriors in the prime of life. There's something crazy mad gleaming in their eyes. It enough to make me shit my pants.

I want to yell, "I shouldn't be here! Hey, I ain't no soldier!" But won't none of them give a damn that I ain't what I seem. There's no way out now.

We been taught strategy. Battle tactics. Attack. We knew how to charge the enemy lines, how to bring our sabres down, slash our way through. We been taught defence too. How to corrall the horses in the middle, make a square around them, two lines of men, the first kneeling, firing his seven shots then stepping back, letting the second man take his place while he reloads. We'd had all that drilled into us, day after day.

But doing something in training and doing it for real are two different things. And these warriors ain't behaving the way they supposed to. They ain't giving us no time to get ourselves organized.

Me, Reuben, Henry and Elijah been riding in our group of four like we done a hundred times before. When we was attacked I grabbed their horses' reins like I been trained while they jumped down, formed a line, started shooting. But holding four sets of reins when you're panicking bad and the horses is panicking worse ain't easy. Abe was throwing his head up, squealing and tugging so hard he has me half out of the saddle. And forming an orderly line of rifles when every bush is hatching out savages is nigh on impossible.

Reuben and Isaiah are shooting at them Indians like crazy. But Henry's slow. He ain't just one beat behind, he's missing the whole damned song. He fire off his seven shots and I don't think he hits a single thing. Elijah take his place and Henry got to reload. But his hands is shaking. He can't do it nothing like fast enough. Indians was pouring down on us like raindrops in a thunderstorm. Elijah done his firing and step back but Henry's dropped his bullets. He bends down. Starts picking them up. One's rolled along the ground and he goes crawling after it.

And now there's a gap in the line. Them Indians come hurtling through. The air's full of tomahawks chopping and sabres slashing and so much gun smoke I can't hardly see nothing. Them savages ain't just going for the men, they going at the horses too. While I'm holding them a big, painted warrior runs up whooping and hollering. He slashes at me but Abe leaps sideways, throwing me off his back, and the Indian opens the belly of Reuben's horse instead. Its guts come spilling out as I hit the ground. The other horses run off and I ain't sorry. Don't want to hear

Abe squeal like Reuben's horse is doing. Don't want to see him down, eyes rolling, legs thrashing. Don't want to see him laying still.

I'm on my feet and I got my carbine. I fire off one shot, missing that Indian by about a mile. And then the lever jam and I can't fire it no more. Well, I know from training that my pistol's about as reliable as my rifle. Besides, it's buttoned down in my holster and I ain't got time to fetch it out. So I draw my sabre. Got it in both hands. Cut it through the air, slice that warrior across the arm so he drop his tomahawk. But he's got a knife in the other hand and he's jabbing it at me. A knife's a whole lot shorter than a sabre so he can't quite reach but he ain't giving up. He's quicker than me, darting from one side to the other, making me twist and turn and I'm getting dizzy. I lunge at him. A sabre's meant for slashing, not stabbing. But I stick that weapon in him just the same.

And that's when I discover what training don't prepare you for: how it feels to push a blade into living flesh. Through skin and muscle and soft insides. How it looks: watching the light go from someone's eyes and knowing you're the cause. Something in me cracked when I seen that.

But I couldn't go thinking on it. There was at least ninety-nine other warriors intent on killing us. The next come at me. And then I discover yet another thing we hadn't been told in training: if you go sticking your sabre right into someone, you can't go pulling it back out. It had gone into the belly, curved on up under the ribs: it was clamped tight. So I just grab the knife from the dead Indian's hand. Pick his tomahawk off the ground. And I carry right on fighting, and I find that there ain't nothing that makes you feel quite so alive as when you're staring Death right in the face and every second might be your last. You savour every breath, every heartbeat. And I find that a rifle ain't half so useful as a tomahawk and a knife when the fighting's this close and this thick and this fast.

Wasn't no time for any of us to shoot, reload. Half them Indians had guns but they wasn't using them neither. Only Henry's still trying to. I got that Indian's knife. I'm screaming at him, "Take this. Use this!"

He turn to see what I'm saying.

And oh hell. Damn! Damn! Damn! While he's looking at me, his puppy-dog eyes full of fear, he takes a tomahawk in the back of the head.

He falls at my feet. His brains spill on my boots. And a scarlet veil come down over my eyes. I'm madder than I ever been. Madder than I ever dreamed possible. I'm taking out Indians as fast as they come at me, and hell, I'm loving it. Ain't nothing I want more than to spill every drop of their heathen blood.

We was holding our ground when Reuben gives a yell. I think he's hurt and I swing round to help. I ain't watching his head split too. But Reuben's pointing at the hill. The air's cleared some and I see a herd of horses stampeding towards us. Figured this time we was going to be pulped under them hooves for sure but it was a whole lot worse even than that. There was men riding them. Warriors. Same tribe? Different tribe? Who in the heck knew? Who in the heck cared? There was a whole lot more than the ones we been fighting for the last hour. Maybe three hundred, coming real fast. Wasn't no way we could fight that many. Captain Smith yell an order. The retreat gets sounded. I sure was glad to hear that call! But then I look around for our horses and my heart sinks down into my boots.

Reuben's animal been killed. Abe done run off along with Elijah's and Henry's. I knew we was gonna be wiped out for sure. Couldn't escape on foot.

I was about to fall on my knees and start praying for that sweet chariot when I see Abe's tail sticking out from a bush. See, he figured if he couldn't see no trouble, it couldn't see him neither. It had worked too, because there wasn't a mark on him. I whistled and he come, nosing for a treat like he always done. His reins was tangled up with Elijah's horse, so Abe brung him along too.

We was up, me and Elijah, quick as we could, but we sure wasn't leaving Reuben to die. Now Elijah was a big man for a horse to carry. Didn't take a whole heap of thinking to work out what to do. I hold out my hand. Reuben grabs my arm above the elbow and he's up behind me, then Abe, true to form, is running after the Captain without a click of the tongue or a kick from me because he don't like being left behind.

But them Indians had us surrounded. Only way to get out was by galloping hard at them, slicing our way through the line, only I didn't have no sabre. Was Abe's instinct for self-preservation saved us. He took off like someone set fire to his tail. Squeezed through the tiny gap between the Captain's horse and Elijah's. Nearly rubbed me and Reuben off his back, but got through them Indians and started heading along the valley floor back towards the fort.

Two people on one horse over a long distance when you're being pursued by more than three hundred hostile Indians ain't no easy ride. Abe had a big heart – the biggest I ever known in any animal – but he was struggling. Them Indians' breath was hot on our necks when we come within sight of the fort. But the prairie is a big old place and though you can see a thing on the horizon that don't mean you're anywhere near it. Abe's puffing like a train and Reuben's clutching onto me but his grip's getting weaker because riding on the rear end of a horse behind the saddle ain't no pleasure at all and by now he's so tired he's near to giving up the fight. Me, I just seem to have stopped breathing altogether.

A warrior rides up alongside us and I still got that knife in my hand but he's on my left side, and with Reuben's arms round my middle and Abe's neck stretched out and bobbing up and down with each step I couldn't see how to get to that Indian without hurting Abe or Reuben or both. The fella's got his tomahawk raised, and it's aimed at the side of Reuben's head and there ain't no way I can do nothing about it and neither can Reuben because he's hanging onto me and he can't get to his sabre and even if he could I'm in the way. The fella brings down that weapon. But right then Abe stumbles, and that tomahawk slices through empty air instead of Reuben's head. We go down in a great rolling mess of tangled arms and legs and hooves. We was moving so fast we just kept going, head over heels across the grass, and I couldn't see nothing but a blur of sky, grass, horse, but I could feel a whole barrelful of pain, and something cracked in my arm – my right arm – so there wasn't no way of defending myself. Or so I thought. But it's amazing what a body will do when it's trying to stay alive. Before I know it I got that knife in my left hand and when that Indian comes at me I'm using it with a skill I had no idea I possessed.

Of course then it ain't just the one warrior we got to worry about. Soon as I got him killed a whole bunch of them descended on us like vultures. Reuben's using his rifle like a club, cracking skulls every which way. Elijah's riding into the distance, and I get a glimpse of him, looking over his shoulder, and I'm thinking, *Keep on going, Elijah. Don't turn.* Elijah don't catch the thought – he wheels round in a great big circle and rides back for us. He don't get as far as me and Reuben. He's lost in a storm of savages.

It's all noise and sweat and blood and rage and fear, and you can't see nothing excepting the man you're fighting.

But the thing about the prairie is that if you can see something – like a fort – you can be pretty darn sure it can see you too. The sight of a bunch of troopers galloping across the plain with three hundred whooping Indians in pursuit was enough to make every soldier in that place spring into action. In two minutes they rolled the cannons out. They aimed them wide. One ball crashed to the side of us, throwing grass and dirt high in the air. Another landed maybe fifty yards to the other side.

Them Indians didn't sound no retreat. Wasn't even no order given, far as I could tell. But them cannon blasts was enough to break up the attack. They ride away and we're left to pick ourselves up, dust ourselves off and get ourselves back to the fort.

We made a sorry picture. Me and Reuben was back up on Abe. Elijah was sunk forward over his horse's neck and his blood was running down, staining its mane scarlet but thank the Lord!, he'd survived.

We didn't look none too pretty. But we was alive. It was a whole lot more than could be said for Henry.

A couple of days later Captain Smith said how he'd been talking to one of the scouts. The word was that them warriors had give us a name: Buffalo Soldiers. The Captain said it was on account of how we fought like cornered beasts and how the buffalo was a sacred animal and it was something of an honour, something we should be proud of. It meant them Indians was giving us some respect.

The General said different. He figured it was on account of our nigger hair being just like hair on the hide of a buffalo. He must have thought it was a mighty fine joke because he kept on and on repeating it.

And maybe the General was right. When a patrol brought Henry's body in he been scalped. So them warriors knew exactly what our hair was like.

Well, we got ourselves patched up, leastways on the outside. Inside I had a wound just wouldn't heal. While my arm was mending there wasn't nothing for me to do but sit brooding. I didn't have no doubts now about being able to fight. I promised Henry I was gonna pay them Indians back for what they done to him, even if I had to kill every last one of them with my own bare hands.

I kept dreaming about Henry. Night-times, he was sitting there on the end of my bed, that big smile across his face. Sitting there, his skull showing, red blood and white bone. He's holding his hair in both hands, twisting and turning his scalp like it's his cap. He's asking, "What was you saying to me, Charley? I didn't hear you. Charley?"

I got me such a lump in my throat I can't speak so he gets to pleading.

"I'm brave, ain't I? Ain't I, Charley? Did I fight good?

I didn't run away, did I? Why won't you say nothing, Charley? You mad at me? Didn't I fight good?"

Now I know I didn't see it happen, but in my mind I saw that Indian taking the knife to Henry's head over and over again. Waking and sleeping, I just couldn't shift it. I heard the noise of it too, clear as clear: his skin coming off the bone. Was the sound of Cookie peeling a possum for the pot. And somehow all that gets mixed up with Jonas and them men, and I dream I'm down there in that yam cellar with Henry asking, "What you doing down there, Charley? You're a soldier, ain't you? You can't hide." But I don't move. I'm curling into a tighter ball and I'm sticking my fingers in my ears, pressing them in so hard it hurts like hell, but no matter how hard I do it I can't block out the sound of Jonas laughing.

18.

The girl I'd been was killed the moment Henry took that tomahawk in the head. "Charlotte" was as stone-cold dead as he was. I wasn't acting like a man no more: in my heart I'd become one. I was a soldier, right through to the core.

Something happened to the men of Company W after we seen our first piece of action. When you're fighting side by side like that, when you're all staring Death in the face, when you're up so close you can smell his breath and count his nose hairs, it has an effect. We wasn't like dust settling after a storm no more: we was packed together, tight as salt pork in a barrel. We didn't go talking about it none: there wasn't no great declarations of love nor loyalty. But we was tied together all the same, closer than if we been family. And me and Reuben – who been clinging to Abe like ticks on a dog – felt closest of all. We was blood brothers.

Captain Smith told us he was real proud of how we

conducted ourselves, but our great courage in the face of the enemy didn't impress General Sullivan none. I had a feeling that the better we got, the less that man was gonna like it. As for them whitey troopers: they was still hell-bent on making fools of us any chance they got.

Oh, they didn't think they was being mean. They were just funning. What was wrong with us? Couldn't we take a joke? Didn't we have no sense of humour?

Didn't a day go by without a heap of "joshing" and "funning" and "playing tricks." I can't even recall the number of "practical jokes" what come our way. There was sometimes so much hilarity we damned nearly died laughing.

The bone in my arm been cracked but not broke clean in two. The post doctor bound it up and it was healing well enough. I was itching to pay them Indians back for what they done to Henry but a couple of weeks after he been killed they packed up their tepees and went off. According to the Captain, they was chasing after buffalo and for now at any rate they was the responsibility of some other company in some other fort.

Things was quiet so the General decides to have himself a day's fishing with some of his fellow officers. But he ain't content for them to entertain themselves. No, he wants to take me along too.

I was minding my own business, giving Abe a rub-down with my one good hand, when the General shows up. He takes a long hard look at the two of us. I'm praying to God that he'll just walk on by, but he points at me and says, "Hey, you. Private! Saddle your mule and come along with us."

Now I didn't much mind what he called me but I took offence to him calling Abe a mule. When a horse carries you fast and sure the way Abe carried me and Reuben you get kinda fond of it. But it didn't take a whole lot of looking to see that the white troopers' animals was a whole lot better than the ones belonging to Company W. Their horses' necks arched and they looked down their noses kinda proud but Abe's neck was bent the other way. Looked like it been stuck on upside down. His hips poked out like a cow's and his back sagged in the middle. Didn't matter none to me how he looked. I liked him and that was that.

But General Sullivan was my superior officer. I couldn't make no objection to him calling Abe names. When you're in the army you does what you're told, no talking back. Thirteen dollars a month: unquestioning obedience. That's the deal. Ain't no getting out of it.

So I saddle up Abe. My arm's still busted too bad to fight, but I can ride all right. Once we're ready the General give me a keg of bait which he says I gotta balance on the front of the saddle. He don't meet my eyes, not once. That thing stinks, seeing as how it's full of minnows that have been dead for a deal of time, but that's part of the good, honest sport them men got planned.

We ride all the way to a bend in the river where the water pools deep under the roots of an overhanging tree, which is about four miles, and we can't go fast on account of my busted arm, so by the time we get there I'm feeling kinda sick.

The rest of the day them men ignored me while they done their fishing. I was less than a rock or a tree stump. Was like being back at the plantation. I'd become invisible to the naked eye.

I ain't got nothing to do so I just sit there watching them string minnows on a line, drag them slow and steady across the pool. All day. By the time the sun was getting low they'd pulled fish after fish out of that river and used up all them minnows. They'd caught a whole heap – way too many to fetch home in the keg.

So here's what them officers do. They cram all the white fishes in the keg and load that on me and Abe as before. These being freshly caught they don't stink so bad, which is something of a relief. Then they tie the catfishes together on two long strings and they fix them to the rings on the back of Abe's saddle.

Well, I'd have figured out what was gonna happen next even if the General hadn't been so near pissing himself with laughing he could barely tie them knots. When I seen the prongs on them catfishes I resigned myself to the explosion that was sure to follow.

"Time to head back to the fort," says General Sullivan,

slapping Abe on the rump. "Lead the way, trooper."

As soon as Abe move off them catfish start banging against his flanks.

Now Abe and me had come to an understanding. We had a bargain: if he does what I ask him, I don't use no spurs. Was what you might call a gentleman's agreement. Soon as Abe feels them prongs sticking in his sides he gives a snort and I swear it's more disappointment than pain – he thinks I done break my promise. What's worse, the pricking don't stop when he speeds up. He's walking, then trotting, and the faster he goes the more them fish bang against him. Soon he's squealing like he's being poked by a dozen arrows and kicking out like he's plagued by every devil in hell. He's bucking – Lord above, there was so much movement everything was a blur. I drop the keg, but not before all them fish come flying out. They soar into the air with the force of Abe's bucking and come down *slap! slap! slapping!* on my head.

Now Abe figures that the bucking didn't work, and he's still got them things banging into his hide so it ain't entirely surprising the next thing he does is try to run away. We're off, galloping between them trees, and for such a funny-looking animal Abe sure has one hell of a turn of speed. All I can do is let him run until them strings break and the catfish go thudding into the dirt. Soon as that happens he slows and then stops dead and by now I know him well enough to predict that the next thing he'll do is stick his head down and eat, so I don't slide down his neck like I done that first day.

But I do dismount, and he looks at me and rolls his eyes and snorts – suspicious, like.

"Wasn't my idea," I tell him quietly. And he flicks his ear, so I know he's listening. "They was messing with both of us." Then I give him a bit of hard tack from my pocket and he takes it so I know I'm forgiven.

I break a branch off of a tree. I gather up them catfish and loop them strings on each end. Abe skitters sideways and looks at them real nasty, like he's figured out what was hurting him. But he lets me get back on up and with that branch across my legs the fish is dangling a long way from his sides so he don't get no prongs sticking in him. And then we got to go back and find them fellas who was all darn near paralysed with the hilarity of the situation.

Well, me and Abe got back to the fort without further mishap, but I had to endure a whole cartload of humiliation as the story of me and my "crazy bucking bronco" got told to them who hadn't seen what happened. Jonas would have loved it. I could almost hear that laugh of his, mixed up with all them others.

Captain Smith wasn't none too happy but he couldn't say nothing. General Sullivan was his superior officer too.

19.

I done a good deal of sitting around while my arm was healing. Guess it was that idle spell helped fill me out some. That, and the fact that I been getting three meals a day while I been in the army, which was more than I'd ever been fed in my entire life. I was still on the flat-chested side – wouldn't no one ever call me well endowed – but them things weren't the itty-bitty bumps they'd been before. One night I took one of my shirts into Abe's stall, cut it into strips with my knife. Wound them around my chest tight, like a bandage. I'd have to pay for the loss of the shirt, but a few cents out of my wages was nothing compared to the danger of getting caught out.

I was back on active duty around about the same time that them Indians start moving onto our patch of prairie again. Soon enough word come in that a wagon train was under attack.

Well, them Chinamen been defenceless enough. But attacking a wagon train? According to Captain Smith, there was decent, ordinary, God-fearing folks on them things, heading way out west into the wilderness to make something out of nothing. They was doing their damnedest to get by the only way they could. There would be babies. Little children. The notion of them being scared out of their minds bring that scarlet veil down again. I was itching to give them Indians a taste of their own medicine.

The General give the orders and the whole of Company W ride out in fours. Me, Reuben, Elijah and a man by the name of Thomas Walker – who took Henry's place. He been slave to a painter back in the old days and was something of an artist himself. Isaiah and George was somewhere behind us.

We ain't exactly sure where the wagon train is so the General tells the Captain to take thirty of us riding on ahead of the rest of the column so we can scout out the land. And that's when I learned a real important lesson: never go riding into no ravine when there might be Indians in the vicinity.

Them prairies was deceiving. When you was in the fort, looking out across that land, it seemed flat as the linen cloth laid on the master's dining table. But when you was in it – when you was moving out across it – it was more like riding on the ocean. There was dips and crests, and sometimes you'd go down into one and be lost from sight.

The thirty of us was heading down along one of them dips when we find the land starting to rise up on either side of us like two great waves. It put me in mind of Cookie's story about the Red Sea being parted by the hand of God. But I don't know if the thirty of us are Moses and the Israelites, or if we're them Egyptians, about to get drowned.

It's getting real tight and narrow. We can't ride in fours no more, so go down to threes. Then pairs. Me and Reuben are riding along, our knees rubbing together.

When I look up the sun's in my eyes so I can't see nothing. But I can hear. Something slips. A foot, maybe. And it ain't wearing no army boot. A little shower of dust come whirling through the air.

And then all hell breaks loose.

We was trapped like rats in a barrel. Arrows and bullets are raining down. It's a stinking bloody mess. In about five minutes flat nearly half the men and most all the horses is dead.

But not Abe. And not me. We're fine. We're wedged under an overhang and can't nothing touch us.

The rest of Company W hear the noise of fighting and start charging towards the ravine to save us. Which is when all them other Indians – who been hidden by a fold in the land – come riding over the crest behind them. Looking down the ravine, I can just catch a glimpse of what's happening. There's this big, barrel-chested red man leading them. Not red in the way the white folks said the

Indians was. I mean really red. Painted red. Scarlet. All over. Like he dipped himself in a barrel of blood. He's blowing this brass horn and that sound is more fearsome than even their war cries. It's like the Devil himself has come to snatch our souls.

Now there ain't nothing much I can do. Abe's pressing himself so hard against that rock he's crushing my leg but I ain't aware of it at the time. I can't fire at no one from here, but they can't get me neither. About two yards away I see Reuben have his horse shot out from under him – the second animal he's lost in less than three months – but he ain't wounded himself. He's using his horse to hide behind, taking shots when he can. Ain't none of us saying nothing. We all concentrating too hard on staying alive. But inside we're all praying our hearts out.

I see Red Barrel Chest riding backwards and forwards trying to break through the cavalry lines. But Company W is fighting real good and he ain't having a great deal of success. By the time the sun start going down we're all still holding out against him.

When the light begin to fade my courage fades right along with it. Fear takes me in its hands and starts to squeeze me tight. I'm dreading what's going to happen when it's dark. The notion of one of them Indians coming slithering on his belly like a snake, knife in his hand ready to slit my throat, ready to cut my fingers off, scalp me, is enough to make me want to empty out my guts.

But that night I learned another important lesson: don't no Indian like fighting after sundown.

Soon as the sun's sinking they make camp at the head of the ravine. There ain't no getting past them. No way out for us. No way in for the rest of Company W neither. They go off to do the job we was supposed to be doing: riding away in a cloud of dust to find that wagon train, leaving me and Reuben, George and Isaiah and the other fifteen of us still alive stuck in that ravine.

As bad nights go, that was one of the worst. I figured maybe dying wouldn't be so terrible, not if it come quick and clean. But Indians was savages. Them white troopers was full of tales of torturings – settlers being roasted on a spit like turkeys, or tied to a wagon wheel and set on fire – and I knew now they wasn't making them stories up. I was about to do what I did when Cookie and Amos was killed: pass out with the sheer terror of it.

But Reuben come creeping out from behind his dead horse and take hold of Abe's bridle. Give him a tug so Abe takes a step or two forward. It's like pulling out the cork from a bottle. That's when I realized how bad my leg was crushed. Once the blood began to flow it had me almost screaming.

We ain't got no more than a canteen full of water each and I had to give some of mine to my horse, wetting his tongue, his lips, his nose. Abe wanders off down a little way. He don't much like the smell of blood and death, but he's hungry so he's looking for some grass to eat. He's fine when he finds some. Me and Reuben get back under that overhanging rock, and he says to me, "You think it was gonna be like this, Charley?"

"What?" I says. "The army?"

"No," he says. "Freedom. Ever figure things would turn out this way?"

"No." I glance down along at them Indians. They got a fire going and they dancing around it. Red Barrel Chest look even more like the Devil now, and he sure sound like it, whooping and hollering in a way that gets my blood about ready to curdle.

Now Reuben could see and hear them well enough but he acted like they just wasn't there. He went right on talking, like we was sitting on the lawn at some fine folks' picnic.

"You know what I figured?" he says. "I figured Master is free, right? And he didn't never do no work. I put them things together. I thought when freedom come we was all gonna be sitting out on the porch sipping mint juleps."

"Eating gingerbread?"

"Yeah. Plate stacked with slices thick as my thumb."

"Watching the sun go down?"

"Sure. Pretty pink clouds all over."

"Me too."

The notion of us, dreaming we could sit leisurely on some old porch watching the sunset while we was actually stuck in a ravine waiting to get skinned alive by savages suddenly gets us smiling.

"I figured it was going to be like the Bible," I say. "I thought Sherman must be Jesus, Joseph and Moses rolled into one. I figured he was gonna lead us out of captivity all the way to freedom. With clouds of glory, and choirs of angels, singing their hearts out."

"Well, there they are," says Reuben pointing at them savages. "This must be it! Heaven on earth. The Land of Milk and Honey. Look at you and me, Charley. Ain't we reached the Promised Land?"

We're laughing so hard the tears come rolling down our faces and it ain't long before Captain Smith come crawling over and tell us to pull ourselves together, for God's sake, and calm down or else he'll have to discipline us for unsoldierly behaviour.

We sit quiet after that. But the fear's gone. With Reuben there at my shoulder, warm and alive, like my own blood brother, my courage comes creeping back. I even manage to sleep some before the fighting starts up again at dawn.

The moment the first shot is fired Abe comes hurtling under that rock, nearly squashing me and Reuben flat. Like I said, my horse had one hell of an instinct when it come to self-preservation.

It seemed that the rest of Company W found the wagon train we been looking for soon after sunup. Them settlers said there been thousands of Indians attacking them, but maybe they was exaggerating some. I wasn't there, so I can't say. All I know is that most of them survived and Company W drove their attackers off without too much trouble. Then they come riding back for us and we proved a whole lot harder to rescue.

We was so fixed into our holes in the rock we'd just about reached stalemate so the fighting went on all day. We was picking off one Indian here, one Indian there, but they was doing the same to us. We was getting tuckered out. Finally our troopers put in one almighty effort and push them Indians just far enough from the mouth of that ravine so we can slip on out.

The day before we gone riding in with thirty men. Thirty horses. We come back out with four. Four horses. Eleven men. All of them injured, bleeding bad, clinging together two, three to a horse. And it still wasn't over. Them Indians was being gunned down but they just wasn't giving up. They're singing songs – singing their hearts out, like death don't bother them none and they can't think of nothing finer or more dandy than being killed right here, right now! They begging for it, almost. They're coming at us again and again, and some of us ain't had nothing to eat and our canteens is empty and our throats is dry. The rest of the company is in better shape and they're driving them Indians back over and over, yet each time it's getting harder and things is starting to look real bad.

But then the sun goes down.

Red Barrel Chest and his men could have killed every single one of us but for their habit of stopping fighting at nightfall. When we start limping back to the fort the Captain says they're scared of ghosts and evil spirits and that starts George off, talking big. He's walking along, leading his horse, because Isaiah and Thomas been hurt and they was slumped across his saddle. "We're superior to them," George says. "We're civilized. We ain't scared of the dark. We ain't superstitious cowards. We're soldiers of the United States Cavalry. We can outwit a bunch of savages."

Turned out them Indians wasn't as dumb as George thought.

We was within sight of the fort when he trod on a rattler. He was so damned surprised to be bit! We'd have all been laughing our heads off, if it hadn't of killed him.

20.

Rattler bite don't kill a man quick – leastways it didn't with George. He died slow and he died painful and I blamed them Indians for that too. When it was finally over George joined Henry in my dreams, sitting there on the end of my bed saying over and over, "We was gonna kick their butts so hard they'd be breathing out their assholes. Why couldn't we scare them, Charley? I don't get it."

Losing all them men and all them horses was real hard. And it didn't endear us to General Sullivan none, even though it was his orders we was following at the time. Captain Smith told him that our conduct was "exemplary" and some of us "had quite literally laughed in the face of danger" but he didn't want to hear none of it.

A lot more trouble came our way that summer. Indians was attacking anyone. Everyone. Railroad workers, wagon trains, miners, ranchers. The Captain said they was even going for them farming Cherokees. Guess Indians had a pecking order too, because them wild warriors sure seemed to hate the tame ones. Before long they'd killed so many folks that the fine gentlemen in Washington give up on the notion of fighting and decide to send along some peace commissioners to talk to them instead.

So Company W was on the move again and this time we fetched up someplace with a lot of tall trees and a river winding round and about. The air was clear and still and it was a real pleasing spot. According to Captain Smith, we was there to keep things safe and peaceable when the smart civilized folks sat down with the ignorant savages to make an agreement. But before that there was latrines to be dug, and Company W was just the men for the job.

Me and Reuben was on fatigue duty, digging our hearts out, standing knee deep in a trench when this scrawny-looking officer I ain't never seen before pass by. I wouldn't have given him a second glance if it hadn't of been for the Captain standing to attention so sudden and flushing scarlet as he saluted.

Reuben's nearer than me so he catches his name. "Charley!" he says out the corner of his mouth. "That's Sherman!"

"Sherman?" says I. "Heck!"

In all them weeks me and Amos and Cookie been trailing along behind the Yankees I ain't never seen him in the flesh. To tell the truth, he's a little disappointing. He was a whole lot smaller than I imagined. Red-haired and kinda scraggy. He reminded me of Abe, only my horse's eyes was kind as kind and Sherman's had one hell of a mean expression in them. If them Indians had any sense, they'd roll over like dogs and wag their tails at him.

See, I'd heard enough officers talking about strategy by now to know that William Tecumseh Sherman was a military genius. He'd marched his troops into Confederate territory, hit the enemy so hard and fast they was knocked out stone cold, didn't have a hope of ever getting back on their feet. And the reason his men had moved so hard and fast was because he didn't have no lines of supply to slow him down: there wasn't no long wagon trains loaded with food trundling on along behind, getting stuck in the mud, needing ten men to pull them out, holding everyone up. Them Yankees had killed Mr Delaney's hogs and cows because they was under direct orders from Sherman to feed themselves on whatever they could find: what they thieved was all they ate.

They been told to make the Confederates howl, and all that burning of houses and smashing of crops been done by civilized white folks to a bunch of other civilized white folks. I figured it stood to reason that Sherman would be a whole lot tougher on a bunch of heathen savages.

Well, along come the government folks from

Washington and along come the Indians. Captain Smith says they're Cheyennes and Arapahoes and Kiowas and Comanches: a whole heap of tribes all led by different chiefs. The only one among them I seen before was Red Barrel Chest. There was thousands of warriors and they bring along their wives and their children and their old folks and their tepees and their herds of horses and packs of dogs. They set up villages along the river and before too long we was sitting right in the middle of them and all you could see and smell and hear was Indians, Indians, Indians in every direction. They may have been different tribes but they looked the same to me. Wild. Dangerous. All excepting this little old bent-backed, grey-haired chief who didn't look like he had the strength to harm no one.

Them Indians had all camped on the same side of the river as Company W. Bent Back was the only one took his tribe to the far bank down aways where there was a bend jutting out like a finger.

One morning Reuben and me was detailed to water the horses. We led a bunch of them out on halters to the river but the only place we could get them in and out easy was down by where Bent Back and his tribe was camped. They was minding their own business. Didn't no one even look at us while we seeing to the horses.

Then all of a sudden my skin starts pricking. Bent Back is coming through the trees on the far bank. I can see him, but I can't hear him. He walks through them leaves so silent he might as well have been floating above the ground.

There something snagging in my head.

"Why's he camped on that side?" I says to Reuben, real quiet.

Reuben has a think. "Maybe he want to make a quick escape."

Bent Back was just about the most harmless-looking Indian I ever seen, but Reuben was right: he'd put his folks in the one place they could run away from real quick. "You figure he gonna attack?"

"Maybe. Attack. Then retreat fast."

"Go tell the Captain."

So Reuben goes, taking his horses with him, and I'm left standing there alone with Abe and holding the ropes of five others while they drinking peaceful. I look across the water at that Bent Back chief, wondering what he's doing, but as I stare at him I gets the strangest feeling. He's standing right by the water's edge, just standing. There was something mighty unsettling about the way an Indian could do that – still and silent, like they was rocks. While I was staring he turn his head and I see them eyes of his. There was something in them that bring Cookie to mind. He look about a million years old. And for one second, maybe two, there was a noise carried in the wind. Seemed I could just catch the faint echo of women screaming, babies crying, tearing flesh and broken bones, the smell of burning. Horses dying.

Then it was gone. The river was running over the stones, the wind was blowing through the cottonwoods and one old, broke, bent-back Indian was turning away and going back to his tepee.

When the Washington folks was ready to begin talking they all sat themselves down but the Indians didn't come and join them, not right away.

Me and Reuben was on guard duty along with Isaiah and Elijah. My rifle was in my hand the whole time, cocked and ready because when them warriors finally decide they're ready to come along in, they kick off with a real fine display of their almighty power and magnificent manly bravery. They come galloping up to the commissioners, screaming and whooping their war cries, looking like they was about to spear then trample down the whole lot of them. But they stop dead about a couple of yards in front of Sherman and let their horses prance while they glare into Sherman's eyes and he glares back at them and they all look so much like dogs squaring up to each other, hackles raised, growling, that for a second I felt like laughing.

Reuben's thinking the same as me, because he says, "Look kinda like mutts, don't they?"

And I says, "Any second now they gonna start pissing on the cottonwoods, see who can hit highest."

That bunch of Indians settle themselves down then

another chief comes riding in. His warriors are all firing their weapons in the air, screaming and hollering and making everyone in the place ten times twitchier than they been before. When they settle down, in come another bunch.

It went on for the whole damned morning and I stopped feeling like we was going to be trampled to death. It was show, was all. A heap of strutting and preening. They was like roosters. Before long I started to get kinda bored. Kinda itchy. Back on the Delaney place I been worked from before sunup to after sundown. And now I been trained for action. Any time I wasn't doing something – even digging latrines – I started to get restless.

All the chiefs was sitting down by the time Bent Back showed up. He rides towards Sherman at a walk, real quiet, real calm. He points to himself and tells the General that he's a good Indian.

Sherman grinds his cigar butt into the ground. "The only good Indians I ever saw were dead," he says.

Well, I was nursing me a bellyful of hate on account of Henry and George and all them others. I figured Sherman was speaking the truth. He was a white man with a heap of book-learning. A military genius. How in the hell was I supposed to know any different?

Well, eventually they're all sitting down and the talking starts up. The purpose of it was this: the government done decide it wants them Indians to go settle down someplace. It wants them to stay put, and not go off killing and thieving. Couldn't nothing be simpler. If they do that they'll be given houses and schools, food and blankets and whatever the heck else is their hearts' desire. As long as they keep south of the river they'll be left alone. Sherman tells them they can hunt buffalo and indulge all their savage heathen ways as long as the grass grows and the waters run. But north of the river, settlers is gonna move in and civilize the place.

Having been on the receiving end of Red Barrel Chest I watched with interest when I see him stand up. I nudge Reuben and Reuben nudges me and we both listen good when Red Barrel Chest opens his mouth.

I'm expecting him to whoop and scream and come out with all them savage noises, but he don't. He starts talking and the interpreter starts translating and it's all about how much he loves the land, and how he likes to roam free on the prairie, and how he ain't planning on giving none of it up to no settlers. Then he starts going on about how he don't want the schools or the churches or the homes the government is offering to build, and I starts getting mad.

I says to Reuben, "Why's the government offering to build houses for a bunch of savages?"

"And why ain't they got the sense to take them?" It's Elijah who answers me. He's real mad. "Ain't no one never come offering to build me no house. Ain't no one giving me no little plot of land to raise corn." I know full well he's got a wife and baby back east and she's struggling along on the money he sends. Elijah spends most all his off-duty days whittling little bits of wood into animals for their baby boy. He was aiming to make him a whole ark full.

Now when you're in the army you follow orders, that's all. We was paid for fighting, not thinking, so mostly I tried to avoid it. But right here, right now, well, I just couldn't help myself.

The way Red Barrel Chest spoke of being free and the way I'd heard white folks speak about it – it was like they was using the same-sounding word but with two entirely different meanings.

I seen them settlers heading out on them wagon trains. To them being free meant getting their own place. Shaping it to what they wanted. Taking the big empty wilderness and turning it into something better. Freedom was ownership. Staking out a plot. Building on it. Didn't matter if it was small. Was someplace to rest their heads. Someplace to call home.

But here's Red Barrel Chest talking about how he wants to wander about, rootless as a piece of tumbleweed, over the whole damned prairie! He ain't gonna make nothing of all that good grazing and all he ever gonna do is follow along behind them buffalo. It ain't never occurred to him or any of them warriors to build a fence so as them animals would stay put.

I was thinking folks got to anchor themselves to something, same as trees. Even grass got roots. Gotta have something to hold you to a place. Gotta leave something to show you was there. Why bother living otherwise? Each time Company W was sent someplace new, I carved my name into the stable wall. Felt good to leave a solid mark. Show that I been there. But them Indians – they vanished like ghosts. A whole village could come down in less than an hour and they was off like they never existed. Like they was just cloud shadows sliding on over the prairie.

Well, then Red Barrel Chest was saying he didn't want nothing to change and he didn't want none of them things the government was offering and I got mad as a hornet. He wanted everything to stay the same – to have his children raised like he was. He was clinging to his old ways same as the master had wanted to cling to his. Them two men was more than twice my age but I figured I knew more than both of them put together: I knew darned well that things is always changing and you got no choice but go along with it. If Mr Delaney had of understood that maybe he wouldn't have ended up dead, burning like a hog roast on his own front porch.

I was mad enough, and then Red Barrel Chest start saying bad things about soldiers and by the time he's finished complaining about how we done cut down his trees for firewood I just about got smoke coming out of my ears.

"His trees? *His* trees?" I says quiet to Reuben. "How does he think we gonna cook? Stay warm?"

Again, Reuben don't answer. He's frowning and his head's on one side like he's thinking as hard as me. He looks kinda sad and sorry for that chief. Goddammit! It's almost like he thinks Red Barrel Chest might have a point. So now I'm mad at Reuben too.

"Does that man think he's president of the whole damned prairie?" I says.

Well, yes, seems he does, because now he's saying he wants to keep it all. He finishes up by telling Sherman that maybe, just maybe, he'll let the government build his folks houses when all the buffalo is gone. But there are plenty of them about so it won't be any time soon.

Then I see the look that passes across Sherman's face. It's the same look Jonas give me that last time I saw him: just before he put his hand to his neck and jerked it up like he been hanged. A cold finger run down my spine. I don't know what it means, but it ain't good. And I figure maybe Red Barrel Chest should have kept his mouth tight shut.

21.

Red Barrel Chest wasn't the only one who was none too happy with what Sherman was proposing. The other chiefs said most all the same things. The talking goes round and round and round in circles. After a few days Sherman gets tired of it. He slam down his fist and tell them plain: they ain't got no choice. Roads is coming, railroads is coming, settlers is coming. He's building a nation here! Something big, something fine. You can see he don't much care whether they settle down peaceable, or whether he's got to kill every damned one of them Indians himself. Either way, progress is marching on and there ain't no stopping it, any more than there is of stopping the sun or the moon.

There's more talking and it goes on into the night and it goes on all the next day, and the next and sometimes me and Reuben is on guard duty and sometimes we ain't. I lost count of how many days it took them to come to a decision but finally them chiefs sign the bits of paper Sherman been waving in their faces and me and Reuben is there to see it.

Bent Back is the first to put his mark down. The moment he done it his folks move off, quick and quiet. On the far side of the river we can see them tepees coming down before the ink's even dry and then Bent Back is off too, looking over his shoulder at Sherman like he's afraid, like he thinks the General might jump up and stick a knife in him. I can't help thinking, Is he crazy? Why's that man so scared? But there ain't no one I can ask.

Red Barrel Chest takes the pen next, but he's looking like he'd rather stab Sherman with it than make a mark on the paper. One by one all them chiefs do the same.

Well, that treaty might have been signed but I got to say things felt about as safe as sitting on a keg of gunpowder with a lighted match in one hand.

I was expecting trouble to break out right away. But it turned out Indians didn't like to do no fighting in the winter, no more than they liked fighting in the dark. As long as the weather was icy cold we had ourselves some peace.

We was moved on again, north and west this time. Ended up in the same fort as General Michaels and his men. Can't say we was best pleased to see them again. Especially when Captain Smith says we gonna be stationed here the whole winter. But he ain't so fussed about it. We was staying put long enough for his wife and child to come out from east to join him. They arrive just before the snow come down.

My experience of white ladies been mostly confined to Miss Louellen. I wasn't in no rush to know whether Mrs Smith had the same notions when it come to my general lack of trustworthiness. But it wasn't like our paths would be crossing. I figured it would be easy enough to avoid her. But that child of his? Seemed there wasn't no getting away from Tiberius Smith.

Now there was other officers' children at that post — enough for one of the mothers to start a school so they could get their lessons. Mornings we could hear them singing out their alphabet while we was on guard mount. Afternoons them kids was free to roam. They be running around all over the place but didn't none of them ever wander over to the side where we was quartered. Was like there was a line drawn in the dirt keeping them out. The only one who couldn't see it was Tiberius.

He been there about a week when one morning the reveille sounded. A groan go around the bunkhouse. On one side of me Elijah says, "Hell, it way too early." On the other Reuben says, "That bugler gone crazy or what? Can't be time to get up yet."

I push my blankets back, step out of bed. It's morning and it's dark in here and I ain't entirely awake until my foot lands on something. Something soft. Something warm. Something alive.

"Goddammit!" It just about scares the life out of me. I jerk my foot back. "What the devil is that?"

I'm up on my bed and I got my feet tucked right up under me and I'm yelling, "There something under there! What is it, Reuben? Can you see, Elijah? That a rattler?"

They both up on their beds too because if that's a rattler come in off the prairie don't none of us want to go nowhere near the thing. Don't none of us want to go the same way as George.

All of Company W is wide awake now and ain't no one volunteering to look so Reuben gets his gun. He starts poking the end into the shadow under me and then the thing starts screaming.

"Don't shoot! Don't kill me!"

It's a high-pitched voice. Child's.

"Come out of there then. Show yourself."

Tiberius Smith come slithering out. He got feathers in his hair and war paint across his nose. He been crawling along on his belly under all the beds in the bunkhouse, pretending he was a warrior come to ambush us. Guess he succeeded.

Well, there been so much commotion, and what with him screaming his head off it ain't entirely surprising that Captain and Mrs Smith come running to see who's killing their boy.

Mrs Smith's hair is hanging loose down around her shoulders. Captain Smith's coat is all unbuttoned. I think there's gonna be hell to pay. It don't matter that Tiberius come in uninvited. He's a white child. We're all of us gonna be in the wrong.

But it don't work out like I'm expecting.

Captain Smith tells us to get on and get up because we gonna be late for Stable Call if we don't get shifting. But before he do that Mrs Smith flush red and apologize for Tiberius disturbing us. She make Tiberius do the same. She tell him to say sorry special to me, seeing as he near scared me to death when I trod on him.

"Hey, it's fine," I says. All this fussing is making me feel mighty awkward.

"Shake on it?" says Tiberius. How old is that boy? Four? Five? He's standing there, hand outstretched and, when I take it, he pump mine up and down like we're both a pair of fine upstanding gentlemen. The feel of that child's small hand in mine – soft, trusting – does something to my heart. I'd built me a shell by then, hard as stone. But he's found a crack in it and wormed his way in.

He looks a whole lot like his ma. He's got the same sandy-coloured hair and the same dusting of freckles across the bridge of his nose. But his eyes are his pa's – clear blue, like the sky on a crisp winter morning.

My insides are flipping right over. Them eyes of his are even more unsettling than the Captain's. The sight of them has made me recall being up in the branches of the cottonwood tree.

I'm small, real small. My arms and legs are wound around the branch and I'm clinging on for dear life to stop from falling. How did I get there? Can't have climbed. Couldn't have reached that far. Someone must have lifted me up. It's mighty strange. But that ain't the strangest thing. The strangest thing is that I'm looking down into Jonas Beecher's face. And there ain't a trace of fear in me. I'm feeling happy. Because he's smiling on up at me with just the same look on his face as Tiberius got right now.

Sweet Jesus! It was almost as if Jonas had liked me!

22.

Back on the plantation winters been on the mild side. I hardly ever seen snow. When I did, it just been a dusting that didn't hang around long. When that snow come down on the fort it was like a big, thick blanket, covering up everything, changing the land so much you couldn't recognize none of it.

I hated even thinking it, but it seemed them Indians had the right idea about not doing no fighting when the snow was on the ground. They was hunkered down in them tepees, sitting about the fire and telling each other stories. While they was snug and warm, we was out chasing damned fool men who was doing damned fool things. Outlaws and cattle rustlers was preying on settlers like vultures. Preying on the army too, when they got the chance. They needed hunting down and bringing in because we was there to keep the peace and bring law and order to the west.

Finding them reprobates wasn't no problem at all – each time they thieved something they left a trail about as wide as the wide Missouri in all that snow. So when they took thirty head of beef from the fort it wasn't remotely difficult to track them down. The difficult part was the shoot-out which come when we caught up with them because when your hands is so cold that you can't feel your fingers and you done forgotten you ever had toes it's real hard to pull a trigger. Was easier to just whack them whiteys over the head with the butt of my rifle. I confess I took a certain amount of pleasure in doing that.

It was hard being out on the prairie chasing reprobates but it was a whole lot better than being stuck inside that fort with General Michaels' men and their foul-mouthed remarks.

If you're fighting for America, you got to belong in America, don't you? If you're good enough to die for your country, ain't you good enough to live in it?

Captain Smith told us we was. But there was only one of him. All them others couldn't never pass any of us by without spitting words which ain't fit to repeat.

And it didn't matter how well we done in the field and how many hostiles we'd gone and killed, General Michaels plain refused to believe any of us could have done good. Wasn't nothing Captain Smith could do about it. He just shrugged his shoulders and had to whistle for his ten dollars.

But it wasn't long before Christmas was on its way and

the Captain was making plans for us to have a celebration in the recreation hall. Me, Reuben, Elijah and Isaiah was put to cutting and bringing in greenery for decoration. Things was going along fine and we was all looking forward to some rest and relaxation but then General Michaels pulled the rug out from under us.

When he seen what the Captain was planning he calls his officers and men together. And the upshot of their conversation is that they refuse to share the hall with "a bunch of mokes".

The Captain can't go fighting a superior officer so he don't say nothing but he sure ain't gonna let us miss out on no festivities neither. He begs and borrows a load of lumber and tells us to go and build ourselves a stage in the barn. He even get hold of a stove so we don't go freezing to death while we do it. Isaiah supervises the construction.

Truth be told, none of us was what you might call surprised about General Michaels and his men. The surprising thing was having Mrs Smith get some old blankets out of the Quartermaster and stitching them up to make curtains for a stage.

It turned out Captain Smith been a music teacher before the war come along. He got the band practising carols and as Christmas Day got closer it was all downright festive and the more General Michaels and his men looked like they been sucking on a bushel of lemons the more we was determined to have ourselves a good time.

Mrs Smith didn't just sew them curtains. She made a heap of real dainty decorations and hung them on a tree. When we walk in on Christmas morning her kindness took my breath away. When it come to singing them carols and giving thanks to the Lord I done it with all my heart.

Back on the Delaney place all Christmas meant was harder work for Cookie and me. We was at it from before sunup to way after sundown for days on end. When we was following the Yankee army, when we was hunkered down in that stinking cabin, when I was all that time on the road walking – I guess two, maybe even three Christmases had passed me by altogether. This was the first time in all my born days I got to sit down to a Christmas dinner.

We had ourselves turkeys and oysters, venison and tinned tomatoes, and plum pudding. Was the finest meal I ever ate. Then there was more singing, and we was banging out carols but across the way General Michaels and his men was trying to outdo us and they sure as hell wasn't singing about peace on earth. They was roaring out the words to "Sam Hall". Jonas used to whistle that tune through the gap in his teeth. I'd never heard the words before, but now they was so loud I could catch every single one of them.

My name it is Sam Hall
And I hate you, one and all
I hate you, one and all,
Damn your eyes!

We know them sentiments is aimed at us. Thomas is near crying with rage over it, but Reuben calm him down. "Hey, this is Christmas! We'll just sing louder to drown them out." Then some of us pick up the band's instruments. Reuben's got a natural talent for the bugle, which pleases the Captain no end. But I can't raise nothing out of none of them excepting a sound like breaking wind. It make Tiberius giggle so much he get the hiccups. Mrs Smith go red in the face, she so mortified. After that, folks got to talking and telling stories.

Elijah was real good at that. He sits there with Tiberius crouching in the dirt at his feet, whittling this tiny little deer for his own boy while he talks. The night was drawing in and the cold come creeping back so we huddle closer to the stove and Elijah's voice just flows along like molasses. He's telling the story of how this fox hates this rabbit so much he done set a trap to catch him. The fox makes a baby out of tar and sets it down on the side of the road where the rabbit is sure to see it. When the rabbit comes a-hopping down the track he stops to talk to the tar baby, which, not being real, can't answer him none. So the rabbit gets mad and he gives the baby a smack, right there on his nose, but his paw gets stuck to the tar so the rabbit gets even madder and he hits it with the other paw and it ain't no surprise that it gets stuck too. So now the rabbit is madder than a hornet and he's trying to pull his paws away but he just can't do it, so he tries kicking it with his back legs.

We was all grinning our heads off at the notion of this rabbit stuck-up with tar. Thomas had took one of them blackened sticks from the stove and was drawing a real fine picture of the rabbit in his pocket book and I was so busy watching the shape coming to life on the page that I didn't see Mrs Smith was behind me.

Elijah goes on with the story. The fox come along and catch the rabbit and he's wondering whether the rabbit would taste better fried or roasted.

But that rabbit's smart. Smarter than that old fox, anyhow. He tricks the fox by begging and pleading. "Oh, please don't throw me in the briar patch! Anywhere but there! Throw me in the fire, throw me in the river, but not there! Don't throw me there! Anywhere but there!" And that fox hate that rabbit so bad that's exactly what he does. He chuck him in the briar patch and the rabbit wriggle through and escapes, easy as eating cherry pie.

When Elijah gets to the end we all laughing like crazy but I hear this big old sigh right behind me and I see Mrs Smith standing there. She ain't laughing. Ain't smiling, even. She's got her hand on her husband's arm and her eyes are looking real sad and she's saying softly, but not so softly that I can't hear every word, "That's what we're fighting, isn't it? A huge tar baby. The more we fight, the more we cover ourselves in pitch."

I don't know what she means, but it give me an uncomfortable feeling inside – that same uncomfortable feeling I got when Reuben looked kinda sorry for Red Barrel Chest. I got enough problems of my own to deal with, and I just don't want to be bothered with a feeling like that. So I take it in my hands and I crush it right down into a ball and then I tuck that ball into the deepest, darkest corner of my head so I don't have to look at it.

23.

We passed a pleasant Christmas but that was only one day in a very long winter. When we was out in the field chasing outlaws time passed quick enough. But in the fort the days dragged bad and the nights dragged worse. On duty we went from one bugle call to the next: reveille, stable call, breakfast call, guard mount, drill call. Sometimes the space between each one stretched out so long it felt like there was days dividing them; like twenty-four hours was twenty-four weeks, twenty-four months, twenty-four years. And when we was off-duty? Well, there ain't a whole heap of things to do at a military post when the snow's thick on the ground. There was whisky to be had from the post store so long as you kept it quiet, but that didn't hold no attraction for me. And then there was the women who done the laundry. Some of them was happy to keep a fella warm for a few coins. Reuben was friendly with one or two but it wasn't exactly the kinda pleasure a man with my attributes could go indulging in. That winter, mostly I was just sat on my butt freezing half to death.

As the weather got colder the world shrunk right down until it was just the stove in our quarters. Was the only place you could feel anything like human. Trouble was, when you was stuck in there what you had to fight was the boredom. That was just about enough to kill a man stone dead. I ain't never known minutes crawl by so slow. Listening to Elijah's stories been pleasant enough to begin with, but he didn't have an endless supply of them. By the time you heard him tell the one about the tar baby for the fiftieth time you got so you wanted to yell. As for Isaiah – he had this goddamned awful habit of cracking his knuckles, one by one. He'd sit there, nights, and you'd be waiting for that sound to come and the more you waited and the longer he went without doing it the more you wanted to lay him out flat when he did.

Times like that I'd take myself off, go be with Abe. Sit with him, that was all. If I had one of them monthlies I'd wash my rags through in his bucket. Didn't no one think twice if I had to keep fetching him fresh water. That horse was so clumsy! He just kept kicking that old bucket over! There goes Charley again, filling it up.

When Abe was done eating he'd lean his head up against my chest, let me rub his ears. Or he'd hang it right over my shoulder, let me wrap my arms around his neck.

There was a spot halfway down he liked me scratching. I'd get my fingers in there under his mane and when I got the place just right his top lip would start twitching, flicking from side to side, and pretty soon he'd start rubbing my shoulder back. Or he'd lift his face to mine, blow clouds of sweet hay-smelling breath all over me. There was a peace and a calm being there with him that used to soothe me right down. Was only the cold ever drove me from there back to quarters. Figure I'd have spent the whole winter in with him if I could have.

Abe was stalled right next to the pony Captain Smith had bought for Tiberius. He'd got the animal off a passing trader – a tired old pack pony that wasn't gonna go running off with him. Wasn't going to go running anywhere much at all, truth be told. But he needed brushing and feeding and talking to and he kept Tiberius out from under everyone else's feet. Tiberius give his pony the name Mighty Spotted Warrior but that animal didn't have no fight in him. Thing he liked best was eating his head off. I guess him and Abe had a lot in common.

They couldn't find no saddle small enough to fit, and in any case them stirrups would have been way too long for Tiberius's legs. So Captain Smith had give him a blanket, Indian-style, and fixed it firm with a strap around the animal's middle. Trouble was, with no stirrups the boy couldn't get up on his own. For the first few days he was happy enough for his pa to lift him up when school was done and he'd sit there most all the afternoon imagining he was leading a charge of braves across the prairies. But then he started to think being lifted up was undignified for a chief of his standing. He needed to figure out his own way on and off.

Didn't take him long to discover Mighty Spotted Warrior's fondness for food. One afternoon I see Tiberius come out the stable with a handful of hay. He put it on the ground in front of Mighty Spotted Warrior. As soon as that pony's head go down to eat Tiberius swing his leg across its mane just behind its ears. When its head come back up, Tiberius is lifted in the air. He slide down its neck and into place. It looked so darned funny I had to bite my lip – I figured Tiberius wouldn't like being laughed at no more than I ever did.

Tiberius come over once in a while to talk to Mighty Spotted Warrior when I was there with Abe. If he come in, I went right on out even if Abe start whickering after me. But one time Tiberius block my way. He stand there, right in front of me so I can't get past and he put his hands on his hips and look up at me and them Jonas-eyes of his is troubled.

"Don't you like me?"

"Oh hey, no. It ain't that."

"Did I do something bad again?"

"No."

"Then why'd you run away every time I come in?"

"I ain't running away."

"You are. You do it every time." There's a catch in his voice. He sounds like he might start crying. And I can't stand to see him cry. That boy brings out the woman in me and I can't allow that.

I says, "You put me in mind of someone is all."

"Who?"

"Just someone."

"Someone who was mean to you?"

"Yep, I guess."

"But I wouldn't ever do that. I promise," Tiberius says, serious and solemn. He turning me inside out again. "Whoever it was must have been a bad person. Ma says it's our Christian duty to be kind to the poor Negroes."

"Does she now?"

"Yep. We got to be kind to the heathen Indians too because they don't know any better."

"That so?" I keep my mouth shut. I ain't saying that maybe she wouldn't feel so kindly if they scalped her husband or stole away her boy.

Lucky for me, Tiberius has done with moralizing. "I saw your horse rubbing your shoulder. Would Mighty Spotted Warrior do that to me?"

"Maybe. If you scratch him right."

"Could you teach me?"

I showed him how to find his pony's ticklish spot and we spent the time pleasant enough. But I couldn't be easy with him. He could promise all he liked. But if I was remembering things right – not dreaming them up – there'd been a time when Jonas had liked me too. Something had changed him. Didn't know what. But if it changed Jonas it was like to change Tiberius too. I didn't want to look at him one morning and see hate in that child's eyes.

Aside from Abe the only other thing that kept me from going crazy that first prairie winter was that one of General Michaels' men had bought himself a pair of bear cubs to tame. I don't know where they was from or how he come by them or what he was planning to do when they grew up. He kept them chained near the stables. Every time I went to see to Abe I had to walk on by. I took to taking some jerked beef, some hard tack, any bits of food I could find to put in my pocket. Made me smile to see the way they stand on their hind legs and take that food in their paws real delicate, like they was folks in fur coats.

But they didn't last long. They got big and they got strong. One time they cuffed a whitey and damned near ripped his leg off. Didn't matter none that he'd been poking them cubs with a stick at the time. The General give the order to get rid of them and they was chased out onto the prairie.

Now, one of the problems the army had in winter was carrying the mail from fort to fort. The prairie's mighty big. It goes in every direction, right up to the horizon. And over it all there's that great dome of sky. In the winter, when the snow lies thick, every single feature gets buried beneath. If you lucky you can just about make out where the river is, but in places it's frozen over and snow come piling in so you can't see its shape. Trails are all wiped out and it ain't like there are roads or signs to follow.

So taking the mail wasn't exactly a popular job. But me and Abe got ourselves something of a reputation for sheer plumb doggedness when it come to doing our duty. One week, I get picked for the task and I ain't none too pleased. I don't know if Abe picked up on my reluctance to go on that ride or if he made up his own mind on the subject. He never was what you might call a natural born leader. Always liked to have at least one horse in front of him. When we was attacked he had the speed of a racehorse, but he kept a neck's length behind the leaders so they was first in the firing line. He had a level of cunning which saved my life on more than one occasion.

We was supposed to ride out but Abe just wasn't having none of it. I strung the mailbag across my chest, but when I click my tongue and urge him on, Abe digs his heels right in. He ain't going nowhere. And me and Abe got an agreement: I wasn't going to use no spurs and I wasn't going to whip him. So I try a little persuasion. Then I try encouragement. I talks to him real nice, and I try moving off again. All Abe does is run backwards so fast he nearly knocks down Captain Smith, who has to jump aside real sharp.

That gets Tiberius stepping forward, offering to do the job himself on Mighty Spotted Warrior. Captain Smith salutes him, thanks him for his brave and courageous offer, but politely declines. Then Thomas volunteers to take my place. Which was lucky, or not, depending on whether you was me or Private Thomas Walker.

Thomas was one hell of a good artist. But he was one hell of a good soldier too – one of Company W's finest. The result was to get himself subjected to a whole heap of them side-splittingly-hilarious jokes, same as me. But whereas I kept my head down and let it slide like rain off a duck, Thomas took it hard. I seen him crying with frustration sometimes. He was busting to prove he was good as them. Figured if he kept excelling himself, sooner or later they was gonna have to give him some respect. So it's Private Thomas Walker who rides off across that snow. It's Private Thomas Walker who don't come back.

Like I said, he been subjected to a whole heap of abuse. Not just words neither. He been given a bloody nose on more than one occasion and he couldn't never fight them troopers back: one of us fighting one of them was always in the wrong. Captain Smith knew the score. It was his opinion that Thomas couldn't take no more. After two weeks, when he don't show up, we're sent out looking for him. But there been more snow so we don't find nothing, no tracks, not even a body. The Captain is real sad, but he lists him as a deserter.

He didn't consider them bears. None of us did.

Maybe Abe had got wind of them. Maybe that was why he didn't want to set foot outside. I guess Thomas's horse didn't have the same urge towards self-preservation.

When the spring come and the snow melt me and Reuben found them lying within thirty feet of each other. Thomas was face down in the river. Guess he drowned. Or froze. Maybe both. His horse been half eaten but it wasn't enough to keep them bears alive. They didn't know how to take care of themselves. They starved. Or froze. Maybe both.

I seen some pitiful sights in my time but that was one of the worst.

24.

When the weather warmed and the Indian trouble started up again, it come as a welcome distraction. We was able to get out in the field, away from that fort and leave General Michaels and his men behind.

Now, which particular tribe was causing the trouble or why they was doing it I didn't know and I didn't care. As far as I was concerned they was all savages: it was in their nature – they just couldn't stop themselves. Word come in of attacks here, attacks there, ranches burned, women violated, children stolen. Seemed the whole of the plains was in uproar. The marks them chiefs made on them pieces of paper didn't count for nothing. They was all liars. Cheats. Thieves. Wasn't none of them to be trusted.

That whole summer them Indians kept us real busy. We lost sixteen men, one after the other in a dozen different fights. In between, there were the long days and weeks of boredom when we had to find our own ways and means of amusing ourselves. Sometimes Reuben would take a stick and stir up a pair of ants' nests. He'd get the red ones fighting the black. We'd all be laying money on which side was gonna win.

Heck, we'd lay money on anything: whose horse would cast a shoe first; whose britches was gonna give out next; how long I could last without needing to relieve myself. The parlous state of my bowels been something of a joke in Company W ever since I gone running off the parade ground.

Towards the fall we was posted back to the same fort as General Michaels. There was a bunch of new recruits waiting for us there who'd come from out east so Company W was back to full strength. Mrs Smith had herself a new baby girl and Tiberius had grown some. Made me smile to see how tender that boy was with his baby sister. He'd carry her around like she was a doll, lift her up onto the back of Mighty Spotted Warrior, hold her there because she was too small to sit up by herself.

The days had been roasting hot, but then there come a sudden change. For a time the air was deathly still, hanging so heavy you could hardly breathe. Then a cold wind starts blowing from the east and big angry clouds gather on the horizon. It was plain to see one hell of a storm was on its way. I was off duty, so I figured I'd go talk to Abe because he didn't care for thunder and lightning no more than I did.

I cross the parade ground but when I get to them stables I see there's a white man in there giving his horse a rub-down. A stranger. Wearing a coat made out of buffalo hide and looking like he been in the saddle for weeks on end, he's one of those frontiersmen who's seen everything there is to see under the sun and don't nothing surprise or scare him. He's come in just ahead of the storm looking for shelter, I guess. Or maybe he's got business with the General. Either way, I don't want to go talking to no whitey so I turn on my heel.

But Abe's seen me. He lift his head and whicker. When I don't come over right away he stamp his foot and squeal, real indignant. The man looks at Abe, he looks across at me and then he does the most surprising thing: he smiles. His mouth splits wide apart in a friendly grin as if I'm just a regular trooper.

"Opinionated devil, ain't he?" he says. "You'd better get on over before he breaks his stall down."

I figured Captain Smith was the only white man on God's earth who could act clean and talk decent but here's this rough-looking fella dealing with me straight. Like it ain't even unusual.

I don't know how to answer him, so I don't say nothing. I don't move neither. Abe stamps again. He's getting mad, and that makes me recover the use of my legs. Soon as I get to him he start nosing in my pockets. He's so eager for a treat he's near ripping my coat apart and that man start laughing at him, but it ain't unkind.

"He's no beauty," he says. "Guess he's fast enough, though, ain't he?"

"Sure is. Got me out of a tight spot more than once."

"I'll bet. Horse like that can turn on a dime; run all day if he needs to. That's what you need in your line of work."

We might have talked some more, but then who should come on by but one of General Michaels' troopers.

Private Creech was fresh out from east and he got golden curling hair like Angel Face. Like Jonas. Turned me inside out the first time I seen him. I'd had to go running for the latrines again.

He been picked on guard mount this morning as the General's orderly for the day. My heart sinks right down into my boots. He's giving me one of them looks: like he's trod in a heap of hog shit.

I'm about to go sliding out of there, back to quarters. But then I see that if Private Creech is giving me that look, he's giving it to the man I been talking to as well. And the man in the buffalo-hide jacket ain't remotely happy about being looked at like that. I can see he's planning on doing something about it.

Now whoever he is, that man is smart. He don't say nothing that will lead to a fight. Leastways, not directly. He just carries right on talking to me. But his words is aimed careful as arrows and they go thudding into Private Creech.

He give me a wink and a smile and then he says to me,

"Been out in the field long, trooper?"

Now I'm treading careful, but I can't help but catch some of his mischief. "Couple of years or so."

"Seen a lot of action?"

"Some."

"Bet you're a fine shot, ain't you?"

"I get by."

"You're too modest. Why, I'll bet you could show some of those raw recruits a thing or two."

He takes a long, cool look at that trooper's new uniform and squeaking boots so it's plain as day who he means. Private Creech give a squawk. Sounds like he swallow a whole chicken without plucking it first.

Now the private has come to the stables for a reason but it takes him a while to remember what it is. He's standing there looking like a fish that been pulled from the river. His mouth is opening and closing and he's mad as hell, but he can't think of nothing to say. Finally it comes back to him that he been sent over to deliver a message. "Mr Cody? The General would like to see you." It's taken him so long that by now the General himself is on his way over to see what's going on.

Seeing the General crossing the parade ground, Private Creech and the buffalo-hide man leave the stables together, but that trooper still looks like he's choking on feathers. He's so red in the face that General Michaels asks, "Is there something wrong, Private Creech?" He don't reply because the buffalo man – Mr Cody – gets in first. "I apologize, General. I think I've just about scared the pants off your orderly. I was just saying I figured that trooper there could outshoot him." He points back at me so the General can't mistake his meaning.

"That's bullshit, William, and you know it."

"Care to make a wager?"

I don't get no say in the matter. The next thing I know, I'm about to have a shooting competition with Private Creech. Word gets around in a heartbeat and every man in the fort – white, black, on-duty, off-duty, officer, trooper, scout – the whole damned lot of them, is pushing and shoving to get themselves a look. The officers' wives has come out too, and all their children. Bets is being made and money's changing hands and I'm carried along on the wave of excitement until we're standing there by the corral and the fear takes me and starts shaking me like a leaf.

This is Mr Cody's show. He give the order for me and Private Creech to go back fifteen paces. He put an empty whisky bottle on top of the corral post and stand back. Private Creech takes aim and fires and the bottle shatters so Mr Cody puts up another. It's my turn.

And I pick up my rifle and it's then that Mr Cody sees what I'm proposing to shoot with. Before I can fire he come over and look at it and he says, "You can't aim right with that. Use mine."

Well, it's true that my rifle ain't what you might call

a fine weapon. Along with us getting the old worn-out horses, we got weapons that been discarded by the rest of the army on account of not being up to standard. When that patrol brought back Henry's body they brought my rifle back too. Even them thieving Indians hadn't had a use for it. But I was used to firing that rifle, like I was used to Abe being so funny-looking, and used to wearing dead men's clothes and boots that didn't fit. And I didn't feel comfortable taking something off a white man. So I says, "I'll use mine, sir."

And he shrugs and goes back to his position.

I take aim. Always needed to point a little to the left on account of my rifle not shooting straight. I fire and the bottle shatters.

So then we move back another five paces and we have another go. Private Creech shatters his bottle, no problem. I'm getting ready to shoot but then my lever jams. It been doing that on and off ever since I been issued that thing. I'd worked out by now there was a way of unjamming it: sharp jerk and a twist and it was sorted. But Mr Cody come over again and he says, firmer this time, "Use mine." He don't wait for me to answer; he just take my rifle away and put his one in my hands.

"1866 Springfield," he says. "Second Allin conversion. You'll do better with this."

Right away it feels good. The weight of it. The balance. Feels like it's alive. Feels like it's part of me. And I swear that thing is purring with pleasure at the notion of what it's about to do.

I raise it to my shoulder and aiming is as easy as holding out my arm and pointing my finger at the bottle. Squeezing the trigger soft, that bullet flies just exactly where I told it to go. Feels like it come right out of my fingertip. God Almighty! There something powerful fine in that.

Mr Cody come on back over and this time he give me his ammunition belt, buckling it around my waist before I can object. He show me how to reload. It take just one bullet at a time, not the seven my Spencer do but this Springfield open so easy, the bullet glide into place so quick, the whole thing snap shut so smooth, I figure I could fire off seven with this faster than with my old rifle. And it ain't got no lever to go getting jammed.

Once I'm done, me and Private Creech got to go back even further.

By now the air's changed from noisy with excitement to hushed with anticipation. The pride of Company W is resting on my shoulders. Reuben's looking at me and I can feel him willing me on. Elijah's lips are moving and I know he's praying and Isaiah is tugging on his knuckles like he's about to pull each and every one of his fingers clean off. Captain Smith's standing there. Just standing, arms folded. He give me a nod. Beside him, Tiberius is white-faced, jiggling nervous like he about to pee himself. I don't want to let none of them down. Not if I can help it.

We fire a third, then a fourth time and I'm loving the feel of that weapon in my hands. Me and Private Creech was evenly matched until the fifth.

The fifth time, Private Creech misses his bottle. His shot goes thudding into the fence post, splintering the wood. The cry that goes around General Michaels' men makes my heart shrivel away inside me. It's more howl than anything. An animal noise. Wild with anger. It's the sound them men made when they come lynching Amos and Cookie. The state of my bowels might be a joke in Company W but right now I feel like I'm gonna fill my pants for real right in front of all of them.

I can feel the weight of Company W's hopes. The pressure of it on my shoulders is getting unbearable. Trouble is, I can feel the weight of General Michaels and his men's hopes too and those folks' wishes seemed to lay upon me even heavier. My hands are shaking so much I can barely reload. I drop my bullet. They start jeering. Whooping. Screeching. Baying for blood. Sound's worse than war cries.

Mr Cody is at my side again.

"Take your time, trooper. Steady as you go. Don't forget to breathe."

He put a hand on my shoulder. A friendly hand that's mighty strong. He grins and says, "It doesn't matter either way. Relax. I win some, I lose some. Been good seeing them all shook up, though, ain't it?" He give me a wink and walks off.

I take a deep breath. I get a hold of myself. I look along the barrel of that rifle and take aim. Them clouds is just starting to shed their load. Specks of rain coming down, drawing my eye off of where it should be.

And now the sweat's beginning to drip down into my eyes and my hands are clammy but my finger's on the trigger and I give it a real gentle squeeze. At that selfsame moment Isaiah give his knuckles a crack. I jerk. The bullet flies.

I swear time slowed right down. I could follow the path of that bullet like it was a leaf floating along the stream, or a feather drifting down to earth. There was silence. I wasn't breathing. No one was. For a second I thought I'd aimed too far to the left. Maybe I had. Maybe it was Isaiah's *crack!* and me flinching to the right that did it. Slow as slow that bullet clip the bottle. It shatter, and it was like seeing a bunch of Miss Louellen's diamonds thrown in the air – all them fragments seemed to shimmer, mixing in with the falling rain like there was millions of them, like the whole world was full of fractured glass.

That quiet continued for one, maybe two seconds longer. Then the men of Company W gives this great cheer. Reuben got his arms around my legs – he's picking me up. Elijah got me too. And Isaiah. They're lifting me up on their shoulders, lifting me up in the air, carrying me around in the rain. Tiberius is whooping and cheering loudest of all. I look at General Michaels and he don't seem none too happy. I can't even glance at Private Creech. But I'm praying I don't never have the misfortune to find myself out in the field with him. Because if I wake up one day dead with a bullet in my back I'd sure as hell know who put it there.

The General give Mr Cody his money but it's like he tearing out his own liver in doing it. And when Reuben and Elijah and Isaiah and the rest of them finally put me back down on the ground Mr Cody walk over to me and slap me on the back so hard I near fall down flat. I hold out his rifle to him.

He don't take it.

"It's yours," he says. "You earned it, O'Hara." He give me another wink as he show me a fistful of dollars. "The General's buying me another. Ain't that kind of him?"

I'm real surprised at myself. I never thought I'd go taking no gift from no white man. But when it come to that Springfield? Lord above! It was just too damned good a rifle to refuse.

25.

Mr Cody's wager didn't improve the feeling in the fort none. Wasn't no concern of his: he was off out of there as soon as the storm passed by, on his way buying, selling, scouting, trading – Lord alone knows what that man did to get by. He shook me by the hand and I wished him well, I truly did. But that was it. He was gone and I was stuck inside, watching my back the whole darned time, expecting to get me a knife between my ribs.

Elijah, Isaiah and Reuben stuck to me like ticks. I was thankful. Kinda. It was real nice of them but it put the fear of God into me: if one of them monthlies come along I was gonna have a lot of explaining to do. As well as the worry of that happening, I wasn't getting no time on my own – to spend with Abe – and it started to drive me crazy.

I guess Captain Smith saw how things was because he had me on every routine patrol, every mail run. Any time he could get me out of the fort and into the field, he did.

Fall turned into winter. Snow settled thick over the prairie. Christmas come and go – in the barn again, not the recreation hall, for the same reasons as the year before. Must have been early in the new year when we was coming back from patrol and I see a little old Indian on a little old pony up ahead. He's heading for the fort, same as us, and we follow in his tracks all the way. When we get there and he gets off his pony I see it's Bent Back, the chief I seen standing down by the creek that time they made that peace treaty. He's the one that camped on the far bank. He was the first to put his mark on a piece of paper. He was the one told Sherman he was a good Indian.

He says he's come in to have a talk with General Michaels. The General come out of his office and shut the door behind him. He don't invite Bent Back inside. He keep him standing out there in the cold and the snow while Bent Back ask if he can move his people closer to the fort. For protection, he says, though he don't say from who or from what because the General cut him off. Bent Back is saying he's heard a rumour when General Michaels snaps out, "No." He tells Bent Back to return home to his people. They won't be attacked.

That's all there is to it. Bent Back don't say no more. He gets on his pony and he heads off without another word. I watch him go. I ain't never seen a man look so beat. And the snow starts falling and the wind's whistling so I can't tell if it's that I'm hearing or if it's people screaming. Or maybe horses.

The next day Captain Smith sends me and Reuben off out again, only this time we're carrying a heap of messages for the fort about twenty, maybe thirty miles along the river. The military is inclined to ignore such things as the weather when it comes to promoting the interests of civilization. Come what may, the mail had to go out.

Me and Reuben wasn't best pleased to be picked for that particular task. Since Thomas been found dead, we rode in pairs. The idea was, we could cover each other's backs. Them bears was dead and gone, but there was always enough young warriors around – crazy from liquor – to cause mail carriers a heap of trouble. So as well as having to cross icy streams and feel the bitter wind blowing right through you there was the chance that you might get yourself killed or captured and, given a choice, we knew we'd both opt for the killing, not the capture, on account of the hideous torturings folks said Indians carried out on troopers.

We set off and that snow looks mighty pretty but it's a freezing hell to ride through. In the daytime, when the sun come up, the surface melt a little. Then down come the night and it freeze hard again. So Abe has to crunch through a layer of ice which can cut a horse's legs clean open no matter how careful he tread. In addition to which there was the risk of a blizzard coming. Me and Reuben knew them things was deadly dangerous. We'd heard of settlers who'd got froze solid getting lost between the house and the barn when they gone out to feed their animals.

Well, we was way out of sight of the fort when the snow starts falling. Flakes as big as my fist. It's heavier than we ever seen it and there's a biting wind blowing it into drifts. I can't see nothing remotely recognizable, can hardly even see Abe's ears ahead of me. And in them conditions the prairie's a real easy place to get lost in so that's what we does. We gets lost. And being as how this is me and Reuben we does it real good. We're riding leg to leg, knees rubbing against each other, so we don't part company because the notion of getting separated out there is too godawful to contemplate, but we got no idea of where we are. No idea of which direction north lies, or the location of the fort we come from or the one we going to. Can't tell the sky from the land neither. We keep riding because if we stop we're gonna be smothered by that big old blanket and we know without saying nothing to each other that we won't get found until spring. So on we go, and we might be riding around in one big circle or we might be heading out into the wilderness, and I'm sure I can hear wolves howling through that wind and I'm scared as scared can be and that sound is coming closer and now Abe's heard it too so he speeds up, or at least he tries to – it's hard moving fast through them drifts. Our animals are jostling together and they're sending each other into a panic or maybe it's me doing it, or Reuben.

Then something appears out of that snow like it been dropped from the sky in front of us. But it ain't no pack of wolves. It's an Indian.

Now I reckon he was surprised as we was. He didn't make no move to harm us. But Abe was real twitchy by then. When that fella come looming out of the blizzard Abe rear up high on his back legs and whirl round away from Reuben and towards the Indian. I was a fair-enough rider – spent two years in the saddle. But I was half froze to death. Guess I was just too chilled to stay put.

I fall, thumping off into the snow, landing in a deep drift. And before I can get myself back up and out of it that Indian's grabbed Abe's reins and took off with him.

He thieved my horse! Was so mad I forgot for a while how cold I was. I pull myself out of that drift and run after them but I ain't got more than a couple of steps before I sink right into another one and they was already out of sight, the snow coming so thick I couldn't see more than two, maybe three feet ahead. When I turned round I saw I lost Reuben too and if it wasn't for him shouting after me things could have gotten a whole lot worse.

We find each other and I climb up behind him, and we start off after that Indian because there's only one of him and two of us and I want my horse back.

It wasn't hard to follow them tracks to begin with but it ain't long before the snow's filling them in and the wind's doing its level best to rub them out and of course that fella knows the prairie a hell of a lot better than we do so come nightfall we was in a heap of trouble. We find ourselves a withered old tree and press ourselves close to it like it was our long lost ma. Wasn't no question of sleeping – fall asleep in conditions like that and you don't never wake up. All we could do was wrap ourselves in Reuben's blanket and huddle up under the belly of Reuben's horse and pray to Almighty God that the snow would stop so by morning we could figure out where in the hell we was.

By dawn the three of us was barely alive. Then the sun come up and there's a mist hanging over the water but we can see we've fetched up on a rise near the river and there are fifty, maybe a hundred tepees grouped in circles down along the valley.

I'm not thinking straight. We're right there by the enemy but all that's running through my head is that it's a real pretty scene, with the sun slanting through the mist, and the snow sparkling fresh, the clouds coloured scarlet and the light on the land kinda golden.

"What you planning to do?" says Reuben and despite the cold that man's managing to smile through his chattering teeth. "You just gonna walk in there and fetch Abe out? Because I ain't going in with you."

Goes without saying that I didn't have no plan. But while I was thinking how best to rescue my horse I see Bent Back step out of his tepee.

Well, that fella seems like a good-enough Indian to me even if Sherman don't think so. Maybe I really can just walk in there and ask him for my horse. He's a chief, ain't he? He can tell the thief who stole Abe to give him back.

But before I can take a step there's a woman shouting. Don't understand the words, but it's some kinda warning. Bent Back steps into his tepee and comes out with his gun. He fires it into the air, and that wakes up the village.

And then I hear the darnedest thing. Music. There's a band playing. Me and Reuben look at each other.

"You catch that?"

"Yeah."

"Figured I was hearing things."

As we look, General Michaels' men come riding along, a hundred or so of them riding abreast in a line like they about to charge and the band's playing and them Indians don't know the words to the song but me and Reuben do – them men been singing it all through Christmas Day same as the year before.

My name it is Sam Hall
And I hate you, one and all
I hate you, one and all,
Damn your eyes!

All of a sudden I'm feeling sick to the bottom of my belly because I know just exactly what's gonna happen next.

Bent Back walks towards General Michaels, and he's got his hand raised and that's a gesture of peace but it don't make no difference. Him and his folks must have done something real bad that I don't know about because he takes a bullet through the neck. Just like that. He falls and they trample right over him. Them soldiers charge, and they're riding through the camp, and I seen it all. All that killing. Women. Children. Old folks. And it ain't enough just to kill them Indians, they're being scalped too, and worse, and it's General Michaels' men doing all that savagery not them redskins. And there's Private Creech right there in the middle of it, golden curls flying, whooping and screaming and laughing like Jonas Beecher. And the words of that song are banging through my head to the rhythm of the shooting and the hacking and the raping and the butchering. Didn't take them long. General Michaels' men was real efficient. And when they finished with the people, they make a start on the horses.

Imagine killing one horse. Just one. It's a big animal so there's a lot of blood. Imagine putting your gun to its head and pulling the trigger. If it don't know what you're about to do it'll stand real quiet and nice for you. But once you kill one, the others panic, and you can't get a clean shot at the next. So you wound it mortal bad and it takes longer to die. Imagine killing one horse. Then imagine killing five. Ten. Fifty. One hundred. And all the time you're shooting they're trying to run but their legs are hobbled so they can't do more than limp and shuffle and scream and scream and scream. One hundred horses. Two hundred. Five. Six. Seven hundred.

When they start in on that herd I start running. Reuben's shouting but all I can hear is them screams. One of them's Abe, I can feel it. He's down there, scared out of his mind, and if I don't reach him he's gonna die along with the rest of them. I'm running, running through snow that's two, three, four foot deep in places so it ain't much of a run, it's more of a stagger and a fall and a stumble and it ain't fast enough, it ain't nothing like fast enough. And I'm too late even before I fall into a gulley full of snow. I'm up to my chest in it and I can't get myself out and I'm thrashing and fighting and yelling at them to stop but they can't hear me none, I'm too far away and even if I could reach them General Michaels' men ain't gonna pay no attention to no goddamned moke.

By the time Reuben gets to me the screaming's stopped but that silence is worse than the noise because I know it's all over and I failed. General Michaels is moving on out, along around the bend of the river. My horse is down there and he's dead. Or he's dying slow. And I gotta see with my own eyes, because there's this killing piece of hope that's telling me maybe the Indian what thieved him didn't come from this place – maybe he come from another tribe, a different village. Maybe Abe's alive and well just over that hill or that one there. Maybe I can still find him safe someplace.

So when Reuben pulls me out of that drift we go down to where seven hundred horses are bleeding in the snow.

Abe's one of them.

And the worse thing is he ain't dead. He's lying there, real quiet, and I know that when a horse is hurt bad he don't make no noise because whimpering would be the surest way of inviting a wolf or a coyote to come get him, so I know he's a goner even before I see the big old wound in his neck. When he sees me he tries to stand but he can't and he tries to whicker a greeting only the blood burbles out instead of any sound because his windpipe is cut through. And all I can do for my horse is end it for him, because I ain't letting him lie there and bleed to death. So I take his funny-looking head in my lap and I take my pistol and I do what I need to do. And then I just stay there, sitting in the snow, because I ain't got the strength to do nothing else.

26.

I was sitting there in that snow, with Abe's head in my lap,
and the warmth leaving him and I was grieving too bad
even to cry. I couldn't move. Guess I'd have sat there until
I froze solid along with the rest of the dead if it hadn't of
been for Reuben. He come wading through that mess of
blood and snow and pick me up by the shoulders and haul
me out of there. And he had his arm around my waist and
was helping me along like I was wounded, which actually I
was, because let me tell you that if you gotta shoot a horse
it ain't especially smart to do it when it got its head in your
lap because the bullet goes clear through and slices you
across the thigh although I was hurting too bad inside to
notice it at the time. And when we get over to his horse
he clasps me in a manly embrace by way of telling me he's
sorry about Abe without having to actually say the words.
His breath's hot in my hair. "Why'd they do that, Charley?

It don't make sense. It don't make sense."

Now, grief is a mighty strange thing. I was so deep down sorrowful that the feeling of Reuben's arms around me had a real powerful effect. One minute my heart's aching so much all I want to do is lie down and die. The next my heart's pounding and all I want to do is lie down with Reuben and get real physical. So I find myself returning his embrace in a fashion that ain't what you might call brotherly.

I didn't do nothing but that. Was a hug, that was all. My arms round him. But men can smell lustful thoughts a mile off and Reuben's sure smelled mine.

He drops his arms. Steps back. He don't say nothing. But the look he give me makes my heart shrivel right up inside me. Makes the words die on my lips.

I don't get up on his horse behind him. I limp all the way back to the fort. He's too good a soldier to abandon me altogether. He keep me in sight, but only just. And he don't say another word to me. Not then. Not later. Not ever.

I guess I could have told Reuben what I was. I ain't entirely sure why I didn't. Guess I was so shook up about Abe I wasn't thinking straight. Or maybe I was. Either way, telling him just didn't seem to be an option. What could I have said?

"Hey, brother! I'm a woman. Yep, I been lying to y'all these last two years. Seemed like a good idea at the time. How d'ya like that?"

217

I'd have been kicked straight out of the army. I was in the middle of the prairie in the middle of winter – where in the hell was I supposed to go?

So I let Reuben go on looking at me like I was some goddamned freak of nature. Soon as we was back he done take himself off for a visit to the laundry. He don't come back to the bunkhouse all night. When the reveille sound, he ain't nowhere to be found. When he don't show for guard mount the Captain says it's official: Reuben's deserted.

Now whether it was because of me, or whether it was because of what we seen in that valley, I don't know and I couldn't ask him. I felt in my heart it was my fault Reuben left.

Shame: that got to be the worst feeling in the world. Eats away at your insides like a bellyful of maggots. Leaves you like a hollowed-out shell. Grief is bad enough. But grief fades. All that sorrow I had for Cookie hadn't gone, wouldn't never go entirely, yet the razor-sharp edges been worn off in time. I knew my grieving over Abe would soften too. Sometime. Eventually. But the shame of hugging Reuben: I knew that would never go away. I might bury it, I might put a lid on it, I might hide it, yet whatever I did it would stay as sharp and clear as the day it happened. It would always be there, waiting to ambush me when I was least able to fight it.

That night, when me and Reuben come back to the fort and I lay awake wondering what in the hell he was up to, I got ambushed by things I'd buried so deep I hadn't thought they'd ever see the light of day again.

Like that time I was in the garden, pulling onions. I been sent there by Cookie again because Amos had turned up and they wanted to be alone. I was crying, tears of rage pouring down my face, and the tears got mixed with the mud and the snot. I was all mussed up. I rub at my eyes with a dirty hand and the grit go right in so I can't see nothing. And I'm so taken up with my own misery I don't hear Jonas coming. I don't even know he's there until his shadow fall across me and the air go cold.

I ain't been stood so close to him in a long time. My first thought is that he's gotten tall. He's taller than his pa. His hair's still falling in them yellow curls but there's a golden down on his top lip now where a moustache is trying to break through.

"Hey," he says. And before I can run he's got both my wrists in his one hand and his arm is around me, pulling my back tight to his chest. My ass is pressed into his groin and I can feel something hard trying to shove itself between my butt cheeks. With his one free hand he's reaching under my skirt, his cold fingers on my warm skin, and he's panting like a dog.

Guess he'd have had me right there in the garden if his pa hadn't been heading to the big house. When the overseer see what his boy's doing he come running. He pull Jonas off of me. He cup his hand under my chin. For a second – just one second – he look right into my face. I see something so strange in his I don't understand it, not even now. He says one word. Whispers it. Sounds like "apple". But it don't make no sense. He orders me back to the cookhouse. Then he turns away and gives Jonas a whack across the cheek with the back of his hand. He don't hit his boy hard, don't redden the skin even, but Jonas is so surprised he fall. He don't make a sound. He lies there, his golden curls in the dust and the dirt, and he fixes me with them sky-blue eyes of his.

Cookie and Amos was so wrapped up in each other they didn't hardly notice the mess I was in when I got back. They thought I'd fallen, was all. And I was too shamed to tell them otherwise. Like I was too shamed to tell them the night one of them Yankee soldiers got me up against a tree when I been trying to take a piss. And that time there wasn't no overseer to go pulling him off.

I thought I'd had plenty enough of being mauled by men. Didn't think I'd ever want to go laying down with one voluntary. Guess I'd changed. Grown up, maybe. That one hug had exposed a need in me I didn't know I possessed. But I'd have to keep a lid on it. Button myself up tighter than ever if I wanted to stay alive.

There didn't seem to be anything to laugh at once Reuben was gone. I missed him bad. But, truth be told, I missed Abe more. My horse been like a rock under me.

With him gone I was standing on shifting ground. There was nothing to hold onto. Didn't nothing seem safe. I got given a new one of course, but it wasn't the same. I didn't give it no name other than "Horse". I was planning on not getting attached to nothing or no one ever again.

A couple of days after I been back in the fort Tiberius come running across the parade ground after school finish and press a piece of paper in my hand. There are two white streaks through the dirt on his face where the tears been running.

In one heartbeat it carry me back to the time I seen Jonas like that: curled up in a ball, being eaten alive with sorrow. He'd wrapped himself so tight he was smaller than I was. I'd edged up to him, my hand reaching out, not knowing what to do, only knowing I wanted to ease that pain. Comfort him.

Soon as my fingers touched his skin: that was when he'd first turned on me. He changed in the space of one heartbeat. In one heartbeat there been enough hate in Jonas's eyes to feed every soul in hell.

Looking down at Tiberius I'm suddenly scared. But he don't say nothing. Don't even glance at me. Just run off before he start crying again. When I look at the paper he give me I see he done me a drawing of Abe. And underneath it he wrote, "Sorry about your horse." Broke me in pieces. Couldn't stand to look at it. I folded it up. Put it in my pocket. Buried it deep. Didn't never take it out.

★ ★ ★

It wasn't long after Reuben took off that one of them laundry women started paying me some attention. Spicy was her name and judging from the way Reuben talk about her she been his particular favourite. I guess that girl was missing the money she got when he come calling. There wasn't nothing loving in the way she made up to me. She just grab me by the crotch of my pants. Leastways she try to. I step aside mighty quick.

"Come on, trooper," she says, soft and silky. "Wouldn't you like some comfort on a cold night?"

I try to be civil. I says, "No", but I don't say it nothing like loud enough for her and she try again.

"Ain't Reuben never told you about me? I can make a man feel real warm." She lunge again and I sidestep but I'm terrified she gonna find out what's in my pants – or rather what ain't in them – so this time I'm shouting when I tell her I ain't interested. Captain Smith hears it all good and clear as he passes by and the next thing I know I'm being summoned to the officers' quarters.

He call me in, and first off he commend me for my fine soldierly ways. See, even though me and Reuben failed to deliver the mail like we was supposed to it hasn't troubled him none. I couldn't tell him about Abe – didn't trust myself to speak on the matter – so he didn't know we'd fetched up in that Indian camp. The Captain done put two and two together and make about three hundred. He figures we was lost in the blizzards then attacked by hostiles and my horse was killed and I was wounded in the course of carrying out my duties – and I just let him go right on thinking it. Next thing I know I'm being complimented for my gallantry. Then he says, "I heard what took place just now, Private. Don't approve of loose women, eh?"

"No, sir!" I says. And he finds the sincerity I put into my reply highly satisfying. It wasn't strictly true. I wasn't in no position to judge a person for the way they chose to get by. I had nothing personal against them girls. But I generally found it was easier to tell white folks what they wanted to hear.

So he goes and gives me a promotion. All of a sudden, I'm Corporal O'Hara and I got me a stripe on my arm. I got me some power. I got me some authority. And there's the Captain thinking I'm a fine, upstanding soldier of unimpeachable moral fibre and there's Reuben running off all on his own across the prairies in the snow because he thinks I'm some kinda freak.

It might have been funny if it hadn't of been so damned sad.

Reuben wasn't the only trooper to desert that year. The winter was terrible bad. A bunch of General Michaels' men run off too. I might even have considered it myself if I hadn't found Elijah in the bunkhouse about a week after I got promoted. He was sitting close by the stove and he was shaking like he got the typhoid fever or cholera or something. I figured he was sick and trying to get warm, but then I seen what he was dropping in the fire.

Them animals. All them ones he carved. Eagle. Wolf. Deer. Buffalo. Horse. Into the flames. They lick round one. It flares. Blackens. Crumbles into ashes. In goes the next. One by one. The whole damned ark full.

The Captain had given Elijah some news. Seemed that about the same time General Michaels been killing them Indians, a bunch of civilized white men been doing much the same to Negroes back east. Only back east it lasted six days. And at the end of it, four hundred was dead. Elijah's wife and son was two of them.

He stayed. I stayed. There was no place else to go.

27.

The fine gentlemen in Washington was sick and tired of trying to fix the "Indian Problem". They had decided enough was enough. The army was under new orders. We got to break the Indians by whatever means possible. That was why General Michaels had took his men down along that valley. It was what he called a "pre-emptive strike". Guess he was doing what Sherman done in the war: destroying everything the enemy cared about. What made Indians happy wasn't big houses and sprawling plantations. It was their families. And their horses.

I didn't like what General Michaels had done but it sure was effective. Come the spring – before Company W could start in on them – hundreds of wild Indians was drifting in off the plains and settling themselves down voluntary where the government told them to. Bent Back was dead. Seemed that the heart been ripped out of the rest of them.

In a few weeks there was thousands camped around the fort.

They been promised food when they signed that treaty – I been there, I heard what been said – but supplies was awful late in coming. We had to sit and watch them Indians getting skinnier and skinnier.

When the supply wagons finally rolled in me and Elijah was detailed to hand out rations. We was giving over sacks of flour when one split. Some spilled over my boots. When I bent down to brush it off I seen that flour was cut with sand. Worse, it was peppered with mouse shit and alive with weevils. Cookie would have screamed the place down if someone had tried passing that off on her.

I look to where Isaiah and some others is giving out meat. They a way off but I see it's green and gristly and even from where I'm standing it don't smell so good. I look at Elijah and Elijah looks at me and we both look at the Indians all standing in line real quiet and don't none of them say nothing. They take what they're given and they go off. Who was they gonna complain to?

Now up until that point I been thinking all the trouble that come their way was their own doing – that they brought it down on their own heads. I guess when misfortune come to someone, folks is always inclined to blame the victim. You get sick? Must have been something you ate. You fall over? Should have looked where you was going. Your baby dies? You didn't look after it good. You get strung up? Well, you should have been running, not standing there singing. Your folks get attacked by the army? Hell, you must have done something to deserve it! Whatever it is, if something bad happens to you, it's just got to be your own damned fault.

Folks don't like change, but folks don't like chance neither. The notion that things can come sneaking up and turn your life on its head without you having done nothing at all? The idea that you could be living peaceable, minding your own business, just getting on with life, and then some stranger comes riding out of nowhere and starts hurting your family, killing your folks? That's way too frightening to accept. Goddammit, no, that just can't happen! You've got to be blamed. You've got to be responsible.

But when I seen that flour, well, maybe it was then I started to think a little different.

The fort wasn't big enough to handle all them Indians camping around it so we get orders that a new one has to be built. There been a big piece of land set aside: a brand-new reservation provided by the government so them wild Indians can settle down peaceful, stop hunting, start farming and become tame like them Cherokees.

The Captain's family stay put but Company W is moved about fifty miles north and we found ourselves sitting in the middle of that new reservation, living in tents what been condemned as unfit for General Michaels' men to use.

We're on fatigue duty on and off for more than a year while we're building that fort. We don't get to see a scrap of combat in months. I'm a Corporal now, so I'm doing some of the supervising which suits me fine because when it come to heaving slabs of stone I just ain't got the same muscle power as Elijah. But I don't get to use Mr Cody's rifle for months and I miss it bad. It's like we been turned from soldiers into labourers. Field hands.

Our third army Christmas is a sad and lonesome affair without Mrs Smith making decorations and Tiberius making merry. But come the following summer we'd made ourselves a fine set of buildings with stables and storehouses and officers' quarters and a strong stone-walled corral, which was something to be proud of, I guess, although I recall thinking that if Reuben was right – if freedom meant not having to do no work – we was as far from having it as we ever been.

When we done building, General Michaels and his men get posted there alongside us, which is real unfortunate. They come riding in like they own the place – like it was them built it up out of the ground from nothing. Their first guard mount Private Creech give me a look that says he ain't forgotten and he ain't forgiven me for being a better shot than him. This time I ain't got Reuben watching my back. But with him gone, with Abe gone, I find I'm caring a whole lot less about getting a knife slid between my ribs. And this time I'm a Corporal. The look I send back to

Private Creech makes him blink, drop his head. He don't look in my direction again.

The Captain's family come along too. The girl's walking and talking by now and they got a new baby boy a few months old. Tiberius is a whole lot bigger and he's riding a different pony because, he tells me, Mighty Spotted Warrior upped and died on him during the winter.

"He was just lying there in his stall one morning. Wouldn't wake up."

I want to say to him, "Sorry about your horse." But I can't get the words out. So I don't say nothing.

One morning Captain Smith send me over to his quarters with a note for his wife.

I'm knocking on the door when I hear a scream. It was a frightened one to begin with. I thought maybe she seen a spider or a mouse. Hope to God it ain't a rattler! But then the tone of it kinda changed. Turned into something like fury. And she start yelling and hollering and she sound real mad.

I already knocked but she ain't said nothing like, "Yes?" or "Come in!" and I know white folks is real particular about such things. But I figured I'd risk going in uninvited because if she was being raped or murdered the Captain wouldn't be none too pleased if I just been standing there doing nothing. I give the door a push and go on in and it takes a second or two for my eyes to adjust to the dark in there and before they do I hear Mrs Smith screeching, "Get out! Get out, you disgusting creature!"

I'm kinda surprised, but I turn to go. Then I realize I can't see her, and if I can't see her, she can't see me. That voice is coming from the other room. So I go on through, figuring I'd better save her from whatever is giving her trouble.

What I see is this. There's Mrs Smith, hands raised in claws looking like she's gonna pounce. Her girl is clinging to her skirts, wailing her heart out but Mrs Smith ain't paying no attention. Because across the room there's this little Indian woman who's wandered off the prairie and into the house. Her hair is mussed up, full of sticks and leaves and crawling with cooties. She's about half the size of Mrs Smith. You never did see a less frightening figure. So why was a respectable lady like Mrs Smith about to scratch her face off? The answer was lying right there in that Indian woman's arms: she was holding Mrs Smith's baby boy. Just holding him. Holding him, and looking into his face like she was starving for something more than food. She was drinking in that baby's softness. Sucking up the infant smell. And the baby was gurgling away, quite happy, so I knew she hadn't harmed him none.

Well, Mrs Smith couldn't go attacking her in case the Indian dropped the baby. The Indian couldn't put the baby down in case Mrs Smith attacked her. Figured it was up to me to break the stalemate, so I walk over to the Indian real slow and careful and says as soft as I can, "Won't you give me the child, ma'am?"

It's a good few seconds before she can drag her eyes off the baby's face. And when she finally look at me it's like she been swimming up from someplace real deep. I see something in that face of hers that turns me right over. It's like someone's taken my heart in their hand and squeezed it tight. I seen that look before. I seen it on Bent Back's face. And I seen it on Cookie's when we was walking behind the Yankee army. What had she said? *If you take away what somebody cares for most ... well, then, they don't have no fight left in them.* I hadn't known what she'd been talking about. But now the answer is right here in front of me.

What a woman cares for most is her baby.

It hit me like a punch in the face. Cookie must have had a child sometime, before I knew her. Must have been taken away. Sold. That was what Amos knew and I didn't. The wound been so deep she ain't never spoke of it. Leastways not to me.

And Bent Back? I can't be sure. But I'm guessing that maybe that wasn't the first time his folks been attacked by the army. He'd likely lost a child sometime. One, maybe. Maybe more. No wonder he'd looked at Sherman like that.

It takes an age for that little Indian woman to hand over that baby because she just can't get her arms to agree with the orders her head's giving them. At last they move, just a fraction, and I hear this cracking sound. Must have been in my head. You can't really hear a woman's heart breaking, can you?

She can't do no more. I got one hand on the baby but I got to slide the other round against her chest to fetch him away.

I look at that Indian and I'm not sure what to do next. Chase her out? Tell the Captain? Arrest her? While I'm wondering, she look at Mrs Smith real pitiful and she hold her hand up. I see the smallest finger been cut off right there at the second joint. Hadn't been long ago, neither. Hadn't healed yet.

Mrs Smith's mouth drop open. She says, "Who did that? Who hurt you?"

That woman shake her head. She put her hand on her own chest.

"You did it? You did it to yourself?" I can see what Mrs Smith's thinking as clear as if she'd writ it in letters right across the wall. *Savage! Taking a knife to her own hand?* "Whatever made you do that?"

The Indian sink to the floor, a small sad heap and she let out this sound that split my heart wide open.

"What is it?" Mrs Smith turn to me. "What's she doing?"

"I think maybe she lost her baby, ma'am."

"Oh! The poor creature!" Mrs Smith – who been ready to kill that Indian with her bare hands – sits right down on the floor next to her, and she pull that woman up by the

232

shoulders. She stretches her arms out to me for the baby and I give it her. The back of her hand slides over the bandages I got wrapped tight around my chest.

The Captain's little girl stop crying and drop down on the floor next to her mother. Mrs Smith lay her baby down in that Indian woman's lap so she can take some comfort from a living, breathing child. And then they sit there for a while and the baby's smiling and laughing and not at all scared of the wild scene that's been going on around him. And finally the Indian woman hand the baby back, get to her feet, slip on out of the door and vanish into the prairie.

I watch her go and for a moment or two I'm thinking, Thank the Lord, that's one grief I been spared from. I ain't never gonna have no child taken from me. I ain't never gonna have to watch my baby die.

Then I recall the feel of that little boy lying there, looking up at me.

I ain't never gonna hold my baby in my arms. Ain't never gonna have no family.

For the life of me, I don't know which is worse.

28.

We'd done what we was told and built a new fort, and
the Indians had come in from the wilderness onto the
reservation, so they'd done what they was told so we
was both behaving real well. But them fine gentlemen in
Washington wasn't. Supplies was always late coming and
when they did arrive they was the kinda stuff you wouldn't
want to feed your hogs let alone your children. I felt shamed
every ration day. All I could do was keep my head down,
get on with my job, be the best soldier I could be. But I
didn't find it entirely surprising when some of them warriors
took off hunting and thieving again. Was all they could do
to keep their families from starving.

Company W wasn't troubled with rounding them up
though, not that particular summer. That year the Indian
fighting was General Michaels' job.

What kept us busy was a bunch of trashy white men

that kept running off the army cattle. To begin with it wasn't too many – a couple of head here, three there, then maybe a half a dozen some other place. Each time it happen we was sent looking for them but it wasn't no easy task. See, when General Michaels' men had ridden out their horses, they was given fresh ones. All we was given was their broken-winded, lame, worn-out mounts and it ain't easy persuading an animal in that condition to gallop off in pursuit of rustlers. Some of them was so old and tired they just give out and it feels real bad pushing a broke animal so hard it ups and dies right under you. My horse gone that way early in the spring. I'd ridden two more to dropping since.

As the weeks went on them thieves got a whole lot bolder. Was like they was watching us, laughing at our pitiful efforts to catch up with them. So one fine morning we wake up to find they driven off one hundred and forty-seven cattle and fifteen mules.

Tracking them was gonna be the easy part. That many hooves make a big impression in the dirt. They was heading south, plain as day. They had maybe twelve hours' start on us but they wasn't moving fast because you can't take off at a lick when you're driving a herd that big.

And there was something them rustlers hadn't taken into account this time. Like I said, our animals was wrecks when they come to us and some of them didn't survive. But Elijah was real good with the ones we got left. A couple of months with him seeing to them had made a whole bunch of difference. They was fed, watered, and tended real well – them things you do with any horse was done by all of us – but there was more to it than that. I don't know how Elijah done it. That man just about lost the ability to speak to us since his wife and child been killed. But he could talk to them horses. Somehow that man whispered in their ears and put the heart back into them.

So when five of us rode off after them thieves we was on mounts that took off so fast and furious seemed like we was on a race track. Them men got a whole lot more than they bargained for.

We was two days out before we caught up with them. We could see a cloud of dust from way across the prairie but by the time we was almost on them the land had done that strange thing of rising up either side of you like a pair of waves. They go right ahead into a ravine.

Captain Smith look at me and I look at him and I know we're both thinking the same thing: if we do this the Indian way then maybe we'll stand a chance of catching them thieves. We ride back aways until the land flatten out again. Then he give the order for us to split up. I take Elijah and Isaiah to the left; the Captain and a private by the name of Jefferson go to the right. Instead of heading down along the trough between the waves we're riding the crests either side. When we get maybe within a hundred yards of the edge of them we hobble our horses and go the rest of the way on foot, because we can't risk them men seeing us coming. We keep low and walk real careful but army boots ain't as quiet as moccasins. It's lucky for us that the cows are bellowing so loud they ain't aware of us coming up on them.

The ravine they gone into runs to a dead end. There ain't no way out but the way they come in. But before it stops it opens out into a wide corral-shaped valley. If you was gonna go stealing cattle it's the perfect place to hide them. They only need to have one man watching the entrance to it – that herd can't go wandering nowhere.

What happened next was more or less up to me. The Captain had said I was to use my judgement and give orders and fire or not as I saw fit. And I saw fit after I been watching them rustlers for about half an hour.

The Captain and Jefferson had come up the other side. I could see their dark uniforms moving through the rocks.

I says to Elijah, "You and Isaiah go back on down. Cut off their escape route if they try to run."

They don't argue. They move quick and when they're gone I keep on watching.

It's easy as eating cherry pie to figure out who the leader is. He's yelling loud as Miss Louellen and his men are running in all directions, doing his bidding. There's a cloud of dirt thrown up by all them hooves so I can't get a good view of him for a while. But soon enough them cattle realize they ain't going nowhere and they settle down to grazing. And that man figures he's done a real fine job, but Lordy, ain't rustling cattle thirsty work and don't he deserve to have himself a drink? He's cracking open the whisky, settling himself for a pleasant rest on a rock, which happens to be under an overhang directly below where the Captain and Jefferson are hunkered down.

They can't get a clear shot at him.

But I can.

Mr Cody's rifle is purring with pleasure in my hands at the prospect. I didn't want to kill him, not outright. The idea was that when we caught up with them we'd bring them in. Show them what American justice meant. I had to fix him so he could still ride, but couldn't run. I aimed for his leg, halfway along his thigh.

But he was one heck of a long way off and I was out of practice. I caught him bang on the knee. He screams. Falls off that rock.

His men was awful yellow. Soon as he done that the rest of them got their hands up in the air and they down on their knees begging for their lives.

"Take the cattle! Don't shoot! Don't shoot!"

They couldn't see any of us from where they was – I guess they thought we was an Indian war party gonna skin them alive. I ain't never seen no one squirm so much.

Across the chasm Captain Smith waves to get my attention. He point. Gesture. There's a thin trail that zigzag down into that place and he's gonna take it. So I keep him covered while him and Jefferson start climbing down to arrest them.

When they see it's the army coming one of them men decides he's gonna fight back. Quick as a flash he pull his gun and shoot Jefferson bang in the chest. Jefferson fall off the rock. Lands in amongst the cattle. Starts them running in rings again. But not before I've put a bullet right through the head of the man who killed him. Guess I ain't lost my touch after all.

Captain Smith's near busting his lungs with yelling at them. "You're surrounded. I've a hundred men up there. A hundred rifles, trained on you. Surrender now, if you want to live."

Three of them have got their hands in the air. They're ready to roll over like puppy dogs and submit. But one of them – a whiskery, weasely fella – is looking up to where I am. I'm pretty well hidden but that ain't what's interesting him. "Both shots come from that rock," he says. "I reckon you only got one man up there."

The Captain stop. There ain't nowhere for him to go. If any of them cut up rough now he's an easy target. He try to brave it out. "You want me to prove it?"

"Yeah. I reckon I do."

I'm cussing myself for having sent Elijah and Isaiah back down along to the entrance of that ravine. At least the three of us would have stood a chance of keeping him covered. I'm a fine shot, but how in the hell am I gonna make out like I'm a hundred troopers? I've reloaded, and I'm taking aim at the weasely fella thinking at least I can take him down.

Then gunshots start ringing out. They coming from way along the ravine but them rustlers haven't figured that out. They think they're under attack.

The weasely fella has his hands up in a second, but I shoot him just the same. Catch him through the shoulder so he drop his weapon.

Captain Smith don't even need to ask them others to surrender. They throw down their guns and let him tie their wrists, meek as lambs.

At which point another hundred or so head of cattle come running in, followed by maybe a dozen mules. I'm wondering what the heck's going on when I see Elijah and Isaiah riding in after them leading a pair of horses with two more captives tied across their saddles.

Turns out they're all part of the same outfit. They gone off to raid the herd from a different fort and this is where they'd all arranged to meet. Elijah and Isaiah had a little shoot-out with them when they come along the gulley.

So without too much trouble, and the loss of only one man, we capture the whole darned gang. And when we ride back to the fort we got ourselves seven prisoners and nigh on three hundred head of cattle and all them damned mules – looking like Yeller and acting just the same – which

I'd have preferred to leave in that ravine if I'd have had the choice.

For bringing them animals safe back we gets commended and I get me promoted all the way to Sergeant, which I'm sure don't please Private Creech none but which please the heck out of me. I earned this one. I'm a good soldier. The best that I can be. Ain't that something to be proud of? And now, finally, finally, finally, the General hands over his ten bucks to Captain Smith. We won the Captain his bet.

Sure wish Reuben had of been around to see that.

29.

Soon after I made Sergeant word come in that yet another bunch of goddamned Indians was attacking yet another goddamned wagon train. Most all of General Michaels' men was already out in the field so he give the order that a detachment of twenty men from Company W was to go after them.

When we got to where they been attacked them warriors was long gone. Most of them settlers was long gone too – they managed to run away because it wasn't no big war party that been going at them. But there was seven of them dead and I never did get used to seeing folks scalped.

We followed the Indians' trail but we didn't find none of them and eventually it give out so we headed back to the fort and the reservation.

Now we didn't have no notion of who had attacked

that wagon train and we wouldn't have never found out if Red Barrel Chest had of kept his mouth shut. But he didn't.

By that time Washington had sent out a civilian agent to the reservation. He was in charge of giving out them Indians' supplies. Come ration day I been detailed to help him so I was there when Red Barrel Chest come riding in to get his provisions.

The agent was the God-fearing, respectable kind and he used to speak to them Indians real polite. Things is going fine but then he says to Red Barrel Chest, "Know anything about the raid on that wagon train a couple of weeks back?"

Well, I figure he was only making conversation to be civil, but the effect was like walking up to a hornets' nest and giving it a big old kick. Red Barrel Chest swell, and he was large enough anyhow, and I was half expecting iron hoops to come busting off his ribs. He pull himself up to his full height, and I was reminded of the way a rattler looks just before it strikes. I take a step back, out of his reach.

As he swell, the agent shrink. Every scrap of colour fade from the white man's face and that was before that chief even open his mouth and this angry voice come roaring out, damned near powerful enough to blow the agent's hair back like he was caught in a storm.

Red Barrel Chest start shouting about how he's kept asking for all them things the government promised but they ain't come, so he done take his best warriors off raiding, one of whom has come riding in with him. He's a skinny little fella with a moustache and that's the first moustache I ever seen on an Indian and I kind of fix on that one little detail. I'm watching it twitch up and down while Red Barrel Chest is yelling. And I'm thinking, Shut the hell up! Hush your goddamned mouth. Just stop. *Stop.* Because I can see if he goes on they're all gonna end up dead and I don't much care about any of them but who knows how many of us are going to end up dead right alongside? But he don't. That savage ain't got the sense he was born with! Hell and goddammit, that man's naming names, listing them warriors that was on that raid like he's proud of it, like it was an honour, and he don't realize how much trouble he's bringing down on all of their heads.

He goes on talking until he's said his piece, and then he rides off. His head was held high. Mine was in my hands because right away – while I'm left standing there – the agent skedaddles over to General Michaels to tell him all them warriors' names.

And the next thing I know, Company W is being ordered to saddle up and stay hidden in the stables in case there's a fight. And I – on account of my being so useful with a gun – have to go right into the General's house with a dozen others and hide in the front room, peeping between the shutters so we can see what happens. And I ain't set foot inside a house so fine since the Yankees set fire to the plantation and it feels real strange to be back in one where there's lace tablecloths and velvet cushions and the smell of women's perfume and fried chicken hanging in the air. We're looking out onto the porch where General Michaels and some of them other officers have summoned all them warriors and are waiting for them to arrive and it's a bit like seeing the master waiting for his neighbours to come calling, only there ain't no mint juleps, nor Irish whisky, nor no gingerbread.

Them warriors come in of their own free will, most of them. One had to be forced in. One had to be run down and dragged in.

But soon enough, there they all was, sitting on the porch and of course they ain't alone. Their squaws and their kids and a whole bunch of other warriors have come along to see what's going on so there's a great crowd of Indians standing there in front of the house.

General Michaels tell them chiefs they being arrested for killing seven settlers on the wagon train. And Red Barrel Chest yell in his big, booming voice that he'd rather die than be a prisoner, and he reach for his pistol.

General Michaels give the command and we throw back them shutters and we point our rifles at all them warriors' hearts and I got mine pointing at Red Barrel Chest and I'm praying he won't do nothing because I don't especially want to fire on someone who's not firing at me, even if he got his gun on the General.

Then the Indian with the moustache stands up and says

he ain't gonna let none of them be taken. Him and General Michaels are gonna die right there on the porch. And then another warrior ride up and he got two rifles and he throw one at one fella then get off his horse and come over and sit down in front of General Michaels and he point his weapon right at the General's head.

And we get given the order, so we pull back the hammers on our guns. It's gonna be the biggest God Almighty bloodbath since what General Michaels done down along the river and I'm right there in the middle of it and I'm wishing I got a death song to mark the occasion like them warriors do because it feels strange being wiped out in someone's house where there's all that polished wood and white lace and a piece of Mrs Michaels' embroidery thrown down on the chair with the needle still stuck in it. The sight of that little piece of cloth makes my mind go wandering off to Mrs Beecher and how her husband been teaching their boy to read when she was off at her sewing circle and I start wondering did she ever stitch anything so fine and dainty? And Mrs Michaels' fancywork is going to be spattered with blood and brains any second now. My blood. My brains. And wouldn't Jonas have laughed to think of me fetching up dead like this on the floor in the middle of someone's parlour?

My mouth's running dry. All them soldiers in the stables come streaming out, half to the left, half to the right and they got the crowd surrounded. General Michaels is looking real mean but Captain Smith takes matters into his own hands. He yell at the interpreter to tell them Indians that violence ain't gonna save none of them warriors from justice.

Our guns is pointing at them Indians' chests. And the Captain tells them, real calm, real quiet, that they're going to be held for trial and there's nothing none of them can do about it.

It's the truth, plain and simple. They don't have no choice, and they know it as well as we do. Only decision is whether they're going to come quiet, or be killed right there on that porch.

We was all balanced on a knife edge. There was this silence so deep I swear I could have heard a pine needle falling to the ground. And it's a mighty tricky thing keeping still when the hammer on your rifle is cocked like that. Your fingers get twitchy. They start to ache because they know the routine better than your head does by now: hammer, trigger, fire. Not doing it is like trying to turn back once you've jumped off a cliff. Only if you fire before the command's given you likely to start up a whole new war. So you don't move a muscle, not even if Mr Cody's rifle is purring in your hands. Not until Red Barrel Chest stands up.

He catch sight of me behind General Michaels and he look me real hard in the eye, a look so full of hate and rage and wild despair that it make my blood boil at the same time as my heart fill with sadness. And he turn away. He put down his gun. One by one the others do the same thing.

So they didn't exactly agree with the Captain, but they didn't put up no more fight. Their families stood there watching, quiet as mice, while we took them warriors off to the guardhouse and locked them inside.

They was held prisoner for a couple of weeks. Then all of them was supposed to be taken off to the courthouse in town to be given a fair trial but the one with the moustache didn't never get that far.

We load them into the wagons, but suddenly he stand up and he call something to Red Barrel Chest. He nod towards the tree on the horizon. Then he start his death song.

Now I heard plenty of those in my time. When the odds was stacked against them, a warrior would start singing. And these wasn't no sweet voices, twining around each other like honeysuckle, rising to heaven. They was chilling things. Strange. Ghostly, almost. Sad, too.

The sound of that moustached man's singing freeze me to the marrow. A death song's a haunting thing. And I was thinking, How's he gonna die? I mean, he was chained to the wagon. I seen Elijah make them manacles. They was fitted around his wrists tighter than a wedding ring around a finger. Was no way he'd get out of them. So what was he going to do? Kill himself just by wishing hard enough?

Well, I wouldn't have been surprised if he'd of done just that – some of them Indians was like witches, the things they could do. Sound of that wailing cry was enough to make a person believe he could summon up the Devil to strike us all stone dead.

Once his song is finished he sits down again in that wagon and pull the blanket over his head. It trundle along, same as before and it's getting further from the fort and closer to the tree and nothing's happened, so I figure maybe he's planning on starving himself to death.

Only he ain't.

Now them Indians was sometimes capable of doing things that made your brain bust with the horror of them. No wonder the US Army couldn't scare them.

Suddenly that moustached warrior jumps up. He's got out of them manacles and the way he's done that is to bite through his own flesh, ripping off the skin with his teeth till his hands is small enough to slide through them. I've known some bad, bad times, but I can't begin to imagine ever being desperate enough to do something like that.

He's got a knife hidden somewhere, though God alone knows how he done manage that because he was searched and searched again when he was arrested. But he take that knife and stick it into the soldier who's driving the wagon – who just so happens to be Private Creech – right under the ribs, straight into his heart. That Indian done me something of a favour.

He grabs a rifle. His hands is running with blood. It's everywhere. He can't get a grip on the weapon. Before he can fire it at the other fella on the box he gets himself shot.

It's a mortal wound but it ain't fatal yet. The General orders him to be thrown in the ditch and the first wagon just carries right on rolling away towards town and the courthouse like nothing has happened.

Me and Elijah have to stand guard over him, make sure none of his folks come nowhere near. That man don't die quick and he don't die clean. It takes more than three hours for the life to finally leave him. He don't make a single sound all that time. If I could have helped him to a faster end like I done with Abe I'd have put a bullet through his head. But that was against orders.

The others, well, they was put on trial and they was found guilty by the white men on the jury in about ten seconds flat. They was sentenced to hang. But some other white folks – including the civilian agent who done report them all to General Michaels in the first place – went to the governor and begged him to show them mercy. They was given life imprisonment instead.

Life imprisonment for the man who wanted to roam the whole dammed prairie? If he'd been given a choice, I figure Red Barrel Chest would have preferred the hanging.

30.

What happened to Red Barrel Chest and them others got all the Indians stirred up again real bad. They was restless and twitchy and that makes them settlers restless and twitchy too and they start complaining to the folks in Washington so before long the government decides it's got to tighten its grip even harder. Orders come in that the Indians got to be kept in line. Each and every one of them have got to camp within ten miles of the fort and they got to come for a weekly roll call. Any who don't answer when their name is hollered out – man, woman or child – is officially classed as a hostile, a renegade, an enemy who's gonna be hunted down and killed.

It felt like we was sitting on a powder keg again and sure enough it done explode into another war. Only this time it was worse because I was beginning to feel like Company W was ants being stirred up with a stick: black folks being set against red ones. We was fighting because we had nowhere to go and nothing to lose. They was fighting because they was about to lose everything. I was starting to wonder if maybe we wasn't both fighting the wrong people.

The Indians got the army telling them they gotta stay put on the reservation, else they'll be shot. But I seen with my own eyes that the food they been promised don't show up the whole of the following winter and the whole winter's a long time to go without eating and them folks start to starve. So off go the warriors in search of buffalo and off we go in search of them but they was way ahead of us and we never did catch up. All we found was the carcasses of hundreds of dead buffalo, laying over that prairie like the droppings of some giant animal. It was one hell of a sight. One hell of a smell too. Seemed that white hunters had got there before them warriors was even close, took off the skins to sell, left the rest to rot. They was crawling with maggots. Wasn't nothing fit to eat left on them. It made them warriors so mad they went off killing all the hunters and fur traders they could find.

But if they was mad, Captain Smith was pretty mad too. He had himself one hell of an altercation with the General when we got back to the fort. We could hear every word over in our quarters. He damned nearly got himself court-martialled for insubordination.

Captain Smith was a deep-down decent man. The way

he saw it, them hunters was thieving what was rightfully Indian property. But the General refused to let Captain Smith take us off in search of them. The way the General figured was that if the buffalo was wiped out, them Indians would be wiped out too, like vermin, sure as night follows day. He told Captain Smith it was an "elegant solution to the Indian Problem". It would clear them off the land for once and for all. Guess he had Sherman's backing on that one.

Seemed wrong to me then, seems wrong to me now. Them buffalo was created by the Lord God Almighty. Wasn't for mankind to go wiping them off the face of the earth. But didn't no one ask for my opinion.

Them Indians hold a sun dance and they get themselves fired up with singing and dancing and sticking arrows and knives in themselves to prove how big and brave they are. And after a few days of this, them warriors go on the warpath. But this time it ain't just the men who go running. Their families follow right along, so thousands of folks go streaming off the reservation. The plains are in uproar and we're the ones supposed to sort the whole damned mess out.

We're criss-crossing the prairies after all them runaways – who now count as hostiles and renegades – for weeks on end and sometimes we find a bunch of them but more often we don't. Then one day we come by a trading post. Seemed white hunters been real busy lately. There are fresh buffalo skins piled high by the door.

We ride towards it and there's some strange-looking carvings on top of the corral posts and a mighty bad smell, but I don't pay it much attention because the trader come out to talk with Captain Smith. He's looking kinda pleased with himself and, after wiping his palms on his apron, he reaches up and shakes the Captain by the hand.

"Well, lookee here! Here come the cavalry!" he says, and I don't especially like the smile on his face. "You've arrived two weeks too late to save us all."

Captain Smith ignores the fella's tone. "Did you have some trouble here, Mr...?"

"Jones," he says. "Sure did. But we didn't need no bunch of mokes to help us out. We killed them Indians all by ourselves."

And he jerks his thumb towards the corral and I realize them strange-looking things on the posts ain't carvings.

They're heads.

And that explains the smell and the fact there's so many flies buzzing and why the horses is all grouped together, nervous in the middle, because they don't like the smell of blood no more than I do.

Mr Jones start telling Captain Smith how Indians come attacking at sunup one morning. He was bragging his head off: he talked the same way all folks done after they survive an attack. From what he said you'd have thought he fought off more than a thousand desperate warriors. Well, they may have been desperate, but there sure wasn't that many of them. I ain't repeating his account – I didn't believe less than half of it. What it amounted to was this: some chief led the charge but Mr Jones and them hunters at the trading post was sitting inside some mighty sturdy walls, and what's more they got themselves new telescopic sights on their guns, which is a whole lot finer than anything the Indians got. Finer than what Company W got, come to that. They could shoot them warriors off their horses from a mile away without so much as breaking a sweat.

Well, the Indians keep right on most all of the day but they ain't getting nowhere and by the time the chief call off the attack fifteen of his men is lying dead. And if you're an Indian you can't go fetching along a bunch of new recruits from out east to replace them. So he rides off, and then them hunters come out and cut off the dead warriors' heads and stick them up on the corral to warn off any Indian who's thinking of doing the same thing.

Now that sight was enough to turn my stomach in any case. But Mr Jones' next words were like having a cold knife slide into my guts.

He says, "Was a mighty strange thing. There was a bugler with them. All the time they was charging he kept playing and shooting. Was the darnedest thing, seeing them all ride along to music."

Before I can stop myself I says, "What was the song?"

Mr Jones looks like he don't want to reply to no question from the likes of me. He's torn between going on with his story and turning his back on us. In the end he can't resist completing his tale, and every sentence is like a twist of that knife.

"'Sam Hall'," he says, and he sings a line just in case the Captain don't know the tune. Which of course he does, because he's heard General Michaels' men singing it as often as the rest of us. He skip right ahead to the last verse. "My name is Samuel, And I'll see you all in hell, I'll see you all in hell, Damn your eyes!" Then Mr Jones adds with that snake-like smile of his, "Was driving us plumb crazy till I brung him down." He pick up an imaginary gun and point it at his imaginary opponent. Pulls an imaginary trigger. "Got ya!" He laughs, long and loud. "Sure was a relief when he stopped. And do you know who the crazy dumbass was a-playing that bugle?"

"Enlighten me." Captain Smith's voice is cold as cold because he was there that first Christmas when we decorate that barn and we all got to messing with them musical instruments.

But Mr Jones don't even notice, because this is the punchline to the biggest joke in history. He slaps his leg, and he's laughing so much he can hardly spit the words out. "A nigger!"

"Do you know the man's name?" asks Captain Smith.

"Nope. Weren't nothing in his pockets worth having.

He was in army uniform, though. We figured he was a deserter. Ain't no one been able to identify him. Want to take a look? Mind you, he's getting a bit beyond being recognizable."

Captain Smith ride over to the corral and it don't take a whole heap of figuring to work out from the look on his face that he knows that last head.

The Captain look across at me and he give the very smallest of nods and my heart feels about as heavy as a stone. Behind me Elijah takes a deep breath and Isaiah gives a gulp but none of us say nothing because there ain't no words what will cover Reuben ending up dead.

31.

Any pride I had in being a good soldier, any belief that I was part of something big, something fine – all that vanish like gun smoke when I seen Reuben's head on that post.

How in the hell he had ended up with them Indians I didn't know and there wasn't no way of finding out. Guess they'd found him wandering alone over that prairie. A soldier, running away from the US Army. A deserter who thought that Red Barrel Chest had a point. Who seen Bent Back shot when he raised his hand in peace. Who was maybe prepared to change sides and fight for a lost cause. They needed all the fighting men they could get. Made sense keeping him instead of killing him.

All I could think was that it was my fault: mine, mine, mine. If I hadn't of scared him off like that, if I'd have just told him what I was. But I'd been too much of a goddamned coward. I'd killed Reuben. Same as I'd killed

Amos and Cookie. Henry. And Abe. Seemed I killed things just by caring for them.

After that, the world seemed a bad, sad place to be. I figured God must be sleeping, else how could he stand to look down on his creation and see the mess folks was making of it? Them Indians was better off out of it. I'd have left it behind too, if I'd have had any choice. But it didn't seem to matter what I did. I could take all the crazy chances I liked, throw myself in the line of fire, go hand to hand with the enemy – there wasn't no bullets out there with my name on them. No arrows nor blades neither. Seemed Death just didn't want to take me. All I got was a reputation for outstanding courage, nerves of steel and excellent marksmanship.

Days, weeks, months, went by. It was the same thing, over and over. Seemed we was going round and round in circles. Fighting. Losing men. Having new recruits come from out east to replace them. Trying to train them up, but losing them even quicker than the old soldiers because they was so raw didn't none of them know what they was doing. Fighting, killing. Fighting, killing. Fighting, killing. Didn't seem there would ever be an end.

The generals was discussing tactics and strategy but down on the ground it didn't feel like there was nothing orderly nor organized going on. A piece on a chequerboard don't know why it's being pushed from square to square and neither did we. They was zigzagging us back and forward, driving them Indians so hard they couldn't hunt or rest or eat or sleep; driving them head first into a noose.

And in the middle of all that mess of blood and stink and pain there was me and Elijah and Isaiah, clinging together like drowning men. None of us was proud of what we was doing. But we didn't make the rules. When you're in a situation like the one we was in you just do what you're told, keep your head down. And when you get ordered to ride into an Indian camp and destroy everything you find there, you ride right on in, you torch them tepees and even shoot the horses, and you shut your mind right off because there ain't no point in thinking. Thinking keeps you awake. Thinking gives you bad dreams. Thinking just about kills you.

It was killing me.

I kept telling myself that we wasn't doing what General Michaels and his men done to Bent Back and his people. He'd lied to that man: I'd heard him. Said he wouldn't be attacked, then gone right ahead and done it. What we was doing wasn't the same. It wasn't the same at all. We was just trying to bring them Indians back in onto the reservation so they could live peaceable. If they chose to die out there in the wilderness that was up to them. It was their choice. Their decision. I told myself that so often I almost come close to believing it.

It went on and on. One year? Two? Ten? I plain don't

know. Felt like a hundred. I didn't care enough to keep count.

Then come a summer when the weather was mighty strange. Seemed like Judgement Day had arrived. We had heat so bad you felt like you was gonna shrivel up. It was a hundred degrees and we was buttoned up in them wool jackets the whole time because there ain't no flexibility in the army when it come to rules and regulations, leastways not for the likes of us.

Finding water was a real big problem and sometimes we had to dig for it and scrape it out of the ground with our tin cups, and sometimes we was days without it, which can make you feel like you're going crazy, and it can make you feel like you want to kill someone for just cracking his knuckles and you'd do it too if only it weren't so darned hot that you ain't got the strength to lift your rifle and pull the trigger. And our mouths was dry and our tongues was swollen so you couldn't eat nothing because you couldn't swallow it, not even eat the sugar that was in our packs because sugar won't melt if you ain't got no saliva.

The sun was burning, and the wind was hotter than Satan's breath. Sometimes the land was flatter than the master's dining table and when the land's that featureless you can't tell distance because there's nothing to judge it by. Ain't no trees, no bushes, ain't nothing but sand and grass and a horizon, which never comes no closer. You can ride for hour after hour and you don't seem to get nowhere, so pretty soon it's like being in a real bad dream where you're riding, endlessly riding, and never getting nowhere and you don't know whether you're awake or asleep or alive or dead.

In the middle of that heat a swarm of grasshoppers come flying down and strip the whole prairie clean. Wasn't nothing left. Not a single blade of grass. A train got itself derailed when it run into a three-foot drift of them and about twenty folks was killed. It was like we was living through them Egyptian plagues and I got to thinking about Moses and the Promised Land again and wherever that place of flowing milk and honey was, it sure as hell wasn't in America.

Next, a freezing wind come down from the north, whipping up the dust, turning the prairie from brutal heat to brutal cold in a matter of minutes. Rain followed, drops so cold they froze soon as they landed, covering everything in a sheet of ice – horses, saddles, troopers.

Then we got floods when every stream and river busted its banks and the whole of the plains was awash with mud and we didn't have no ark to come and save us. Ain't pleasant making camp in them conditions. Ain't pleasant fighting in them neither, but we done plenty of both.

After the fall floods come the winter snow, and I already said how that could be.

But if it was bad for us, it was worse for them Indians. We hounded them so hard that in the end they just couldn't keep on running. When they finally give up – starved, broke and beat – it was one hell of a goddamned almighty relief.

The relief didn't last long.

As soon as the last of them prairie Indians come trailing in we get sent out. Company W was moved again, way out west, further from civilization than we ever been.

This time we was supposed to be rounding up Apaches.

I didn't know nothing about them. None of us did. They was just Indians, as far as we was concerned. Cheyenne, Sioux, Kiowa, Comanche: didn't matter none what tribe they was – Indians was Indians, and they was all one big old pain in the ass.

There I was. Still alive. The good Lord been protecting me all this time and I guess I should have felt grateful. But I didn't. I was like something mechanical. Had as much heart and soul as a steam engine. Everything human inside of me been shut down. I didn't feel nothing. I didn't think about nothing. As for living or dying: I didn't care what happened either way.

But soon after we arrived in Apache territory I laid eyes on a man who changed everything. After that, I cared. I cared a lot. He was my saviour. Or he was my downfall, depending on how you look at it. Guess maybe he was both.

32.

Company W was sent along into Apache territory with a scout by the name of Bill Hickey. He passed the time along the way telling tales about the enemy. We had a bunch of new recruits along and he was scaring them half out of their minds. If Captain Smith had of been with us he'd have found a way of hushing that man's mouth.

But he wasn't.

Captain Smith had got himself a promotion. He was being sent back east with his family to set up some kinda new school. He was gonna bring the benefits of education to the Indians. Take their children, cut their hair, put them in white man's clothes and teach them all to grow up civilized. I don't know if their parents was willing to part with them. Don't suppose no one asked.

Saying goodbye to Captain Smith was one of the hardest things I ever had to do. I never thought I'd care so much about a white man. The morning Company W moved on out west he went down the line shaking his soldiers by the hand, wishing us luck, saying he was proud to have served with us, and how there wasn't no better company in the United States Army. When he stopped in front of me, clapped both hands on my shoulders and said that I'm a truly fine soldier and he'd never known anyone so recklessly courageous in combat, well, he cut me up bad. All I been doing was trying to get myself killed. I didn't deserve his good opinion.

It cut me up even worse when Tiberius come to say goodbye. That boy had grown tall as me and his hand was big as mine when we shook, but there was tears in his eyes like he still just a boy inside.

Truth be told, there was tears in mine too. He looked me in the face and I saw his expression was the same as the first day I'd laid eyes on him. There wasn't no hate there. Not a trace of it. Wasn't nothing but open-hearted honesty.

As we mounted up and rode on out of the fort a question started nagging at me: if Tiberius hadn't changed when he got bigger, why in the hell had Jonas? It banged against the sides of my head like a fly against a window pane. I couldn't shake it free. Not until Bill Hickey started talking, and then I had other things to think about.

Without Captain Smith I felt like a turtle whose shell been ripped off. I was a mess of raw meat, and Bill Hickey was a bird pecking bits off of me. I kept wishing the

Captain was there. But he wasn't. So I had to listen to Bill Hickey's ramblings. It was like standing in the bottom of a latrine, letting the shit and piss rain down on my head.

"Now an Apache warrior can't look you in the eye, man to man. They're liars, cheats, thieves, every man jack of them. If you ever get talking to one, why then, you'd better not believe a single word he says. Their tongues are more forked than a rattler's. And when they start a fight, you'd best look sharp. They won't ever come at you straight."

Bill was riding beside me, but he was making damned sure his voice was loud enough to carry on down the column. "Listen to me, boy, and listen good: I'm telling you now they are the slipperiest varmints in all creation. Wily as coyotes. You won't know they're there until men start dropping dead all around you. I've seen entire columns of troopers wiped out before they had time to fire a single shot. When they've finished fighting, why then those braves vanish into thin air – it's like they can make themselves invisible! They don't leave a trail, not so much as a footprint.

"And whatever you do, don't ever let them catch you alive. If you're ambushed, if you're ever in a tight spot my advice is this: save one last bullet for yourself because you're going to need it, boy. If they get hold of you they'll give you over to their women first. I say 'women'. Huh! She-devils is more like it. They'll peel the nigger hide off of you inch by inch with their flint knives. Then they'll let their kids have their turn. By the time they've finished sticking their spears in your back you're going to have more spikes than a porcupine. If you're still alive after that the men will tie you up by your feet. Hang you from a tree, cut off your dick and stick it in your mouth. Then they'll light a fire under your head and cook you real slow. Yep. I'm telling you, boy, you don't ever want to get yourself caught by an Apache."

Bill had what looked like a strip of beef jerky wound around the pommel on the front of his saddle. He was fingering it while he talked, and when he notice me looking a slow smile start spreading across his face.

"Of course, I've never had a problem with Apaches myself. I showed them who was boss a few years back. A group of them came thieving. Ran off fifty head of cattle from a friend of mine. We got ourselves up a posse and caught them when they got back to their camp. We showed those redskins what a white man can do. Killed the warriors. Had the squaws. Sweet Jesus, that was some party!"

I don't know what manner of a trophy he had there on his saddle. I didn't care to ask. But I knew deep down in my belly that man had done something so ugly to them squaws it made the red veil come down over my eyes.

It's men like him made me sign up for the army. Men like him keeping me in this goddamned uniform. Men like him mean there ain't never been no place else for me to go. Hell and goddammit! Ain't there nowhere in this whole godforsaken country I can get away from men like him?

Across my back Mr Cody's rifle starts purring. My fingers are itching. Wasn't nothing I'd have liked better than to pull out my gun and use it on Bill Hickey.

But I can't. I got to bite my tongue. Hell, I got to do it so hard my mouth fill with blood. I'm spitting drops of scarlet, leaving a long trail of them in the dirt all the time we're riding west.

The fort we was posted to was different from them ones on the plains. I guess there wasn't much timber to be had in these parts. Not much stone neither, from the look of it. The little low buildings was made up of mud bricks set around a hard-baked parade ground. There was dust everywhere, a fine sprinkling of it coating everything. Horses, officers, troopers – whiteys and niggers – it turned us all the same colour.

If the fort was different, the men inside it was much the same. The General was a man by the name of Howker, but he might just as well of been called Michaels or Sullivan because when it come to how he felt about Company W they was all blood brothers.

We was on the apprehensive side when we finally come riding in and it wasn't just on account of Bill Hickey's bone-chilling tales. We could see with our own eyes the territory was a tough one to be fighting in. We'd come through deserts criss-crossed with gulleys plenty deep enough for hostiles to hide in. There was whole mountain ranges, sitting in the middle of flat plains like islands in the ocean. And there was ravines. Plenty of ravines. A whole world of them.

But the worst part was not knowing who was gonna replace Captain Smith. That man had always stood between Company W and the General Michaels, and the General Sullivans, and the General Howkers of this world. Without him I guess we all felt kinda fearful of what was gonna be coming our way.

Well, we didn't have time to sit around twiddling our thumbs, worrying and waiting for our new Captain to arrive. We was given a man by the name of MacIntyre to tide us over and pretty much as soon as we arrive we get sent back on out. Seemed a band of hostile Apaches been running wild, raiding ranches and thieving cattle, until they gone and got themselves captured. They was being held as prisoners someplace. We got the job of escorting them – along with a whole bunch of peaceable Apaches who been living nice and quiet – to a new reservation.

Didn't none of us know one end of the territory from another so we get given scouts to show us the way and Bill Hickey's one of them. The others are Indians. One's squatting down in the dirt and he got his back to us until Captain MacIntyre calls him, "Hey you! What's your name? Jim. Get over here."

He stand up. He turn around. And suddenly I'm in a whole heap of trouble.

He the finest-looking man I ever did see. I stare at him and two seconds later I'm hurting so bad I got to bite my lip to keep from yelling.

When you're frozen in the snow there's a numbness that come after the shivering and it's a kind of blessing. Before too long it'll send you right to sleep so you won't never wake up. The pain only start if you survive, when you get back by the stove and the blood gets flowing.

I been frozen solid for months. Years. I'd forgot I was a human being, let alone a woman. Seeing that man made a melting warmth spread through me. So now I was in pain and I didn't like it. I didn't want it. But it seemed I didn't have no choice.

My heart was thumping and my head was screaming inside. I was praying. Begging. God Almighty, stop this. Make this stop. Who you messing with? This ain't funny.

I mean, Lord above, why? Why that man? Why that *particular* one? I been surrounded by men for years. Ain't hardly seen nothing but men. I was adrift in an ocean of men and didn't none of them affect me in that way, excepting maybe Reuben. Why here? Why now? Why *that* man? Why him?

To answer that question I got to look again. And when I look again I just can't tear my eyes away.

It wasn't just that he was fine-looking. Though, sweet

Jesus, he was a beautiful sight to behold! But there was a stillness about him. Was like gazing into a deep, deep pool. And all I wanted to do was dive on in.

I'm sitting there staring at him and as he turns his head his eyes meet mine. And I swear at that moment I feel my soul detach itself from my body and fly right into his.

How much does a soul weigh? Must be a heavy thing. Because I'm as light as air without it. When Captain MacIntyre give the order to move out I'm floating a good two inches above my saddle. Wasn't a pleasant feeling. I was like a broke-down paddle steamer. Suddenly I was drifting. Didn't know where the current would take me. Could be heading onto rocks.

I was so occupied with what was going on inside me I couldn't think straight. Couldn't hardly hear neither over the blood pounding in my ears. Captain MacIntyre thought I was just about the most damned fool sergeant he'd ever encountered. He had to give his orders twice, three times over before I followed them. Took me so much effort to keep my eyes from wandering over to that scout I was nigh on useless for anything else. Every step my horse takes it's beating out that man's name on the ground. Jim. Jim. Jim. Jim.

We ride all day and according to Captain MacIntyre we're still about fifteen miles from where we're headed. So we make camp and I stick right close to Elijah and Isaiah to stop myself walking over to Jim, who's with them Indian scouts, keeping themselves to themselves a long way away from the rest of us. It ain't entirely surprising seeing as Bill Hickey has started off on one of his tales.

As the sun goes down I discover I got me another God Almighty problem. One of them monthlies has started. Soon as I'm able to, I head off to find a bush.

There was the light from the fire and there was a full moon besides but there ain't no bushes nearby. I head on out, away from the camp just as a cloud come scudding across making everything ten times darker. I squat down behind a rock to sort myself out hoping there ain't no rattlers gonna come biting me on the ass. When I'm done I put my hand out to push myself up.

The rock's kinda warm. And kinda soft. And then I realize it ain't no rock. It's an Indian. The cloud slide off the face of the moon and I see it's *that* Indian. Jim. And he's seen just about all there is to see.

His eyes are black as pitch in any case. In that light I can't read nothing in them. He don't say a word. Neither do I. What is there to say?

I button up my pants and I walk back to where we're camped. I wrap myself up in my blanket and lay down looking up at the stars. After a while I shut my eyes. But I don't sleep a wink all night.

33.

In the morning I figured maybe I'd dreamed it. Everything went on the way it should. We ate our beans and bacon, we drank our coffee, we broke camp, we moved on. Didn't nothing unexpected happen. But once or twice I felt him looking at me. His eyes, brushing against my skin. Each time I turned my head he was staring in the other direction.

About noontime we ride into a real pleasant spot. The hills come rolling down to meet in a valley where a river flows slow and steady between them, the banks lined with tall cottonwoods. The only thing that wasn't pleasing to the eye was the government buildings, squatting like dung heaps at the foot of the hills. And what was even less pleasing to the eye was the civilian agent who come out to meet us.

His face was burned red as the wattles on a rooster. And I ain't never seen no one strut so much. He was what, nineteen? Twenty? Something like that. He was so young and ignorant he didn't know how much he didn't know. He was acting like he was the biggest toad in the puddle. Seemed to think he was just about the smartest and the most important man in the whole of America. And the way he talked about his Indians brought to mind the master talking about his property.

"My Indians don't mind leaving here, not now I've explained it to them. They're like children: they require a firm hand. They know it's for the best. They're glad to be heading somewhere new. It's a fresh beginning for them. They're loyal creatures, you know – they'd follow me to the ends of the earth. It's absurd, sending an army escort. I told Washington I could manage quite well without you."

See, it turned out the place we'd arrived at had been a reservation. Only it wasn't one no more. I guess the government had decided the spot was a deal too pleasant for a bunch of heathen savages. Them Apaches had been living quiet, doing what they been told, but it wasn't enough. Their land was being given over to settlers. We got to escort all them Indians to a new reservation. I didn't especially like it, but orders is orders, and we got to follow them.

We have all them folks line up and Captain MacIntyre says we got to take everything off of them before we leave. Knives, belts, ropes, itty-bitty bits of twine: anything they got has to be taken. I'm going on down along the line and them folks is handing over their things peaceable but then

I come to a girl maybe four, five years old. She got a little pouch tied to her waist with a piece of cord. When I cut it off her she start crying. She don't make no sound at all but them tears splash on my hand as I get that pouch free. It's light as a feather. There ain't nothing in it. Nothing at all. I turn it inside out and there ain't even a speck of dust. And I figure, What in the hell does it matter if one little Indian girl gets to keep her pouch? It's probably all she got in the world. I take it off the cord. Fold the pouch real small. When Captain MacIntyre ain't looking I pick her hand up, shove it into her palm, fold her fingers over it quick so don't no one see.

Excepting Jim does. He give me a look. But I can't read what he's thinking.

When we done taking them folks' possessions off of them we fetches out the prisoners from the guardhouse and load them onto a cart.

"Dangerous hostiles," the agent calls them. Then he tells the Captain, "You know, I captured them single-handed."

"Yep. Sure you did." I say them words so quiet I can hardly hear them myself. But Jim look at me. And sweet heaven above! he come on over.

He nod at Red Face. "Gobbling Turkey."

"That what you call him? Figures." My heart's thumping so loud I'm sure he can hear that too. I'm trying to cover it up when I says, "This here's a mighty pleasant spot."

"I was born here."

"These your folks, then? Your family?" I'm looking to see if there's a wife. A sweetheart. But there ain't no one looking at him special.

He nod. Don't say nothing more for a while. But then he says, "My mother was Mexican. She was – how would you say? – a captive." He don't mention his pa.

"You mean like a slave?" That hit me like a kick to the chest. "Hell!" I breathe it out between my teeth. "So where is she?"

"She died. I don't remember her."

"I don't recall mine neither."

Silence come down between us, but then he glance about at the rest of Company W and he says, "Do any of them know?"

And I don't say, "Know what?" because it's plain as day what he means.

"No."

"Just me?"

"Just you."

He looks at me and there's an understanding passes between us. It's like something deep down inside recognizes one another. There's a bond, fastens us together like the buckle on a belt strap. I don't need to explain myself because he knows why I'm here. And I don't need to ask him what in the hell he's doing working for the army either because I know. We're both getting by the only way we

276

can. When it come down to it, we're the same.

We get them Indians ready to move on out. Didn't none of them make no sound. There was no weeping, no wailing, no complaining. Gobbling Turkey thought they was fine: that they wasn't making no fuss because they plain didn't care. As far as he was concerned they was happy as hogs in muck.

I knew what was keeping them so quiet. Hadn't never thought much about a people's pride before. But that was what I seen then. Pride. And grieving so deep it was way beyond words.

The cart with the prisoners rolls out first and the rest of them follow along. Silent. Sorrowing. Like folks walking behind a coffin.

But Jim hangs back. When I look over my shoulder I see he's flat on the ground, lying in the dirt, taking handfuls of that earth and squeezing it in his fingers. Rolling in it. Different directions. Head pointing north, south, east, west. Then he's back up on his feet and he got his arms around one of them cottonwoods. His face is pressed to the bark and he's breathing deep, like he trying to fix the smell in his head.

Then he come on after us, running to catch up.

I guess maybe it was having my soul stuck in his body that done it. When we left that valley I felt something tearing. I could hear a sound like a clod of grass being pulled up or a tree falling. Roots, ripping from the ground.

34.

There was around about a hundred of them Indians and a hundred of us and didn't none of them give none of us any cause for alarm the whole way so maybe Gobbling Turkey was right about not needing no army escort.

When trouble come, it didn't come from them Apaches. It come from the good and noble citizens of America.

Ain't nothing some folks like more than kicking a person who's already down. We was passing through a little town. There was maybe one blacksmith, one general store, one bank and about twenty saloons lining the street either side. Bill Hickey should have known there was sure to be trouble in a place like that. Maybe he did. Maybe he was even looking forward to it. Because he steered us right on through.

Each and every one of them citizens who come out to watch the fun was mean, ugly drunk.

To begin with watching is all they do. But then they start whispering. Once one starts, the others get to joining in. Soon they're yelling out. Before too long they're baying like a pack of hounds. I ain't repeating what they said.

Now most all of that yelling is aimed at them Indians. But some of it is aimed at us too. They're screaming and one or two are making monkey noises and pulling faces and thinking they're just the smartest and the wittiest folks in the whole of creation. Don't none of them seem to have grasped the notion that Company W is here to protect them. That we're the ones who are civilizing the place so they can live peaceful in it.

But if they was being bad to us and them Indians they was even worse to Captain MacIntyre. Hell, he should have been ashamed of himself, leading the likes of us! Didn't he have no self respect? How could he call himself a man? What did he think he was doing?

Now while they was just shouting and staying put, we carried on riding and them Indians carried on walking. But then five of them citizens step out in front of the Captain, blocking the way, and he ain't got no choice but to stop.

One of them men look the Captain up and down. He got a straggly beard. His coat is torn and he look real rough but it don't seem to bother him none. He got a length of rope coiled in his hands and I can see precisely what he's planning to do with it. He spit at the Captain's feet. Then he says, "Where y'all heading?"

"Step aside, man. We're escorting these people to their reservation."

"They ain't people." And he's looking straight at Jim when he says, "They're Indians." He walk on over to the wagons. "And these here are thieving, murdering, savages." He start uncoiling the rope. "Time we had ourselves a hanging."

"These prisoners are in my custody. You will do nothing to harm them."

"You sure about that? We don't need no help from no army. Give us the prisoners. Then you can ride on out."

Captain MacIntyre's tempted. You can see it in his eyes. But he tell them men to back off, to move away, to let us proceed.

Now we was all stone-cold sober and them men was staggering drunk. If it come to a fight it was clear as day who was gonna win.

But drunk folks don't see nothing clearly. They don't back off and they don't back away. They all come on over to the wagons. They start pulling out the prisoners.

Or they try to. The minute one of them lay a hand on the first, Captain MacIntyre fires a warning shot in the air. They're drawing their guns but they all too slow from the whisky. Before they can get a finger to the trigger me, Elijah and all them nearest to the wagon has our guns aiming at their heads. The rest of Company W is pointing theirs into the crowds watching on the sidewalks.

It still don't stop the man with the beard. He's way too fired up. He's reached in, got the end of his rope around a prisoner's neck. When he gives a tug the Captain fires.

He's aimed low. Hit the man's boot, was all. Just through the toe. But that man fall to the ground like he dead. He lay there for a second or two then he start hollering about how he been murdered.

It seemed to have something of a sobering effect on the rest of them. They drag him to the side, and we go on our way, rifles trained on the citizens as the Indians get clear. Me and Elijah was detailed to sit tight until the last of them was free of the town.

As the column of prisoners disappear over the horizon them good folks start advancing on us. We was outnumbered and they knew it. When we turn tail and gallop after the rest of Company W we got a hailstorm of bullets fired after us. Was lucky they was all too damned drunk to shoot straight.

We was ten days marching them Indians to that reservation. Some of them got sick and about eight of them died so we left a line of graves across the desert marking the way we come. And all the time Gobbling Turkey was telling them he's leading them to the Promised Land, like he's Jesus, Joseph and Moses all rolled into one. And all the time I'm aching from thinking about Jim but there ain't nothing I can do about it. I wanted to go on and talk to him, but

I knew it wouldn't stop there. I wanted so bad to touch him it scared the hell out of me. I couldn't do that, not if I wanted to stay in the army. And there was no place else to go. So I kept away. And he didn't come and find me.

When we arrived at that reservation my heart sank right down into my army-issue boots. It was the most godforsaken place I ever did see. I figured the only reason the government had given it to them Indians was because no settler would ever have a use for it. The river water was bad. Wriggling with worms. Stinking to high heaven. The rest of it was desert. Couldn't nothing live there but rattlesnakes and scorpions. And what was them Apaches supposed to do all day? Couldn't grow nothing, like they been told to – was just a heap of dry dust. Couldn't do no hunting. Couldn't do nothing but sit. Lie down. Die. Which I guess is precisely what them fine gentlemen in Washington had in mind when they sent them there.

Looking at that godawful patch of sand put me in mind of when we been riding through Indian territory all them years ago. For the first time I admitted to myself that them Cherokees wasn't the simple-minded crazies I'd once took them for. They hadn't given up their land to the Delaneys voluntary. They been forced off of it, same as these Apaches had. Being civilized – being tame – hadn't benefited them any more than it had benefited Captain Smith's turkey chicks. Any more than it had benefited them bears. Hell and goddammit! They wasn't the dumbass fools. I was.

Why had it taken me so long to work that one out?

Captain MacIntyre tells them Indians that if any of them moves so much as a toe beyond the reservation boundary they'll be shot as hostiles. Elijah was hanging his head. So was Isaiah. I couldn't even look in Jim's direction.

As far as I could see them Indians had a choice. Die on that reservation. Die on the run. I figured sooner or later most of them would prefer to die running. I could see them Indian wars was a long way from over yet.

I reckon the whole of Company W was feeling bad. Then Gobbling Turkey starts telling Captain MacIntyre how we won't have no more trouble from them Apaches. All his Indians is real happy now, and wasn't it a wonderful journey – a migration to the land of flowing milk and honey, just like the Israelites coming out of Egypt?

If Reuben had of been there, he would have pissed his pants laughing.

35.

If the Lord been playing games when it come to Jim it was nothing compared to what he had in store for me next.

After we deliver all them Indians to their reservation the scouts take us back to the fort. When we arrive we get told our new officer has come in. Captain MacIntyre is relieved of his command, which put a great big smile on his face. We was told to get ready for inspection.

Wasn't none of us expecting no second Captain Smith. We all knew how lucky we been with him. I wasn't expecting much. But I was hoping for something other than what we got.

When he walk out of the officers' quarters I catch a glimpse of golden curls out the corner of my eye. Right away I get that familiar clenching in my stomach. Come on, Charley, I tell myself. Don't be such a damned fool. Get a hold on yourself. Your bowels can't go turning to water every time you see a stranger with that colour hair.

But the closer he get the more my stomach's churning. Because as he come nearer that shape don't resolve itself into a stranger. The closer he come and the nearer he get, the more familiar he look. I know that walk. I know the way he flap his hands when he's all uptight like he is now. I know every line, every look, every gesture. It ain't no stranger. It ain't Angel Face. It ain't Private Creech. Hell and goddammit! It's him. This time it really is him. Hellfire and damnation! Damn his eyes! It's Jonas Beecher.

My stomach's clenching so bad I want to bend double. I want to run. Not just for the latrines. To run and run and never stop running.

"You all right, Charley?" Elijah's seen the look on my face.

"Nope."

What in the hell Jonas is doing in the army is anybody's guess. Suppose it ain't no stranger than Reuben ending up with them Indians. No stranger than me being here.

"You know him?"

"Yep."

"That ain't good, right?"

We can't say nothing more. I give the order and everyone's stood to attention. Jonas is gonna come down the line. Starting with me. Because I'm his sergeant.

I got a burning sensation now. I'm clenching my butt

cheeks together tight as I can but they about to give up on me, I just know it.

Jonas take a look at me. He don't do much more than glance in my direction. I was used to meeting Captain Smith's eyes. I spent years holding my head up. All that pride vanish in a heartbeat. My eyes fix on the dirt at his feet.

He can't know me, not after all this time. I been a child when he last laid eyes on me. It was before the war! There was no way he could put together that little girl with the sergeant in front of him. Was there?

His eyes has moved on. I start to breathe again. But there's something in me that he finds interesting because he look back. Then he ask the worst possible question. "Ain't I seen you someplace before?"

"No, sir. I don't think so, sir."

"What's you name, Sergeant?"

"O'Hara, sir."

"Where you from?"

I don't answer. Don't have to.

Because that's the moment my butt cheeks give up on me. Ain't much go leaking out. But Jonas catch the smell.

"You goddamned dirty, stinking nigger," he says. "Get outta here."

I clean myself up as best I can. And then I find I'm on report. The rest of that day I'm on my hands and knees, scrubbing out Captain Beecher's quarters as a punishment for having gotten my uniform soiled.

★ ★ ★

"Who is he, Charley?"

"Overseer's boy."

"They letting Confederates into the army now? Dammit!"

"His pa was a Yankee."

"You had a Yankee overseer?"

"Crazy, ain't it?"

Elijah shrug. "No crazier than anything else, I guess. He figure out you know him?"

"Nope." He can't have. I'm still here, after all. Wearing my uniform, not a dress. "He didn't say nothing. Guess he figures we all look the same." I mean, we had plenty of that over the years: General Michaels' men, roaring with laughter, "How do you tell your men apart, Captain Smith?"

"He look like a mean cuss."

"Yep. He is." But even as I'm saying it, I'm thinking, He wasn't always that way. I was sure, now I'd seen him again, that them pictures in my head of him happy, smiling, was things I'd recalled, not dreamed up. He'd lifted me into that tree because I'd asked him to. I'd wanted to see for myself what the world looked like from up there and he'd obliged.

It was a damned fool notion but I started wondering if I could figure out what had turned him mean. If I knew what it was, maybe I could figure out a way to turn him back again. Jonas was a train heading off down the track, full steam ahead. But if I could find the points, if I could make them switch? Maybe, just maybe, Jonas might change direction.

I told Elijah, "He was different when he was a boy."

"Don't mean nothing. Me and the master played together when we was small. Didn't stop him whipping the hide off me when his horse gone lame."

"What you do to it?"

Elijah is suddenly madder than I ever seen him. "You think I done something? You think I deserved it? Hell, Charley! You crazy? White folks is mean! I ain't never met one who wasn't, excepting Captain Smith. They don't need no reason to act that way. It in their blood. In their bones. It the way they born!"

Elijah was talking sense and I knew it. Yet I couldn't shake that notion. Until I seen that sack of flour full of weevils; until I smelled that stinking green meat and seen them slaughtered buffaloes, I thought them Indians been savages who liked fighting and thieving for the sheer hell of it. I knew different now. And if they had reasons for doing what they done, well, maybe, just maybe, Jonas did too.

36.

Things wasn't looking good for Company W even before a bunch of Apaches gone running off that godforsaken reservation. Truth be told, when we was sent to bring them back in they was the least of our problems.

We been told to pick up their trail and keep on right after them until we catch up. Only that was a whole lot easier said than done. We wouldn't even have found the trail in the first place if it hadn't of been for them Indian scouts. We'd be looking at a patch of land and there wouldn't be no sign at all that anyone had passed that way, but then one of them would give a shout because they see a stone turned over here, a broken blade of grass there – things only an Indian, or someone raised by them, would notice.

To begin with, them runaways been travelling together but when they got a mile or so from the reservation boundary they'd split up into five or more groups and headed in different directions. There was no way of knowing which one we was supposed to follow so them scouts picked the strongest trail and off we went.

Now I didn't much care if every one of them got clean away into Mexico. They be someone else's problem then. Let the Mexican Army deal with them! I had other things on my mind. First was Jim, of course. Second was Jonas Beecher.

That man could cuss powerful bad. I ain't never heard such a stream of it. He didn't speak to none of us without saying we was apes or baboons or goddamned dirty monkeys and worse. Much worse. Every single order he give was followed by a cuss. And all the time there was Bill Hickey, cussing right alongside him. When Jonas wasn't cussing he was whistling "Sam Hall" through the gap in his teeth and Bill was singing right along, singing his heart out.

We been issued with six weeks' supplies but from what Bill Hickey been saying about the godawfulness of trying to catch Apaches it looked like we might be out in the field a whole lot longer than that. Them army rations kept body and soul together but they wasn't what you might call good eating. When we been with Captain Smith – unless we was hard on the heels of hostiles – if a turkey or jackrabbit or some such thing cross your path you was expected to treat it as an act of divine providence. So when a big, fat turkey fly up in my horse's face I shoot without giving it a thought.

Only this ain't Captain Smith we're riding with, it's Jonas. And he's madder than a nest of hornets about me acting without his permission. He goes crazy. He take his knife and he cut off my sergeant's stripes. Just like that, I'm demoted all the way back down to private. He decides that it ain't enough punishment. He take a lariat and he rope that bird onto my back. And I ain't allowed to ride no more. I gotta walk along at the back end of the column until the whole damned turkey rots off.

Well, what with the flies and the stench and the feathers and the heat – it got bad. Mighty bad. But it would have been a whole lot worse if Jim hadn't come over real quiet and give me a wad of something to chew on. It tasted so strong it took most all that stench away. Don't know what it was. Didn't ask. Didn't look too close at it neither. My mind was more taken up with the way his palm pressed against mine. Set my blood racing. Sweet Jesus, it was a powerful feeling!

Thinking on him was a whole lot more pleasing than thinking on Jonas Beecher. I didn't want to be too near Jim – that was way too unsettling – but I watched him from the corner of one eye.

So when something shift in him, I can't help but see.

We was in the middle of one of them flat plains. The

haze was rising off the dirt and there was buzzards circling way above. Guess the stench of that old turkey was drifting up to them and they was hoping for a piece.

We're heading in a straight line right across towards the mountains and Jim's just off to one side near some low-grown scrub when Jonas call a halt. Seems he ain't so used to the heat or the hard riding as we was and he's near to dropping. We're waiting for him to take in water and recover some when I notice Jim.

Now why it made the hairs on the back of my neck stand up I plain don't know. He didn't do nothing. Didn't say nothing. It was like watching that deep, dark pool. The surface is still, but way beneath there's a current whirling. You can just feel it. And I couldn't help myself. I had to go on over and see what was stirring him.

I told Elijah I needed a piss. Headed for that little patch of scrub. When I got there I see there's one of them deep gulleys. It's a crack in the ground and you can't see it until you about ready to fall in. Wasn't visible from where Jonas was. Which was maybe just as well. Because there was a little old Indian woman in there and two kids. One was the girl I give the pouch back to. The other couldn't have been more than two years old. All three was scrawny as hell. Sitting, still as rocks. Not even blinking.

What I should have done was train my rifle on them. Call for help. Take them in. That was what I was being paid for, after all.

But what would have happened next unfolded in my head like a blanket. I could see the pattern clear as day.

Jim hadn't said a word. If I spoke up the first thing I'd do would be to land him in a whole heap of trouble. And Jonas would claim credit for picking up three hostiles. Whether they'd reach the reservation alive was anybody's guess. The thing with the turkey showed that he was crazier and madder than I ever known him. And I figured he was the trigger-happy kind. If any of them three made one wrong move they'd be shot, and Jonas would say they was trying to escape whether they was or not. Alive or dead, it didn't matter none to him.

I had a bird's stinking carcass strung across my shoulders. Right then I wasn't feeling inclined to give Jonas Beecher nothing to brag about.

So I turn my back on them three Indians. I unbutton my pants, make like I'm taking a piss. When I'm supposedly done I button up again. Out of the corner of my eye I see Jim's back stiffen. He's scared about what I'm gonna do. I don't even glance his way. I look over at Jonas, and I says real quiet but loud enough for Jim to hear, "I ain't handing no one over to that cuss."

Me and Jim was strapped together tighter than ever after that. Couldn't neither of us move without the other one feeling it. We couldn't go sitting around talking to each other for hours at a stretch. Wasn't no chance of that. Jim kept himself to himself mostly and so did I. Yet there was moments, here and there, in the days and the weeks that followed. Enough to keep me going. I learned so many things off of that man. I started looking at the territory through Jim's eyes. I got to notice them small patches of green in the wide, flat desert where you could go digging for water. Which cactus leaves you could split and bind to a wound to heal it. Which rocks would be hiding rattlers.

What had seemed an empty patch of nothing started to look full of life, full of colour. Lord above, that stretch of sand started to look beautiful! Sunrise. Sunset. The whole place would be flooded scarlet and gold. I'd lie on my back just looking, marvelling at the splendour of it all. Was half expecting a crowd of angels to appear.

As for them mountains: Jonas would be cussing that the trail was too steep, the way too hard-going but I'd be sitting there, listening to them birds, watching the pattern of light dancing through the trees, thinking no wonder them Apaches didn't want to give this land over. If I'd have been one of them I'd have fought to the death to hang onto it too.

37.

That first time we rode with Jonas we was out in the field for eight weeks or more. He has us on half rations and then quarter rations and when the supplies finally give out we got to turn back. We ain't caught up with no hostiles. Didn't even get within sniffing distance of them, leastways as far as he was concerned.

Sometimes we'd pass a ranch or come across a wagon train and we'd be told they been seen someplace, but by the time we got there they been seen again, this time back in the place we was before. They was running rings around us. And we was going in circles, chasing our tails. So Jonas was in a mighty ugly mood. Guess he was wondering what he was gonna tell his superior officers. And this time it's Elijah who crosses him.

Now when we been on the prairie there was times we had tents rolled up with our blankets and tied to our saddles. They wasn't no more than a square of canvas and a couple of poles. When the weather was dry didn't none of us bother with them. They mostly all had holes in any case and at the end of a hard day's riding it was easier just to roll up your coat, shove it under your head and lie right down on the ground. Out here, this was one tough old territory to be riding in and all them tents would have done was weigh down the horses, make the going harder on them. So we didn't have none. We was well used to sleeping out under the stars and – since I'd laid eyes on Jim – I'd come to like seeing the sky spread so big above me.

But Jonas Beecher didn't follow the same line of thinking. He had to have himself an officer's big tent and a nice camp bed and a whole heap else besides.

One morning Elijah been ordered to take it all down, get it packed. We didn't have no wagon to load it onto on account of us being up in the mountains and the trails being too narrow and too steep to go driving a wagon along. Elijah has to load everything onto a mule and that thing has the same godawful temperament as Yeller done. It's trying to snatch bites out of Elijah's leg so I give him a hand, grabbing its halter to stop it wheeling around.

Now Elijah was a thoughtful man. Everything he done was slow and thorough – I never did see him do anything sloppy.

But Jonas starts up complaining that Elijah ain't

loading them tent pegs right and how he ain't never seen no moke do a decent job.

I'm keeping my head down and my mouth shut. But Elijah finish what he's doing and then he look at his Captain. That's all he does. Look. But he look him in the eye. Direct. Straight. Man to man.

Jonas regard that look as an act of insubordination and he shout at Elijah, "You worthless dog! Don't you stare at me like that."

Elijah hadn't hardly spoke a word to a white man since his family been killed. But he break his silence now. Couldn't have picked a worse time to do it.

Elijah put his shoulders back and he says, "Captain Beecher, I ain't no dog and I sure ain't worthless. I'm a soldier in the United States Army."

Now if Elijah had left it at that, maybe, just maybe Jonas would have let it go. Maybe not. Didn't get a chance to find out. Because Elijah says, "I'm a soldier, sir. Same as you."

Well, that drive Jonas right over the edge. He give Elijah a lick across the face with his whip, hit him so hard that Elijah fall down in the dirt. His whole face is near split in two. Jonas kick him in the throat. Once. Twice. And I can't do nothing but stand there, screaming inside, watching and praying for it to stop. Then he order Elijah to be gagged and handcuffed and tied behind the back end of the mule. He only just out of the reach of its hooves.

Elijah stays chained like that the rest of the time we're out and when he was too tired to walk, the thing just drag him along all the way back to the fort.

When we get there we find the place in uproar. A couple of settlers have come riding in and they're shitting their pants, which ain't surprising because Indians have attacked a ranch a couple of miles away. A family of seven been killed, they say. Mother. Father. Five kids. They found one of them hanging from the wall. A little yellow-haired girl. Dangling from a meat hook punched through her head. She was still alive and twitching when they fetched her down.

Them men say they seen the Indians' trail and they was heading in this direction. They must be real close.

Now the General ain't about to go sending none of his men out when night's drawing in: there just ain't no point. Instead he calls Jonas over and wants a report on what we been doing the last eight weeks.

The fact we ain't had no success finding them hostiles ain't Jonas's fault, of course; it's ours. We can hear him telling the General we're a goddamned useless bunch of monkeys and how in the hell is he expected to make any progress? We're cowards and incompetents and, according to him, can't none of us even shoot straight.

General Howker don't disagree, but he ain't exactly impressed either. He ain't saying much at all. So Jonas Beecher's mood is blacker than pitch when he tell us what we've got to do. And whether the idea was his or whether it was the General's I don't know. All I know is that we're done for.

Now it didn't take much for us to work out that there's only one reason them hostiles would come so close to a fort. They're short of guns. Short of horses. They're coming thieving. And Jonas Beecher decides to make things real easy for them.

He don't let us corral the horses. They been worked hard the last eight weeks, he says; they need a good night's grazing. He give the order that they've got to be turned out. They ain't hobbled, they ain't on picket pins, they're wandering loose. And then he set three of us watching them. Just three. Me, Elijah and Isaiah. Everyone else – including Jim and the rest of them scouts – get confined to quarters. Ain't none of them allowed to move a muscle.

We wasn't given no saddles nor no rifles. Jonas take Mr Cody's Springfield off me. He said I wouldn't be needing it if all we was doing was watching horses. We was riding bareback and all we got to defend the whole herd is one pistol each.

We know them warriors are gonna come – it's as predictable as the fact the sun's gonna rise the next morning. As predictable as the fact that we won't be alive to see it when it does. We got no choice but follow orders. If we don't we'll be court-martialled and end up shot in any case. Either way, we're dead.

"You still think he can be turned good?" says Elijah. The cut on his face has scabbed over, but the back of his head is rubbed raw from being dragged along behind that mule.

"What?" says Isaiah. "Who we talking about?"

"Captain Beecher. Charley here know him from the old days."

"Guess he was a crazy cuss then too, wasn't he?"

"Mostly."

"Charley think the Captain got a heart of gold, deep down."

"That so?"

"He just keeping it well hidden."

"It in there, all right," I says. "Maybe I need a pickaxe and shovel to find it."

"Hell, it gonna take more than that. That heart of gold buried so deep you gonna need to dig a mineshaft to fetch it out."

"A hundredweight of dynamite."

"Team of mules."

We're laughing so much I get to thinking, Hey, well, maybe if I got to die, doing it here, tonight, with these two either side of me, ain't gonna be so bad. If it wasn't for Jim, I'd have welcomed it.

It was a long night waiting for that attack to come. The moon was big and bright, shining almost like day. On the prairie they'd have called it a Comanche Moon. A good night for raiding.

Guess them Indians thought it looked too easy. Probably figured we had extra men hidden someplace, ready to ambush them. By the time they done creeping around and seen it was truly just the three of us it was almost dawn.

I already said how fear is inclined to loosen my bowels. I was off shitting my insides out when them Indians finally come crawling on their bellies through the scrub.

First I knew of it was when the hairs on the back of my neck stood to attention and I could feel deep down in my belly that things was wrong. I froze, still, not moving, and then one of them warriors slithered right by me, so close I could have put out my hand and touched him. And in the moonlight I see hair that's silvered grey with age and I see that man's scrawny as hell. My throat goes so tight I can't breathe. I'm there, pants down about my ankles, and all I can think is, Folks will see. Folks will know. Bill Hickey will know. Jonas will see. The notion of dying, my privates exposed to the sky, was too much to bear. My bowels turn to water all over again.

I couldn't get to my pistol, couldn't do nothing. That warrior turn and look straight at me and I see it ain't a man at all. It's that little old woman. The one who been hiding in that gulley with them kids. The one I never told on. She got a knife, gripped between her teeth. Any second now, I think, she's gonna stick it in me. But she don't. She give me a look and slither on by. And I'm so goddamned surprised I don't do nothing. I don't even call out a warning. She grab Elijah's foot and tip him off his horse. I see her cut his throat. And still I don't yell. I try to. But my tongue ain't working. I can't get no noise out.

Isaiah gets his throat cut too. They was both dead before they knew we was even under attack. And then all them horses get driven off real quiet and orderly and there wasn't nothing I could do about none of it.

I lay down beside Elijah, pressed myself up against his back and tried to keep the life from leaving him. Didn't work. I took Isaiah's hands in mine thinking if I could only hold them tight enough I'd keep him here, get him cracking his knuckles again. I'd have given anything to hear that sound one more time. I wept and I prayed and I begged the Lord to take me instead. But He didn't. So I called on the Devil, told him if he'd only give Elijah and Isaiah back their lives, he could take mine. He could throw me into the deepest pit of hell, roast me, burn me, punish me for all eternity. But that didn't work neither. The Devil didn't want me no more than the Lord.

Come the dawn, I was still sitting there in the blood and the dirt when Jonas Beecher come strolling out from the fort.

He call me a coward and says I'm damned lucky not to get myself stood before a firing squad and shot for deserting my post. Because there sure as hell couldn't be any other explanation for the fact that I didn't have so much as a scratch on me.

He had me banged up in the guardhouse.

Solitary confinement. It's small and cramped and dark. Made of mud bricks. A solid wood door at the front and the only light coming from a tiny little hole at the back which ain't even big enough to stick a hand through. I can't see the sky and it's like being in that yam cellar for days and nights that just go on and on. I want to holler and bang on the door and beg to be let out, but I don't. I want to scream and tear at my flesh with my teeth, cut my own finger off, but I don't.

I don't because Jim come by at night. I'm lying on the floor and my thoughts is bleak as they come. If guilt and shame can kill you, I'm dying.

I didn't hear him. Was too busy beating my brains out with my own misery. But there's this tiny movement at the back. Something's swinging from side to side like the pendulum on a clock. When I get up I see it's his belt. He's taken it off and poked the buckle through that little hole. I take it in my hand and give it a tug.

He hangs onto the other end. It's pulled tight between us. I lean against that wall knowing he's there on the other side, doing the same. We stay like that until the sun come up.

That's all there is to it. Can't neither of us speak: there's a guard on the door and Jim sure as hell shouldn't be associating with me.

Probably couldn't find words in any case. But he come, night after night, the whole time I was in there. He was the only thing that kept me from going crazy.

★ ★ ★

After two weeks, when I was finally let out, we was at war all over again. I was so sick and tired of it I felt close to shooting my own head off. With Elijah and Isaiah killed, all the men I signed up with was dead and gone. Company W was a whole different outfit. There was strangers' faces all around me – young and fresh and ignorant as hog shit. I just didn't have the strength to speak to any of them. Then there was Jim, who was ready to be leaned on. Who I wanted to lean on. I wanted to lean on so bad I could hardly stand it. I wanted to rest my head on his chest, have him wrap his arms about me, take all that load off my shoulders.

But the moment I did that – the moment I give into it – was the moment I'd have to let them know who I was. The second they knew I was a woman I'd be out on my ass. In the middle of Apache territory. In the middle of a war. Where every settler I seen looked on us like we wasn't no different to the heathen savages we was clearing off the land for them. Where men like Bill Hickey could go raping a woman and taking his knife, cut a trophy off of her, fix it to his saddle, and no one think twice about it.

Broke my heart, but I had to hold myself together, keep myself apart. There wasn't nothing else I could do.

38.

Things happened the way I figured they would. Groups of Apaches kept running off that reservation. Different families, in different directions. Then they changed their minds and come back in, or they was caught and dragged back in. Either way, they'd sit tight for a few weeks and then they'd do it all over again. Warriors got themselves killed, and the kids couldn't grow up fast enough to take their places. Each time there was less and less of them. Soon it would all be over, like it was back on the prairie. What would happen to me and the rest of Company W then was anybody's guess. I didn't like to think too far ahead.

But then a medicine man started having a heap of visions and that changed everything, leastways for a time.

The first we heard of it was when Company W was given our marching orders and we was sent back to that godforsaken hellhole of a reservation that we'd dumped all them Apaches on.

Seems to me the one thing white folks find more troubling than a dark skin is a religion that's different to their own. Mr Delaney been raised a Catholic and when he was fired up on drink he'd take to roaring and raving about Protestants and how hellfire was way too good for the whole damned lot of them.

If you put them two things together – dark skin, heathen religion – you got something that gets whiteys jumpier than a jackrabbit.

When we get to the reservation we find Gobbling Turkey ain't in charge there no more. Don't know where he'd gone; never found out. Maybe one of "his" Indians lost patience and stuck a knife in him. Wouldn't have blamed them. But the agent he been replaced by was even worse.

We happen to ride in on ration day so all them Indians is lined up, waiting. The man that come out to meet us is the shiftiest-looking piece of white trash I ever did see. The word "Asshole" is writ across the sky above his head in letters about a mile high. You can tell just by looking at him that he's running all kinds of tricks, cheating them Indians out of what they're due. Cutting flour with sand would be the least of it.

But he come towards the Captain bleating about how he's concerned for the Apaches' safety. He want us to save them from themselves because a medicine man is whipping them up into a frenzy, and he thinks any second they're all going to break out, every single one of them.

And maybe he's right, because when I look about me the place is still a stinking hellhole only it ain't miserable the way it was when I first seen it. Them folks in line isn't hunched and dejected. They standing tall. Looking proud.

Now I seen how Elijah could take a broke, beat-down horse and make it want to live again. Seemed that medicine man was doing the same thing. Somehow he was putting the heart back into them folks – you could feel it beating hard and strong. No wonder the agent was shook up.

Our orders is to keep the peace. That's all. So at night – when them folks start to drift together from all the corners of the reservation to meet up with the medicine man – we're told to watch. Just stand. Just watch. Nothing more.

It's late by then and it's getting dark. Jonas is tucked up nice and cosy in his tent. Me and Jim is up on a ridge with a couple of others. Bill Hickey's down to the left with five troopers. The rest of Company W is strung out along this shallow valley.

We're all on the skittish side, not knowing what to expect. Sometimes Indians would go on a drunk and get so crazy they took to killing each other. When that happened you never could tell who might get caught in the crossfire.

But these folks was stone-cold sober. They start arranging themselves, dozens of them standing in lines, like the spokes coming out from a wagon wheel. I can feel Jim

307

beside me and he's wound tighter than a spring. But we ain't alone, so I can't go asking what's bothering him.

When them Indians have taken their positions the medicine man come along.

I was expecting some savage-looking fella, with rolling eyes and teeth bared and a belt bristling with scalps. What I see is a little white-haired man, almost bent double. He ain't no kind of threat. There ain't nothing remotely impressive about him. And yet Jim look like one of the shepherds at Christmas time staring at the angel Gabriel.

The medicine man start sprinkling all them Indians with something yellow.

"What's that?" I says. But Jim don't answer. He's closed himself off. And I feel that belt that binds us is loosening off. Slackening. I'm so scared I start to shake.

That medicine man start chanting and the sound is haunting as a death song. And together – moving like they one being – them folks shuffle along in this slow, solemn dance. It goes on and on and it last all the hours of darkness. Two steps forward, one step back, one to the left, one to the right and it ain't what you might call pretty but it's powerful hypnotic to watch even if only because there was so many of them concentrating so hard on it. And the reason they're concentrating so hard is because that little old holy man is singing and I don't understand the words but Jim does. When I grab him by the arm – because I can't stand to watch and not understand nothing – he come out of himself for just long enough to tell me that the medicine man is saying that all the dead warriors is coming back to life and they gonna fight and get the white men off the land so they can live free again.

"And Company W?" I says. "What about us?"

Jim don't reply. He don't even look at me. It's like I ain't spoken.

Just before dawn that dancing stops. And that medicine man give a great shout and all them dancers take two, three paces back, which clear a path for him to walk through and he goes to the ridge – the one opposite to where I'm standing. The sun's beginning to rise over it and there are the first rays breaking through the mist so it's clear as clear to see what happens next. He lift his arms and he call out something that can't be anything but a prayer because it sound so sad and desperate and hopeful all at the same time. Them dancers raise up their hands and give a yell of joy that underlines just precisely how deep in despair they been until that moment.

And then, while I'm watching, I see three men – three ghosts – rise up out of the ground on that ridge, and if that wasn't strange enough to make me almost soil my pants one of them turn his face and look right at me.

Or maybe he's looking at Jim.

Because Jim give a cry that just about tears me apart. His hand goes out but the ghost melts back into mist and air.

I don't have no idea what any of it means. But it's like Jim's gone into a different room. I can hear the door between us slamming tight shut.

39.

Well, them ghosts didn't hang around for more than a few heartbeats and most of Company W had their backs to them. All they saw was a bunch of Indians getting themselves stirred up. The troopers with Bill Hickey was too far away and the two with me and Jim had fallen asleep.

If I'd have had any sense I'd have kept my big mouth shut, but sense don't seem to be a quality I possess much of. So when Jonas wake up and call me down I tell him all about it and he look at me like I've surely lost my mind and for a while I was thinking I'd get myself shut in the guardhouse again. But then Jim back me up. He says the medicine man raised the dead. And those are the last words I hear him speak for one hell of a long time.

Jonas gets real fidgety and I can't say I entirely blame him – I was feeling mighty twitchy myself. Mostly it was on account of Jim but it was also on account of the notion that fighting a living, breathing warrior is one thing but fighting one that's risen from the dead is an entirely different matter, and I'm thinking can you kill a man twice?

Now half the settlers in the territory was laughing at them superstitious heathen savages and the other half was filling their britches for fear of what they might do and even the half that was laughing was doing it real nervous. So there ain't no way that medicine man can be allowed to carry on putting hope into them people. Jonas wires the General and the order come back loud and clear: he got to be arrested.

And we got to bring him in.

That little old white-haired medicine man been told to report to the agent's office but he don't do it. We sit from sunup to sundown and there ain't no sign of him. It's the same the following day. And the one after that. When he ain't shown after five, maybe six days Jonas Beecher's patience is all wore-out. So he take along the whole of Company W to fetch him in. We had about twenty scouts with us too, and Jim was one of them, and I ain't never seen him so jumpy. He was in the army – he got to follow orders, same as the rest of us – but more than a hundred men going along to bring in one little holy fella? This was pushing him way too far. Looked like he was gonna snap. Looked like all them Indian scouts was. We was sitting on a powder keg and Jonas was about to light the fuse.

It wasn't a very happy ride across the reservation to that man's camp and when we get there he's sitting outside his shelter and he's looking peaceable enough but the fifty or so Indian warriors surrounding him ain't and the air is so thick with raging feelings you could slice it open with a knife.

Jonas tell him he got to come along to the agency and the medicine man smile and nod and says he's got to eat first and that's what he does, only he does it real slow and all the time he's chewing the tension is cranking itself up and up.

Finally that medicine man take his last swallow and he set down his bowl and get up and off we go, heading back down the creek. Them warriors is following right along with us and we ain't gonna make it back to the agency before nightfall because he's taken so long with his eating. So Jonas decide we got to make camp. He want me to put up his damned tent. And that's just what I'm doing, only them warriors come crowding in too and soon there ain't enough room for it. There's more and more Apaches coming in and I don't know where all them folks is coming from because pretty soon everywhere you turn your head there's Indians. The women and the kids is all rushing in and every single one of them is mighty angry about what in the hell the United States Army is planning to do to that medicine man who been filling their hearts with hope. They're scared too. And scared folks is mostly always dangerous.

Jonas start flapping his arms at them like they a herd of beef he want moving and he's yelling at them to go back, but the sound of him screaming don't do nothing to cool feelings down, no – they building up a whole head of steam by now and are ready to blow and there ain't no stopping what happens next.

I'm right in the middle of that crush of folks and they all looking so wild I'm scared they're gonna tear me apart with their nails, rip me into pieces with their teeth, peel off my hide, spill my guts.

A shot ring out. Just one. I don't know who fired it. Indian? Trooper? I ain't got no idea. But the second that bullet hits the air it kills all them Apaches' dreams and visions stone dead.

"Kill the medicine man!" Jonas screams and Bill Hickey obliges, but he don't do it clean.

First he shoot him in the legs and that little fella tries crawling off, so Bill Hickey take his pistol and he shoot him in the head, only he still don't die, so Bill bring his rifle butt down, over and over, and I can hear the splitting of that man's skull but Bill Hickey goes right on until his head is a scarlet mess of bloody pulp and he don't move no more. And I see all that from where I am because I'm hunkered down next to a rock but I ain't shooting because the light's going. Everyone's running every which way and Indians is mixed up with troopers and there are little children all over the place and I don't want to go hitting none of the wrong folks by mistake. I'm feeling sick to the pit of my stomach.

Then this Indian woman come riding bareback on a pony, hair streaming out behind her, and she done run off our horses. So we're stuck there and all we have to do is wait for them to finish us off and I figure this is the end because the scouts who been working so hard for Company W have turned against us. The killing of a holy man is just too much for them to take. Jim's there, right in the middle of them. He's changed sides, just like Reuben. I can't tear my eyes off him. He's leaving me, like everyone else done.

But seems them Indians changed their minds about wiping us out just then. They decide to run instead. Off the reservation and out into the night.

Jim ain't following. Not yet. He's looking for something. Someone. He's looking for me.

His eyes catch mine. I'm still hunkered down there by that rock and he ride straight at me. His hand comes down, like he gonna sweep me up and onto the back of that horse. My hand's up, reaching for him. Only there's Bill Hickey, with his rifle raised, pointing it right at Jim's head.

So I don't take his hand. I throw myself at Bill Hickey's back instead. And the rifle goes off and Jim's horse rears right up, then bolts after the others. My heart's screaming. I'm being ripped in two. He's trying and trying. But Jim can't turn that horse.

★ ★ ★

315

I was lucky, I guess. Bill Hickey didn't know what had hit him. There was so much going on along that creek he never thought it was anything but an accident. What was left of us limped back to the agency.

The next day some of them scouts had second thoughts about running off and come back in, voluntary, to surrender themselves. Jim wasn't one of them. At the time I was mad. But soon I was glad he'd stayed away. Because them scouts found out all about American justice.

Some got sent to prison for desertion. Some got themselves hanged for it. Bill Hickey said they was good Indians now. Hadn't the noose seen to that? He near split his sides over it.

Well, by now the whole territory was in swooning hysterics, settlers screaming that the army wasn't doing enough to save them from the wild, murdering Apaches. Some citizens banded together and went out looking for hostiles to round up and kill. Only they couldn't find no hostiles, so they killed the ones that was living peaceable on their reservation instead. More and more soldiers was brought into the territory and we was all running every which way and getting nowhere real fast.

When I seen some of the things them warriors done I guess it wasn't surprising folks was scared witless. Them Apaches been backed into a corner and they turned ugly. We saw plenty of settlers killed, carved up like sides of beef.

Saw plenty of soldiers that way too. Them Indians was leaving a long trail of destruction but we didn't see none of them, excepting once.

We was out in the field, chasing after hostiles same as always. We'd made camp right by a spring when a bunch of them come by. What was strange was that we could see them, clear as day.

Now Jonas Beecher had done as much listening to Bill Hickey's tales as the rest of us. He squint at them and says, "I thought you said we wouldn't ever meet them face to face."

Bill Hickey ain't ruffled. "That is unusual," he says. "They must be desperate. Look there, Captain. Their horses are close to dropping. They need water badly."

"What are they gonna do?" says Jonas.

"I'm guessing they'll try getting us to chase them. Our best bet is to stay right here."

The next thing that happens is that some of them warriors come out in the open and, oh Lord, one of them's Jim and my heart does this flip and my stomach turns right over and I'm so mixed up inside I want to spew out my salt pork. If I'm ordered to fire at him I'm gonna have to do it. I'm the best shot in the whole of Company W and even Jonas knows that because he asked me how I come by Mr Cody's rifle after he give it back to me, and I had to tell him. So it ain't like I can miss.

But Jonas don't give no order. He can't make up his

mind what to do. We ain't firing. Neither are them Indians.

"I suppose they're low on ammunition too," says Bill. "You're holding all the cards, Captain. We've just gotta sit tight."

The warriors dance along, then they run towards the rocks, real slow, real tempting. Bill Hickey's right: they're trying to get us to go chasing after them so as the women and the children can get to the water.

Jonas is following Bill Hickey's advice. He's getting madder and madder because them warriors is flipping up their loincloths, flashing their privates at him and making lewd gestures but we can't move from our position until he gives the order.

Them warriors is getting mad too because we ain't doing what they want us to. Two of them come back towards us and one's Jim and he got himself in range. The second man start making signs at Jonas and they're so particular you can't miss his meaning. My insides are turning to water. Jonas don't know precisely what he's saying because his brain's about the size of an army-issue bean and he says, "What's he doing?"

The Apache's got his hands cupped against his chest like he's holding a pair of melons. And then he's pointing at me. Or maybe at Jonas.

When Jim sees what he's doing he smacks the second man's hands down. For a moment I think he's told on me – he's told them Apaches what I am. And I feel so betrayed I almost want to shoot him myself.

Bill Hickey says to Jonas, "He's calling you a woman, sir."

"What?"

"A woman."

Seems they don't have a whole heap of cuss words in Apache. According to Bill Hickey a woman's about the most insulting thing you can call a man. Struck me as kinda funny because I seen with my own eyes that some of them women was real good warriors and wasn't none of them cowards.

Jonas Beecher lift up his weapon and he fire at Jim but he's so mad he miss by about a mile. But Jonas ain't shifting from the spring. So neither can we. And now he give the order for me to fire. I raise my rifle.

Jim look straight at me and he put up his hand, kinda like a salute, and I figure it's a greeting, or maybe a farewell, because before I can fire a shot he and them others duck behind rocks and the next thing we know the whole lot of them have gone, melting away into that land like they never been there. And I'm left wishing I could have melted right along with them.

40.

Bill Hickey been right about staying put by the spring but Jonas didn't thank him none. He was an officer, he needed to report dead hostiles. He was itching to shed some blood. The longer the whole damned thing went on and the more desperate he become, the harder he pushed us.

We was high in the mountains, someplace right down by the Mexican border, when we see smoke rising.

Seeing smoke rise in them days was never a good sign. It didn't never mean logs burning in the hearth or peaceful campfires. It meant raided homesteads. Torched tepees. Dead settlers. Dead Indians. When I seen it my heart sank.

But Jonas is looking happy. His hand is flapping against his leg. He got an idea in his head and there ain't no shifting it.

"That's got to be an Indian village," he says. "There aren't any settlers hereabouts, are there?"

He look at Bill Hickey and Bill just shrug. What he mean is that he don't know, but Jonas think Bill's agreeing with him.

So Jonas give the order. We gotta dismount and go on foot. He split us into four. Some of us are to go to the left, some to the right. Some take the higher ground, some take the lower. We gotta go quick and quiet and surround the camp. When he give the signal we gotta attack.

We done what we was told and Jonas was right: there was signs a little Indian village been down there with a group of maybe thirty people. But they wasn't there no more and Jonas never did give no signal. Because when we was close enough to see the camp, it was plain someone been there before us.

The brushwood shelters was just smouldering ashes. Whether it was the army done it, or whether it was civilians, there was no way of knowing. They hadn't left no note. What they had left was five dead Indians. Two men, one woman, two kids. All five had fingers, ears, hair missing. Trophies been cut off of them as keepsakes. The woman had her skirt pulled up around her waist. Whoever killed her had violated her first. She been left lying, legs apart, privates exposed to the sky.

It was real unusual to catch Apaches by surprise so I figured whoever had done it had just got lucky, but when we walked into that camp for a closer look it seemed that maybe they'd had a helping hand.

There was a flagon of whisky lying on its side under a rock. Guess it had rolled there when they been attacked. Another was right by the stream, still half full. If those Indians been on a drunk they wouldn't have heard no one coming. They sure paid one hell of a price for that liquor.

Jonas give the order that we're to make camp right there for the night. In the morning we'll see if we can't pick up a trail, catch up with the ones that got away.

I went to cover that woman up. Pull her skirt over her legs. Didn't seem right letting her lie like that. But Jonas scream at me to leave her, leave her alone, don't touch her. He's madder than he ever been so I do what I'm told.

I'm gathering wood to make a fire, and I'm so bothered by the sight of that woman I'm whistling "Sam Hall" between my teeth. I don't hardly know I'm doing it until Bill Hickey start saying something. I'm behind him, so he ain't seen me, just heard me whistling. He says, "Captain, do you think…?" When he turn around and sees it's me he give a grunt and don't finish his sentence. He shrug and go on with what he's doing. He ain't troubled by his mistake.

But I am.

I'm so troubled I drop the firewood I'm holding. Because that ain't the first time someone's took me for Jonas.

I'd clean forgotten it, but now the memory hit me like a bullet straight between the eyes. My head's reeling with it.

The other time was way back, before Miss Louellen

even arrived on the Delaney place. Way back, before Jonas turned mean. He been trying to teach me to whistle. He been at it for weeks and I couldn't get it. My baby teeth had come out and there was this big old hole in the front of my gum. I couldn't get my lips to hold their shape. But then my new teeth start coming through. One day I'm on my own and I'm leaning against the cottonwood, trying my damnedest to make a sound, and all of a sudden it burst out shrill, clear as a bell. Not just one note, neither. I can make a tune!

Then I hear this shout, "Why there you are! Jonas, honey, I been looking all over for you." And around the tree come Mrs Beecher.

She was pretty back then – not like the scrunched-up dishcloth she become. When her eyes fix on me, the pink bloom fade from her cheeks. Her lips thin into a tight line.

"You goddamned clumsy nigger!" Jonas jerk me back to the here and the now. He's come across the camp and is looking at the wood I dropped. "Get on and pick that up, boy."

I do what I'm told again, eyes to the ground, following his bidding without a murmur. My mind's racing. All them shadows in the mist is coming together. I'm beginning to see them clear. I don't like the shape they taking. I don't like it one bit.

While the sun's going down Jonas and Bill Hickey share what remains of that whisky. And all the time there's

323

that woman, lying there. Sooner or later they was bound to come around to discussing her.

"You ever had one, Captain?" Bill Hickey is at the talkative drunk stage. He lean across and point to that woman, just in case Jonas don't catch his meaning.

Jonas don't answer but Bill's way beyond needing anyone to reply. He carries right on talking. Hell, he just wouldn't hush his mouth! "You know, I was married once to a white woman. Norwegian. She had golden hair, red lips, pale skin: she was pretty as a picture to look at. But she was cold as ice in bed. Just about froze my dick right off. I had to get rid of her, I couldn't stand it longer than a year. I reckon a white skin just doesn't lend itself to passion. But Indians, they know how to treat a man right. The darker they are, the sweeter they taste. I had a nigger woman once, black as the ace of spades. She was wilder than a bobcat. Biting. Scratching. She was hotter than hellfire! Raked up my back with those nails of hers…"

Bill shuts up, real sudden. Because Jonas has got him by the neck. He's straddling Bill's chest, pinning Bill's arms to the ground with his knees. All the time Bill's been talking, Jonas has been drinking. He's reached the ugly mean stage and he's squeezing the life out of his scout. And he's screaming, screaming, screaming in Bill's face, "Don't you ever! Don't you ever say that, you hear? You hear me? You hear me, you sonofabitch?"

Bill can't answer because he's choking. He can't nod his

head. Can't do nothing. So Jonas goes on, and on. "You're lying! Ain't no nigger better than no white woman! Don't you ever tell me they taste sweeter. Don't you ever! You hear me? Say it! Say you're lying!" He let out a stream of cuss words and with each one he's shaking Bill. Shaking and shaking till his neck's almost broke. And can't none of us stop him because Jonas is the Captain and we can't lay a finger on him.

He's raving now. "Do you know what Pa liked for dessert? Apple Charlotte. Apple Charlotte! Asswipe! He'd have Ma bake it for him. He'd sit there eating it, smiling at her, licking his plate clean. And all the time he was laughing up his sleeve at Ma. At the two of us."

Bill's face is scarlet. He can't draw breath but Jonas ain't finished yet. "Pa had himself a nigger whore, see? Name of Apple. Kept her bastard bitch of a daughter right there under Ma's nose. D'you know what he called her? Charlotte! It was his idea of a joke. Him and his whore. They'd made their own Apple Charlotte. I saw Ma crying when she found out. But I baked that bitch for her. Soon as I got the chance. Yeah. I baked that bitch good."

Bill has gone limp. Jonas drops him. There's a crack of his skull hitting stone. Then silence. Don't nothing break it. Not a bird. Not a cricket. Nothing. There's nothing but the sound of Jonas Beecher's ragged breathing.

Then Bill give a groan. He curl himself into a ball, put his arms up, cradle his head like it's a baby.

Jonas don't say nothing to him. He just goes into his tent, lays himself down to sleep like it ain't happened.

I was awake most all of that night, remembering, piecing things together.

I only seen Mr Beecher's face up real close that time he save me from Jonas. His two front teeth didn't meet in the middle. Neither did Jonas's. Neither did mine.

I'm guessing it was the gap that done it. His wife hadn't known who he fathered until she seen me there by the cottonwood.

There must have been one hell of an altercation in the overseer's house that night. Guess Jonas heard it all. Was right after that I found him crying his eyes out. That was when he turned mean. He turned so mean I'd forgotten he was ever different until I seen Captain Smith. A pair of blue eyes, looking at me kind. What a heap of worms they turned up!

I want to say to Jonas, Is that it? I mean, really? Hell, is that it? Is that all? Is that the only reason you got for the poison you spitting? That the reason you join a lynch mob? Burn me? Rape Cookie? Kill her? Amos? Isaiah? Elijah? Lord above! Is that it?

I want to scream it out loud, scream it so loud the whole world can hear it, scream it so loud it makes the stars rattle: *Jonas Beecher got a nigger for a sister!*

It might have been funny, if it hadn't of been such a goddamned, godawful, miserable, pitiful mess.

41.

Jonas must have broke something inside that head of Bill's. By the time the sun come up the next morning, the only scout we got left is lying dead.

We don't even bury him. Jonas carries on as if he's a stranger. As if he don't mean no more to him than any of them dead Indians. And I carry on like Captain Beecher ain't my brother. Like I don't know about any of it. Because what else can I do?

Jonas don't need to say nothing to none of us. If it come to it – if anyone asks why Bill ain't with us when we go back – he can tell the General that Bill was killed by hostiles. Can't none of us say a thing. Wouldn't no one take the word of a black soldier over a white officer. We leave them all lying there, food for the buzzards, and follow the trail.

Or at least we try to. There was a few tracks to begin with. I'd learned enough from watching Jim to see that when that Indian village been attacked they'd scattered in different directions fast, then come together again. But after maybe quarter of a mile they'd split into two groups. Whoever had surprised them in the first place had gone after one. Jonas Beecher decided to take us after the other.

It wasn't long before them tracks faded to nothing. Without a scout we didn't have a hope in hell of working out where they'd gone. And by now we was well and truly lost. The only man who might have had the faintest notion of where we'd fetched up was having his bones picked clean by birds.

Only thing we could do was keep going. And we did. All that day. All the next. The whole of the one after that. Then one morning we come down the side of a mountain into a flat valley that stretches for maybe a mile before them rocks rise up again on the other side. And there – right in front of us was footprints, clear in the dust. They was fresh made. You could see the whole shape even down to the stitching at the toe of the moccasin that made it.

It was a small foot, so it didn't take a heap of figuring to work out it belonged to a woman. One woman. On foot. Out all alone. Heading out across the valley in broad daylight, where there was no cover, nowhere to hide.

You might have thought that one woman wasn't much of an enemy to go chasing after but Captain Beecher thought different. Far as he was concerned he could report one hostile dead.

I felt uneasy. Struck me as being mighty strange them tracks was so darned easy to see. So darned easy to follow. And I can't keep my big mouth shut, same as ever, so I says to Jonas, "Ain't them tracks strange, Captain?"

His eyes narrow and he look at me like I'm a hunk of dog dirt and he says, "Strange?"

"They're mighty clear."

"Well, that makes our job easier."

We set off, following them footprints. And that uneasy feeling don't go away, especially when we round some rocks and see her maybe one, two hundred yards ahead.

She turn, and I can see her belly's curved like a full moon. And I think maybe she's heading out on her own to have her baby someplace quiet. Or maybe she ain't. She look at us, and she's facing a whole company of soldiers but she don't do nothing. I can't be sure of it, but she look a whole lot like the woman that run our horses off when we was sent to arrest that medicine man. We eye each other across that sandy scrub.

"Ain't that strange, neither?" I says. "She's just standing there."

"What are you? A coward?" says Jonas. "You scared of one squaw?"

"She's with child, sir. Maybe she's about to have her baby."

"Then we'll get ourselves two hostiles, won't we?"

"We gonna attack a baby?"

"Nits make lice."

The hair's standing up on the back of my neck and my flesh is crawling and it ain't just because we're going after a woman in that state – though God alone knows that should have been enough to make the Devil think twice. It's because she's so darned *visible*. I knew you could ride right by an Apache and never know he was there until after he put a bullet in you. So seeing her standing there so clear, staring right on back at us, was downright terrifying.

She start running towards the rocks on the far side of the valley. Now her belly was big – I could see that with my own eyes – but that pace of hers struck me as being strange too. Apaches move quiet but they move fast. I seen an old woman run down a turkey once and catch it with her bare hands. There was something mighty wrong about how slow she was going. Was like she was a minnow on the end of a line being gently pulled across a creek. Somewhere, someone was fishing: waiting for us to take the bait.

We're following her at a trot as she heads towards the rocks, but as we start to catch up I see there's a crack in them and she's almost there.

Jonas wasn't the kind of man who was gonna take advice. But I can't stop myself yelling, "Looks like an ambush, sir."

And he start screaming at me about how I'm a goddamned coward and a baboon and a gibbon that's scared to fight. He's mad, crazy, ugly desperate to do some killing.

So he give the command and though I know we're dead men riding we obey because this is the army and you can't do nothing but follow the orders of your superior officer. We have ourselves something of a charge at them rocks, but when we reach them we see the ravine she's gone down is too narrow for us to ride in fours. We have to go along in single file and we can't do no more than walk because it twists and turns so much. And Captain Jonas Beecher send me in ahead so I'll be the first to fall. He bring up the rear and in we all go, one by one, into that cool ravine and I know there's an Indian behind each goddamned tuft of grass and each scrubby bush. And I know they won't do nothing until the last of us is in and they can cut off our retreat and kill us all as easily as shooting rats in a barrel. And I ride and I ride until there ain't no more than a thin ribbon of blue sky above and I can't hear nothing but the thud of my heart and the hooves of my horse and I can't smell nothing but my own fear. It's only when I come round another twisting corner and I see that woman ahead of me that I feel death coming down on me like a big, warm blanket.

Facing the end is a mighty strange thing. The idea of it coming calm when you're in bed asleep don't trouble you none. Sometimes the notion of crossing the line into the blackness and not waking up seems welcoming. But knowing it's gonna happen in a heartbeat or two and it ain't gonna be gentle and it sure ain't gonna be painless – generally there ain't nothing like that for making you want to cling to life with both hands and I been in enough situations like that when I fought like a cornered bear to keep myself this side of the line. But there in that ravine it was different.

Now I can't explain exactly how I felt. I just knew in my heart the time's come. I'm giving up. I've had enough. More than enough. This is it.

I was about to die. When them bullets started coming I didn't do nothing. Didn't make no attempt to fire back. Wasn't no point. Can't see no one up there. Was like we was under attack by the land itself. The notion of them rocks turning homicidal amused me some. Guess I was a little crazy by then. I started to smile.

See, there was just me and her there. The ravine come to a halt. Behind her was a rock face that she might have climbed and I guess that was her plan, only she'd gotten herself clipped by a ricocheting bullet that had torn across her wrist.

My horse getting shot from under me woke me up some. Sank down with a dying wheeze, blood burbling from its throat. When we was on the plains a horse dying wasn't no bad thing: you could use its body to give you cover. Sometimes we had to kill horses for just that reason. But that day all that horse did was block the canyon. Them warriors was so high above me wasn't no protection to be had, not from the horse nor nothing. Wasn't long before I took a bullet in the thigh and the pain made me pass out.

When I woke up it was quiet. Or at least the firing had stopped. That woman was still there and I wondered why she wasn't moving – she only had a hurt wrist, after all. But then I seen the sweat on her brow and I figured her baby had started coming for real, which made me want to laugh because it was so darned crazy. Having a child there in all that death? What in the hell was that baby gonna breathe in when it sucked air into its lungs for the first time?

Well, I couldn't walk none on account of that wound to my leg so I figured I'd die real slow of hunger or thirst or maybe something worse if the coyotes found me, let alone them Indians. Hadn't Bill Hickey said that when they was feeling mean they got to hanging folks upside down and lighting a fire under their heads, roasting them alive? That they'd cut off a man's privates, stick them in his mouth before he was even dead? Then I thought what a goddamned surprise they were gonna get if they tried that on me! I started laughing all over again, only then I heard something that wipe the smile off my face.

Footsteps. Coming up behind me. They're so loud I know they ain't no Indian's. They're army boots.

Hellfire! Look at that! Would you believe it? Jonas Beecher has survived that massacre and come looking to see who else is standing. He's injured his right hand, is all.

Company W been wiped out. It's just the two of us now. Me and him. Just the two of us. Him and me. I'm so crazy with the pain in my leg it's turned my head inside out. I'm sitting there, thinking, Hey, now I can talk to him. I mean, God Almighty, we're family, ain't we?! I can tell him who I am! Ain't no one listening now. I can ask him all those things I been wondering. Like, what happened to my ma. Did she die? She get sold, or what? And what about Cookie? Did she know who my pa was? Why didn't she never say nothing? And what in God's name been happening to Mr Beecher all these years, anyhow? Is he still alive, even?

I got my mouth open to speak, but Jonas get in first.

"Shoot her."

"Sir?"

"Shoot her, you goddamned, filthy, stinking nigger!"

Shoot her.

My mouth's dry and my tongue's sticking to the top of my mouth and I can't seem to get out no words. I'm gonna kill a woman who's trying to bring her baby into this big, bad, crazy old world and that baby's gonna die before it's even seen the light of day or drawn a breath of air or felt its ma holding it tight; it's gonna die in the dark of her belly – darker than night, darker than solitary, darker than a yam cellar – and I can't stand it. I can't get up on account of my leg, but I can fire my rifle, Mr Cody's 1866 Springfield Second Allin conversion, and this is the army

334

and he's my superior officer and orders is orders and I don't make up policy I just has to enforce it and it ain't like I got no choice – I ain't never had no choice about nothing – and if I raises an objection he'd have me court-martialled and I'd get myself hanged or shot before a firing squad for insubordination and he's screaming at me to wipe her out or else he'll do it with his one good hand and he's cussing and calling me a damned moke and a worthless ape and I can't do nothing about none of it so I cocks the hammer and my finger's on the trigger and I takes aim because when all's said and done I just ain't got no choice…

Excepting that I have.

I take aim. I pull the trigger. I blow half a human head clean away.

Only that head don't belong to no Indian woman.

It was Jonas Beecher's brains I blasted over them rocks.

42.

"Got ya!"

I lay my rifle down. "Got ya!"

I'm done. Don't much care what happens now. Not until I see Jim, slipping and sliding down the rocks towards me.

He been up there the whole time. He was the reason I hadn't got killed stone dead in that attack. The bullet I been hit by was one that bounced off the rocks. No one was aiming to get me. Because of him. He been protecting me. Watching over me. Like an angel.

For a long time we just look at each other.

I was bleeding bad and I couldn't move and there wasn't nothing for it but to let Jim fix me up because I was getting real dizzy. He kneels on down beside me.

We keep our backs turned on that woman, baby coming being kind of a personal matter, but she don't make no noise. When the baby's here it don't neither. While Jim's seeing to my leg that baby take a breath, take a feed and gets on with living. Seeing that tiny thing in its mother's arms was like having a wound ripped open in my chest. I was so thankful it didn't die before it been held like that there ain't nothing I can do to stop myself and before I know it I'm sobbing like a child.

Jim stare into my eyes like he just can't pull himself away and I guess I must have been something of a sight, swollen-faced and runny-nosed. Yep. I sure must have looked appealing.

But then that man done something that knock the breath clean out of me. He pull off his headband and bunches it into a ball and he wipe my face, real gentle. He trace the outline of my cheek with his finger, running over the diamond scars Miss Louellen give me all them years back. And I been so long on the frontier by then and ain't no one never touched me, leastways not like I was a woman and now here's this man being so tender it just about turn my heart inside out. I want to grab him and never let go but after what happened with Reuben I'm too darned scared to move so I sit there, looking up at him.

Slowly – like he thinks I'm a wild horse that might go skitting off – he leans forward and he press his lips on my forehead and I guess it might have been a kiss, only I ain't never felt nothing like that so I didn't rightly know what to make of it – other than the feel of his mouth bring a lump to my throat so big I was like to choke on it.

Jim start to laugh. He laughs so hard the tears are rolling down his face. Now whether he was laughing because he figured I played the biggest God Almighty joke on the US Army or whether he was laughing because I'd blown the head off of Jonas Beecher I don't know and I never did ask – my leg was troubling me too much. I just watched them tears sliding down over his cheeks and I remember thinking what a heavenly, beautiful sight that man was and about three seconds later I passed out.

By the time I come around again Jim had made a carrier for that tiny baby and it was strapped tight to its ma's back and she was about ready to move off. There was one horse and three mules left alive and the horse was Jonas Beecher's. That woman loads a mule up with as many guns and as much ammunition as it can carry and she climb up on that horse and she ride off to join the rest of them Apaches, and for some reason that I can't entirely fathom Jim decides to stay with me and for a while I just sit there trying to figure out what to do next.

See, I knew if anyone found Jonas it was gonna be real easy to tell he been shot from below at close range. Wouldn't take a whole heap of figuring for someone to work out it ain't been done by no Apache, not when all them other men been killed by bullets raining down from above. And seeing as I was the only trooper left alive, well, you can see why I wasn't keen for my brother to be found quick.

So when Jim hold out his hand I take it, and he pull me up, or at least he tries to – I can't stand good on account of that bullet wound. He fetch one of them mules instead and it's painful getting up on its back but I do it, and then, well, seemed to me the simplest choice in the world was to follow wherever that man led.

The weather helped us by blowing up a big storm later on that day. It wiped out all them tracks leading towards that ravine. If my luck held, wasn't nobody going to find them bodies in there until after the coyotes and the vultures done their work. We had time to get away.

We was both wanting to put distance between ourselves and that ravine so he take us deeper into them mountains.

We didn't say hardly nothing that day. We didn't need to do much talking. There was a mighty powerful feeling between us and it was enough to ride along on that mule knowing it wasn't just the loss of blood that was making me feel so light-headed. I been yearning towards that man ever since I first laid eyes on him and when you been wanting someone that bad for that long – well, the way you feel when they actually touch you is enough to make it seem like the whole world's changing shape or changing colour or something. And if I been feeling all that desperation, he been feeling it too, which seemed to me to be some sort of

339

miracle then and it still does now.

We was moving between rocks and some of them are so tight together that we have to get off the mules. Jim lift me down tender as tender and help me through and then go back for them mules who have to scramble and squeeze and it take some persuasion but they manage it. Then Jim go back again, picking traces of mule hair off them stones and rubbing out hoof prints because if we get followed those are the kinda things that are gonna lead scouts straight to us. I ain't never been nowhere so high and suddenly we're riding along where there ain't no path, just sloping rock, and on one side of us the land falls away down maybe a thousand feet or more. I keep my eyes fixed firm between that mule's ears because if I start staring into that ravine I'm like to lose my balance and if that mule sets a foot wrong we're both dead. For the very first time in my life I'm real grateful to a mule for being so sure-footed.

Jim's ahead now and he's going over a ridge and while I'm watching he disappears sudden and for a second I think him and his mule have fallen and when I come up the ridge on my animal I can't see him nowhere and panic just about drowns me. My mule start sliding down the slope and it's so steep the thing's sitting on its haunches like a dog and there's no stopping it and I can't see Jim or his mule. And that's it, I think to myself, we're gonna end up broke to pieces at the foot of that gorge and that's what you get for killing your commanding officer. I don't mind for myself but the notion of Jim being bloodied and broke is enough to make me weep. Only then I see him and he's on foot. He reach out and he tug at the reins of my mule and he's pulling it to the left and when it feels level ground under its feet it gets up. Then I see we're under an overhang and behind Jim is a cave big enough for both them mules and both of us. It's darn near invisible from above – you'd only know it was here if you was an Apache – and I wish to God the army had never recruited none of them scouts because if it wasn't for them we could stay hidden here for ever.

He lift me off that beast and I ain't never felt so downright female as I done then. He lay me down and he check on my wound which is bleeding and hurting bad but not smelling, which is something to be grateful for. Then he does some praying and chanting and he wipe yellow dust on me like that old medicine man done. Turns out that yellow dust is pollen and it's sacred because I can feel the power of that charm working right away.

At the back of the cave he lights a real small fire because night is coming on and it's getting cold and he gives me a strip of dried meat and I ain't never tasted nothing so good as that before or since.

When we done eating he unbutton my jacket and he lift up my shirt and he take his knife from his belt. Lay it flat against my skin and slide it up under them bandages I been winding round my chest all these years. With one cut he set me free.

It was like beginning a whole new life, in a whole new body. There ain't words big enough to describe the deep-down joy I had in loving that man, touching him, feeling his warm skin on mine, breathing in the smell of him. That night, when we lay wrapped together, our bodies twined so tight you couldn't tell whose limbs was whose, I swear I could feel the earth's heart beating under us and hear the stars singing up above.

Come the dawn, I watched him sleeping, his hair spread across my belly and I was so thankful I would have fallen on my knees and praised the Lord, only that would have meant moving and I couldn't tear myself away from Jim.

The days, the weeks, that followed, I learned so much. Not just practical things, although in time I could chip an arrowhead and fashion a bow almost as well as Jim could.

All my life I been wondering what in the hell folks meant when they talked about freedom. I'd fetched up thinking the notion of liberty was one big damned lie.

Well, it wasn't. With Jim, I was free. I was whole. There was no hiding. No pretending. No keeping a lid on things. No pushing thoughts away where I couldn't see them. I could think. Feel. Laugh. Cry. I could be me. All of me. Each day I could feel my soul expanding, getting bigger. I was transforming into something better and brighter than I'd ever dreamed possible. It was like I was finally growing into the person the Lord intended.

I wasn't alone no more, just me, struggling to get by. But it wasn't just the two of us helping each other along neither. We was more than that. Much more. We was part of something: something big and something truly fine. Jim rooted me to the land: I saw every blade of grass, felt every breath of wind, heard every chirruping cricket – sweet Jesus, even the solid rocks seemed alive! I began to think that maybe freedom wasn't owning land or making a mark on a place: it was being one tiny speck in this God Almighty huge and wondrous world, with everything in its place, everything bound together, everything fitting, everything making sense. Freedom was something in your mind, in your heart, in your soul.

We didn't never talk about the past. There was too much pain in that for both of us. Didn't never talk about the future neither – there was too much fear in what might lie ahead. We just lived right here, right now, with this breath, this heartbeat, this pressing of skin on skin: there wasn't no place else to be. I ain't never known happiness like it.

But we was running. Couldn't never forget that.

Weeks turned into months and months turned into years. We was always moving on, never stayed nowhere for longer than three, four days. One time we come to where the land give out altogether and there's water as far as the eye can see. Jim ain't never seen the ocean before, but I had. We'd reached the western shore and I realized that in my time I'd gone all the way from one side of America to the other. And I was only just beginning to feel it was where I belonged.

Mostly we slept out under the stars and when it got too cold on the mountains we moved down onto the plains and all the while we was both watching the horizon for clouds of dust because that's a sure-fire way of knowing where the army is. For three years we kept one step ahead of them, just one step. None of it was easy but it was the best time I ever had.

Maybe we'd have stayed living that way, just us. If I hadn't done such a damned fool thing we might have hid out there for ever. All I had to do was tend that fire. Tend that fire and stay awake. Couldn't have been nothing easier. Only I didn't manage to do neither.

43.

I guess our baby must have started growing inside me although I didn't know it then. I recall feeling sick most all the time and so darned tired I could barely walk ten steps before I wanted to lie down and sleep again. I didn't know what was ailing me so I was scared as well as tired.

It was the time of year the mescal plants come into bloom and if you take the hearts and bake them they make good eating. Jim was telling me that before the white folks come the men would dig a real deep pit maybe seven feet across and three, four feet deep and the women would go out harvesting all the plants they could get and they'd stuff them in there and bake them for days on end and you could get enough that way to feed the tribe all winter.

But there's just the two of us and we're keeping ourselves quiet, not wanting to get noticed by no one, so the hole Jim dig is a small one and he just cut a couple of plants that won't get seen by no scouts. Jim set the fire burning and he cover it over and leave them things to steam themselves into being edible. And then he go off to see if he can't catch us a jackrabbit and all I have to do is sit there on my haunches keeping still and silent and making sure that fire don't get out of that pit. Only the sun is warm and I'm feeling real sick and I can't help myself. I lie down. And I pinch myself and I slap my face to keep from sliding under but it don't do no good because the next thing I know is Jim's back and he got a rabbit dangling from one hand but I can hardly see him on account of all the smoke because that fire's escaped and it's spreading over the grass and it's rising high and it's like a goddamned signal fire and if there are soldiers anywhere near by – and just about the entire US Army are all out looking for hostiles, so of course there are – there ain't no way they can miss it. We're out on the plains and there's nowhere to run and nowhere to hide and this beautiful, magical, precious life I been living is all over and it's my own damned stupid fault and I feel so heartsore I want to weep and wail and scream and cut myself the way that little Indian woman done.

But Jim takes me in his arms and holds me against him like it's for the last time. I rest my head on his chest and press my face into his neck and shut my eyes because I don't want to see the end come, and we're standing like that when the troops ride on up.

My uniform's real threadbare by that time and my

pants is more holes than anything else but I'm still wearing it so the shock comes off them in waves because they don't know I'm a woman – not yet. It don't occur to me how bad it looks to them to see two men holding each other the way we was – one of them a deserter and the other a hostile – and I guess we was lucky we wasn't shot down right there and then, or worse, because the one thing the crazy, fool army hates more than deserters and hostiles is men who happen to love each other. The look on their faces!

Some captain come riding up on his horse and he holler, "What in the name of God is going on here, trooper?"

And I can't find no words to explain so it's Jim who does the talking and it's back to them big things and little things. The little thing is that I'm a woman who fought for the US Army – and the lie that I been living all that time is so colossal it swamp just about everything else. That captain didn't do no laughing. He wasn't remotely amused. He look like he want to tie me to the back of his horse and drag me along until the life's scraped out of me. But there ain't no army protocol for this situation so he was real confused what to do. In the end we get taken along with them and Jim's a prisoner and finally we fetch up back at some fort and it's only then that someone thinks to ask about what happened to Jonas. And the shocking nature of me and my true self has so blown everybody's minds away that when I tell them I been sent on ahead to scout and I encountered hostiles and got cut off from the rest of the force and I plain don't know what happened to Captain Beecher and the rest of Company W because I got so lost and I been trying to find my way back ever since, they was all so shocked about my being a woman they go right on and believe me. So I get away with murder, which I guess is lucky, or not, depending on how you look at it. But I lose Jim and of all the losses I had to bear in my life it's the most painful.

Well, they can't discharge me fast enough. I get given the pay due to me. One of the officers' wives give me an old dress. Then I was told I was free to go. All I could think was, Free to go where?

See, that same day me and Jim got brought back to civilization was the day the last of them Apaches finally give up. They couldn't run no more and when I seen this little group come trailing in – wasn't no more than forty of them – I knew it was the end of everything: for me, for Jim, for all them Indians.

The white folks couldn't stand to have them in the territory no more. Before I left that fort them Apaches was all rounded up and loaded onto a train and sent off east – even them ones who been keeping peaceable and starving to death on that goddamned reservation. They was prisoners of war, every single one of them down to the tiniest newborn baby. Even them Indian scouts. Working loyal for the US Army didn't save none of them.

And if they wasn't gonna be let alone, what in the hell chance did a man like Jim have?

They tell him to get on that train and all I can do is stand and watch. The government had told them Apaches they'd have two years' imprisonment, that was all. After that they'd get their very own brand-new reservation and it would be someplace real fine and things was gonna be just dandy.

Well, that parting was about as bad as anything could be. I was so choked up I couldn't hardly speak. And I wasn't the only one. None of them Indians was making a sound: some griefs go too deep for any kind of noise.

"Two years' time, I'll come find you," I says to Jim. "You gonna be free."

And them words seem as substantial as a piece of tumbleweed blowing across the prairie. We both of us know how good them fine gentlemen in Washington are at keeping their promises. But I look at him and I put my hands up to hold his face so he's got to look back at me and I says it again, only louder, like by wishing for it hard enough I can make it true, "You gonna be free."

Jim rub the back of his hand across my cheek to wipe away the tears that won't stop falling and then cups his hands behind my head and our foreheads is pressed together and I can feel he's thinking the same as me.

When?

44.

I walked behind that train until it was out of sight. Then I carried on, walking on the tracks, because there wasn't nothing else I could think of to do.

I wasn't alone. Them Indians wasn't allowed to take their dogs with them. They run along ahead of me, trying to catch up with that train, yapping and crying for their folks, and they run until they couldn't run no more and all I seen as I headed east was a trail of broke-down mutts, starved and dying.

The first thing I'd done with the pay due to me was buy ammunition for Mr Cody's rifle. A whole heap of it. And two six shooters. A knife. Used most of the bullets putting them dogs out of their misery. And all of them was in my head like all them horses, and poor old Abe, and them dead children and babies, and Henry and Reuben and Cookie and all the others, and some nights I was scared to sleep for fear of what went running through my dreams.

I walk east. I'm in a dress, and I know what men in this territory are capable of doing to a woman. I'd rather risk a rattler bite than come face to face with the likes of Bill Hickey. So I walk by night and I rest up by day. I'd learned to sit still as a rock by then. Like an Indian, I could make myself invisible to the naked eye.

I walk and I walk and I walk. Until finally, one day, I fetch up in a town. A big town, with fine tall buildings and wide streets and horse-drawn carriages and more folks than I ever seen in my life. I'm thinking, Can I get work here? Would any of these smart dressed folks take me on? What as? What can I be now? A maid?

A woman who'd been in the army? Who knows how to kill but who's forgotten how to cook? Who's got a baby coming, but no husband? A baby who been fathered by a hostile? A renegade? A prisoner of war? I don't even know how to begin trying.

But I do. I take my courage in both hands and I start knocking on doors. Each and every one of them gets slammed in my face.

I'm starting out again the next day, figuring maybe I'll have me more luck someplace else. There got to be other towns; there got to be someone who'll take me on. It's just a matter of finding them, is all.

Somewhere down along the road I can hear there's a

band playing and before I know it I'm caught up in a crowd of folks pushing and shoving, a whole tide of them flowing in the same direction. I'm so tired I get carried right along.

When the crowd stop moving I find I'm pressed up against a fence and before me is a square about the size of a parade ground.

And, hey! Well, would you look at that? There are two bright-painted, covered wagons making their way, slow and steady, across it, like two little ships afloat on the ocean. The oxen pulling them have got ribbons tied to their horns; there are bells around their necks and they all brushed and curled, their hooves oiled. The settlers driving them are being followed along by their very own band. And listen up – what's that? Why them plucky folks are singing! Over the creaking of the turning wheels an uplifting hymn rises heavenwards. As they come closer to where I'm standing I see their faces are clean-scrubbed, their clothes fresh starched and new pressed. Crisp white shirts; pretty gingham skirts. The women are dazzling blonde, hair in ringlets, the men square-jawed and clean-shaved, the children cute as cherry pie.

I start to smile because I know no settler never looked so clean nor smelled so sweet. Never knew no settler to sing in tune neither. This ain't for real. This is some kinda joke, ain't it? They play acting, is all. This a pageant, or what? What in the heck is going on?

A voice is proclaiming aloud to the crowd that these

fine-looking folks are setting out to carve a place for themselves in this brand-new world. They're making a little piece of heaven right here on earth: it's their manifest destiny. They ain't got nothing but courage by the barrel-load and an unshakeable belief in the goodness of the Almighty who done give them this big, empty land of America just as surely as he give Paradise to Adam and Eve.

The crowd give a cheer. They're clapping and clapping.

But about a minute later they start gasping in alarm. Folks all around me is clutching each other's arms because – oh my! Lordy! – what's that godawful noise? What are them whooping screams that freeze your blood and set the marrow in your bones a-jingling? God save us all, it's war cries! Dozens of them. These settlers are gonna be butchered right in front of our eyes! Because – God above! – look over there!

From around the corner – riding in perfect time to the music – they come galloping into the square, half naked, riding bareback on spotted ponies, feathers in their hair, tomahawks in their hands, scalping knives at the ready.

To my eye they're tame as they come, but to the crowd – oh my! A troop of lions wouldn't seem half so wild, nor tigers half so savage. A pack of bears would be less frightening than that host of painted men: animals in human form, devils made flesh. They circle the wagon and them square-jawed men is fighting valiantly back but there's too few of them and too many Indians. One of them

353

plucky pioneers takes an arrow in the chest. Well, kinda. There ain't no blood and I figure he's holding it in place. But don't no one in the crowd mind that.

His golden-headed wife runs to his side. He dies, his head cradled in her gingham-skirted lap. And now one of them savages has his eyes on her. He's off his horse and he's getting closer and he's licking his lips and it don't take much imagining to figure out what's on his mind. A thrill of horror runs around them people watching this thing unfold.

The wild whooping goes on and on, and them plucky pioneers can't fight them savages off. Before too long the men are lying still in the dirt.

The women are trying to shield the children, who are hiding behind their mamas' skirts, weeping prettily – ain't none of that red-faced wailing from these cherry-lipped cuties.

The bare-chested redskins are coming for them real slow. They enjoying this, that's for sure. Everyone's on their tiptoes, straining to see, because they know what's gonna happen. The men's gonna be scalped. The women violated. Them kids are gonna be taken captive. Living with the Indians? Well, hell, everyone knows that's a fate worse than death.

One of them savages jumps off his horse. He about to take his scalping knife to the head of one of them square-jawed pioneers. Another got his arms around the waist of a woman. Her son runs to her but the little lad is pushed away. He fall, sobbing, to the floor. "Mama! Mama!" His cries are pitiful. And now that Indian's dark hands are on her pale skin and the sight's enough to make the crowd want to spew their guts out. Smelling salts are being pulled from purses. Some of the watching ladies look like they about to swoon. But before that devil can raise so much as the hem of her petticoat there's the sound of a bugle.

A bugle? A bugle! I swear I can see relief coming off that crowd like the haze off the desert.

Praise the Lord! Here come the cavalry! Riding in on snowy-white horses, uniforms clean and blue, neckerchiefs of deep scarlet, buttons polished, boots shining, sabres gleaming, and there's redheads and blonds and brunettes but not a single black face amongst them.

The cavalry slash at them savages until every one of them has fallen on the floor. They give a rousing cheer and the folks watching start clapping and screaming and jumping up and down because, glory, alleluia, them white women's modesty is saved and civilization's preserved!

And I just throw my head back and laugh. I laugh and laugh until tears come rolling down my face. I'm thinking what crazy fool has took all that godawful mess of blood and burning I lived through and turned it into a … a concert party for folks to scream and cheer at? What crazy fool is making money out of this?

The answer come riding right into the square in front

355

of me. No one notices them dead Indians quietly getting up off the ground and slipping out to get ready for the next show because a man on a beautiful white horse has come prancing in. He got the whole crowd near wetting their pants with excitement. He's wearing a gleaming white buckskin jacket with a fringe about a mile long. His hair is brushed and curled under a white hat. His moustache is waxed and his beard is combed. He look a whole lot cleaner than he did the last time I saw him, when he come riding in off the prairie ahead of a storm and turned the whole fort just about upside down. He look a whole lot heavier too. Why that man's belly is almost as round as mine!

Aside from Captain Smith he was the only white man I ever met who spoke to me civil and straight. I can't hardly believe my eyes. Would you look at that? It's Mr William Cody. He's turned himself into a whole new man. Now he's Buffalo Bill. And this here's his Wild West show.

Me laughing like that causes something of a stir in the crowd. Folks are looking at the "crazy nigger woman" but I can't stop myself. I'm still doing it when Mr Cody come riding over. He look me up and down, his head on one side.

And then he asks, real polite, "Don't I know you, ma'am?"

I look him in the eye. "You surely do. I won you a bet way back. Out west. A shooting competition. Only I looked a little different then." I hold up my Springfield.

"You give me this."

"O'Hara?" His eyes are just about ready to pop out of his head. For a moment he look at me like I'm some kinda freak of nature. A trooper in a dress? He can't get his head around that at all. Then he notice the size of my belly. His mouth drop wide open. I can see his thoughts making their way slow and steady through his head. When he finally figures out I been a woman all along he darned nearly shits himself laughing.

"What in the world has been happening to you, O'Hara?" he says, shaking his head.

"Long story."

"You'd better come and tell it me after the show."

So I do.

And after I done telling it to Mr William Cody he hires me. For which I am truly, deeply thankful.

He don't give me no job as no performer. It don't matter none that I'm a good rider or a fine shot. White folks don't want to see the likes of me out there and this ain't history he's giving them. Heck! We was being written out of the pages of that all the while we was making it! Nope. This ain't no history lesson: it's show business. He take me on as a stablehand. I'm stuck out back in the dark and the shit. But in my condition, hell, that's plenty good enough for me.

Well, Mr Cody's show gets real famous. We tour all over America and then them fancy Europeans start clamouring to see it. Dukes, princes, even the queen of England: seems everyone's hankering after a piece of Buffalo Bill's Wild West. So over the water we go.

I had my baby right there on the boat. Named her Liberty Belle. She took her first breath in the middle of the ocean, halfway between America and Europe, when all that water was heaving so much that most everybody was real sick. Them cowboys in the show was spewing their guts out and hollering and screaming to the good Lord to give them some relief and them Indians was singing their death songs.

So that's it. Ain't nothing else to say. I'm sticking with Buffalo Bill until I get word about Jim. Meantime I'm holding my baby tight, keeping her safe, loving her enough for the two of us. Some day soon, we all gonna be together. It less than two years' time now. Then we can go live up in them mountains. The fighting's over. There won't be no one chasing us. We gonna be a family. And we gonna be free.

The folks in Washington didn't keep their word. It shouldn't have surprised me. Hell, they broke every promise they ever made to every bunch of Indians in the country – why in the world did I think it would be any different with them Apaches? I had too much riding on it, I guess: I wanted to believe them so bad it hurt. But it wasn't two years before Jim was freed. It was twenty-seven.

Twenty-seven years. I'd had me another whole lifetime of wanderings. By the time I get to see Jim again we're both grey and grizzled and our baby girl is all grown-up and married, with children of her own.

But that don't mean me and Jim ain't mighty pleased to see each other. And, oh sweet Jesus, that powerful feeling is burning as strong between us as it ever was (which is something of an embarrassment to Liberty Belle, but we ain't apologizing: we got too much catching up to do).

We're all living in America, Land of the Free. Guess I'm still struggling with that word. If it means choice — choosing which path you go down, which road you follow, which door you push open — well, for me and Liberty Belle, for her husband, her children — there are still way too many paths blocked, too many roads closed, too many doors getting slammed in our faces.

As for Jim, he ain't a citizen of the country he was born in. He ain't a prisoner of war no more; he's a ward of the government. Don't know how we're supposed to tell the difference. We can't go back to them mountains because he ain't allowed. The white folks are still too scared and too mean and too sore to let a single Apache set foot on the land that rightfully belongs to them.

So some days freedom feels about as far away as it ever been. Some days I want to hang my head and weep.

But then I look at Jim and I feel the weight of his hand in mine, and I look at Liberty Belle and I see our grandchildren growing up fine and strong and I know that I'm free where it counts: free in my heart, free in my head, free in my soul.

And for the rest of it? Well, me and Jim: we're warriors, ain't we?

As long as the grass grows and the waters run, as long as we got breath in our bodies, we'll keep fighting.

AUTHOR'S NOTE

There are some ideas that take hold of you, some characters that seize you by the throat and don't let go. Charley O'Hara is one of them.

Some years ago I wrote *Apache*, a novel set in the American west in the late nineteenth century about a girl warrior determined to avenge her brother's death.

While I was researching for that book – reading the first person accounts of Native Americans who had lived through truly terrible times – I came across references to what they described as 'Negro soldiers' who rode in the 'Blue Coat' uniforms of the US army against the Apache nations.

I was intrigued. And I was uneasy.

It was just after the American Civil War and African American slaves had been freed. What were these so-called 'Negro soldiers' doing? Why were recently emancipated men fighting to take the freedom away from people who had always had it? What were they thinking? Feeling? How did they come to be in Apache territory?

Further reading led me to the Buffalo Soldiers, and in particular the men of the 9th and 10th United States Cavalry Regiments. Many were former slaves who found that, when liberated, there were few, if any, options open to them. They had nothing, and to survive there was no choice but sign up. When I started to read more about their background and history I was struck by the bitter irony of the situation.

And then I came across the story of Cathy Williams, a freed slave who disguised herself as a man and joined the US army as William Cathay. Her true identity was revealed two years later but I began to think that if she had done that – if she had been desperate enough to take that risk – surely there were other women who had done the same and got away with it? Someone like … well, Charley O'Hara?

Cathy Williams opened the door to a world that I felt compelled to write about. It's taken a long time to complete this book. I headed up dead ends, blind alleys and took a lot of wrong paths. There were times I put the manuscript aside thinking it would never be finished, but every time I gave up Charley appeared, standing at my elbow and nudging me along until I'd finished writing her story.

I was in my fourteenth summer when the Mexicans rode
against us. Twelve moons later, I took my revenge.
And though Ussen has drawn visions of a terrible future
in my mind, I will not be vanquished. I belong to this
land: to the wide sky above my head, to the sweet
grass beneath my feet. Here must I die.

But first I will live, and I will fight. For I am a warrior.

I am Apache.

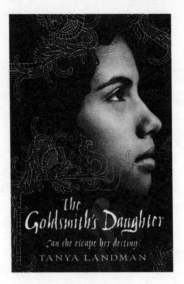

In the golden Aztec city of Tenochtotlan,
people live in fear of the gods.

A girl born under an ill-fated sky, Itacate is destined to a
lifetime of submission and domestic drudgery. But she has
a secret passion, one which she can tell no one for fear of
death. When she falls in love with a Spanish invader and
her secret is endangered, Itacate must fight for her life.

Can she defy the gods and escape her destiny?